Callie's TIME

Callie's TIME

Basalt Bay 1

Mary E. Hanks

www.maryehanks.com

Suzanne D. Williams Cover Design

www.feelgoodromance.com

Cover photos:

Natalia Andreychenko @ istockphoto.com

Background Master @ depositphotos.com

Visit Mary's website:

www.maryehanks.com

You can write Mary at

maryhanks@maryehanks.com

To Hope

Thanks for loving my brother and nephews so well.

May love, peace, and grace be yours forever.

To Jason

My best friend, walking companion, and dream sharer.

Here's to our great Third Act!

"There is a time for everything."

Ecclesiastes 3:1

Chapter One

"Callie, we need to discuss your weight problem." Doctor Isabel met her gaze with a look of authority Callie Cedars had come to expect and dread.

Discussing her weight meant more than talking about the extra pounds she carried. Based on similar conversations, the doctor was about to railroad her by listing some horrible consequences that would happen to her if she didn't lose weight.

Callie gritted her teeth, tempted to tell Doctor Isabel what she thought of her advice. She was sixty-three years old. This was her body. She'd put into it whatever she wanted! And, yes, she would accept the consequences.

She liked pastries. Enjoyed red meat and mashed potatoes swimming in butter. Ate a burger and french fries a couple times a week at Bert's Fish Shack. The cinnamon rolls at Paige's gallery were to die for. Not literally! She swallowed hard then coughed as if she were choking.

"Are you all right?"

"Uh-huh."

"So, what have you done to lose weight since your last annual checkup?"

"Nothing. What's the use? I've tried dieting before and failed!" Callie's voice rose quickly. So did her heart rate.

"You must treat your body better, especially your heart." Doctor Isabel patted Callie's hand like the gesture might ease the sting of her words. It didn't. "You have high blood pressure. High blood sugar levels that border on your becoming a diabetic if you don't change your ways."

Callie gulped. Her brother, Pauly, took insulin daily, and he wasn't close to her size.

But at her age, she was set in her ways. She didn't like taking advice from anyone. She preferred doling out pearls of wisdom. But in this tiny patient room, her opinion didn't matter much.

The doctor explained about high cholesterol and high blood pressure often running together, quoting risks that Callie quickly tuned out. Those things wouldn't happen to her!

"I want you to consider going on a whole foods diet."

"Huh? A what?"

"Whole foods. Eating fresh food. Not packaged. No fast food. Also, you need to take daily walks and do weight-bearing activities."

"You've got to be kidding me!"

"I'm not joking. I've warned you for the last few years, but you haven't taken my warnings seriously."

"Doctor—" Callie groaned. "This is how I've been since the seventh grade. I'm a little overweight. No reason to change at this point in my career."

"Callie. We're not talking about you being a little overweight." Doctor Isabel's lips pressed together in a grim line. "This is serious. I warned you about your heart last year."

Callie clenched her hands together.

"If you were to lose five to ten percent of your body weight, you would be doing your heart, and your blood, a big favor." Doctor Isabel pegged her with one of her doctorly stares. "I can't say this strongly enough. Change your lifestyle. Eat healthily and exercise daily. Also, I'm increasing your medication."

"But—"

"I want you here next year. And the next. You have your one-month-old great nephew to think of." The doctor's eyebrows rose as if to emphasize the importance of her concern. "Another baby on the way. Don't you want to be around for them for a long time?"

"Of course, I do! And that's two babies on the way." Callie exhaled a breath, picturing Paige and Ruby who were both pregnant. "My nieces and nephews are my world. But that doesn't mean—"

"Yes, it does," Doctor Isabel said sternly. "You need to lose some serious weight, Callie. Your health requires it. Your heart demands it."

A rush of hot air hissed through Callie's lips, deflating her lungs and her emotions. "This is exactly why I don't like coming in for my yearly exam. We go through this every time."

"Then let this be your year of change!" Doctor Isabel smiled in an all-knowing manner that bugged Callie. "You can do it."

"Why should I go through all the effort of a fad diet? It's a little late for my 'happily ever after,' wouldn't you say?" Callie stretched her lips over her teeth, grimacing. But then she thought of James Weston, the man who lived across from her family home. Hadn't she dreamed of a happily ever after with him for fifty years?

Sigh. Too bad she gave up on that dream a long time ago.

"It's never too late to go after what you want." The doctor smiled slightly as if she were offering Callie breadcrumbs.

The thing she wanted to go after right now was a double cheeseburger and fries from Bert's. What would the doctor say if she brought up her favorite food choices? Her stomach growled loudly.

"Paisley and Paige need you to be around as a fill-in granny."

"I know." Wasn't she already a fill-in mom to them? Since Piper and Tanner were born, she stepped up to being like a grandma to them too. A twinge of appreciation for the doctor's concerns went through her. But just as quickly, she brushed it away.

"All it takes—"

"Don't give me the 'all it takes' speech. You don't know how many times I've attempted a diet. How many times I denied myself treats or eggs or bread, or whatever the current dieting rage was. And how many times I failed." Callie groaned and hot air filled her mouth like she might be sick.

"Are you talking about dieting in the last decade?" Doctor Isabel raised an eyebrow.

"Maybe not in the last ten years." Callie blew out a long breath.

Getting her annual checkup was physically and emotionally exhausting. She needed some comfort food. Maybe not a burger, this time. A thick cinnamon roll slathered in cream cheese frosting from Paige's coffee shop would do the trick.

"Things have changed," the doctor said, her tone placating. "How we view weight loss has changed. It's about developing an active lifestyle. Eating better. Not just avoiding certain foods."

Easy for her to say, since she was thin. Avoiding food was never easy for Callie.

The doctor slid a pamphlet across the counter. "I want you to read this material, including reading some information online. I'm not talking about starving yourself. You'll be filling up with nutritious food every day. Five or six small meals."

As if eating healthier allowed her to eat twice as many times and not gain weight? *Oh, happy day!*

"I like my food the way I like it," she grumbled.

"Don't we all?" Doctor Isabel chuckled. "Doesn't mean it's beneficial."

Callie tapped the pamphlet. "What would I have to do for this healthy lifestyle?" She wasn't agreeing to anything, but asking didn't hurt.

"Like I said, eat natural food. Smaller quantities more often. No added sugar. Make better food choices."

"Are you suggesting I survive on vegetables and fruit?" Callie felt like gagging on the mental image of cooked spinach sticking in her throat.

"Along with healthy fats and meat." Doctor Isabel shrugged a couple of times. "Skip dessert. Eat more berries."

"My housemate, Kathleen, is a fabulous cook. I can't ignore her baking."

"I mean it, Callie. You've been overworking your heart." Her voice deepened like she was saying something extremely meaningful. "You've gained weight this year."

"Yeah, yeah." Callie let out a long sigh. *Yada, yada, yada.*

"Take this as a significant warning. Otherwise, you might find yourself in the hospital having surgery. Or worse."

What was worse than heart surgery?

Doctor Isabel wagged her finger. "Those nieces of yours would grieve terribly if you weren't here for them."

Way to guilt her.

"I'll consider what you've said. Thanks, Doc." Callie shuffled toward the door, eager to get out of the exam room. The place made her itch. Made her hungry too.

"Oh, Callie?"

Hand on the knob, Callie clenched her teeth so tightly they hurt. Slowly, she turned back to the doctor. "Yes?"

Doctor Isabel held up the pamphlet. "You forgot this."

"Right." She trudged back and grabbed it.

Doctor Isabel patted her arm again. "You matter to me, Callie Cedars. Your health matters. Eat better. Exercise every day. Take your meds."

"Okay." She picked up the pamphlet and left the office, grumbling all the way to her Uber ride.

Change my diet, my whole life, to make myself a few pounds lighter? You've got to be kidding me! I've tried this before. Dieting never worked. It won't work now, either.

"Where to, Ms. Cedars?" Marcus, the mid-fifties driver, asked.

"The art gallery in Basalt Bay."

"Yes, ma'am. Miss Paige has the best cinnamon rolls within fifty miles."

"Don't I know it?" She groaned.

Chapter Two

Callie chose a table near the window in Paige's art gallery and coffee shop where she could view the ocean waves outside and observe her niece assisting a customer. How an eight-month pregnant woman nearly ran around the place conducting business and toting so much extra weight intrigued her. Paige thrived in this environment of beautiful art pieces and delicious scents. And she glowed of motherhood.

For a moment, Callie felt a smidgeon of regret. Looking back on her life, she wished she'd had a child of her own. Too late for that now. Still, at the oddest times, a sense of loss pressed down on her chest. Like now.

"What can I get for you, Auntie?" Paige asked as soon as the customer left.

"Plain tea. Thank you."

"Plain? What about your usual sweet tea?"

"Not today. I'm uh, well, that's how I'll have it from now on." Callie fought the urge to cave in and say never mind, she'd have sweet tea just like always. "I'm changing a few things." She thrummed her fingernails against the tabletop. "Reducing sugar, that's all." She downplayed her decision. Why bother her pregnant niece with her burden?

"That's a switch." Paige lifted a dark eyebrow, giving Callie a skeptical glance.

"I'll still have a cinnamon roll. To go." She could throw it away when she got home. Yeah, right. If she brought a warm cinnamon roll into the project house, she would have the whole thing eaten in a minute!

Maybe she'd give the frosting-laden pastry to Marcus. Although her sweet tooth cried out for some delicious comfort food after her trip to the doctor and the bad news she received. She would diet tomorrow. Or the day after. Next week at the latest.

"Sure thing, Auntie." Paige bustled into the prep area. She fixed a cup of tea, then put a mouth-watering cinnamon roll in a to-go bag.

Forget bringing the treat home, Callie wanted it right now. She focused on the tea Paige set in front of her. Taking a sip, she grimaced. Sugarless tea would take some getting used to.

"Are you all ready for the baby to arrive?" she asked, focusing on her niece instead of the bland tea or her cravings.

"I am so ready!" Paige smoothed her hands over her enlarged stomach. "This little one is doing gymnastics in my stomach. Moving all the time. But I couldn't be happier."

"I see the joy on your face. I can't wait to hear that he or she is on the way."

"Me too. Everything is set for Sarah to run the gallery while I'm on maternity leave." Paige picked up a cloth off the counter and wiped down the tables. "Piper is so excited to meet her sister or brother."

"I bet." Callie took another sip of tea and felt like sticking her tongue out. "I should get going. I have errands to run. Then Marcus will drive me back to the house."

"Are you okay, Auntie?" Paige's brow furrowed as she peered down at Callie.

"Fine as rain in October."

No reason to dump her worries about an overtaxed heart or about lifestyle changes on her niece. She'd go home and read the pamphlet and check out some websites like the doc recommended. The dieting business was her concern. No one else's.

Later, in front of an apple display inside Lewis's Super, she scowled, perusing a pile of Fuji apples. Never her favorite fruit, she passed by the red and golden apples and grabbed a cluster of green grapes instead. She located a stack of carrots and then chose a few to be cut up for snacks. Although not appealing to her, they'd make a healthy alternative to the cinnamon roll. Why couldn't the colorful fruits and veggies look as appetizing as pastries?

A large brick of cheese was what she needed. She'd melt cheddar and dip veggies in the softened cheese. She wouldn't mind the raw vegetables so much then. Rats! Cheese probably wasn't on the approved list of foods. If it tasted good, it was bad for her, right?

Absorbed in her frustrations and hunting for a yummier-sounding vegetable and failing, she turned and ran smackdab into James Weston. Why did she have to crash into the very man she had avoided, and craved seeing, and hoped to marry, every day since her twelfth birthday?

"Cal! Excuse me." Even more handsome with his cheeks hueing burgundy, James stepped back and adjusted his derby hat.

She had the strongest urge to straighten his hat for him. Maybe run her fingers through his white silky-looking hair. Silly infatuations.

"Sorry. I wasn't watching where I was going." Callie inspected a head of broccoli as if the cruciferous vegetable fascinated her. She'd do anything to not meet James's gaze right now. Otherwise, he'd surely recognize the attraction she carried for him like a banner.

"No problem."

Her skin tingled with the throaty sound of his voice.

At the spinach section, they both reached for a bundle of vegetables at the same time, their hands bumping into each other's. Callie pulled her hand back. So did James.

"What's this? Are you going healthy, Cal?"

He didn't have to act quite so shocked! She didn't eat unhealthy food all the time.

"What if I am?" She heard the gruff tone of her voice. The man set off her emotions faster than any other human, other than her brother, Pauly. Here she hoped to shop discreetly and get away from the fresh veggie section without anyone noticing her. James not only saw her fruit and vegetable selection but teased her about it!

"I didn't mean anything personal by it." He tipped his hat toward her then scurried away like she was a rabid dog who might bite him.

She didn't want to talk with him about her food choices, anyway. What she ate was none of his business!

However, she felt remorseful for snapping at him. There was a time how she spoke to him wouldn't have mattered to her at all. She yelled at him plenty of times when they were young. Back then, he ignored her. So if she lambasted him, she would have been proud of it. But in the last year or so, things were changing between them. Snail slow. Yet whenever she and James were in the same room, the atmosphere seemed to shimmer with expectation, hope, or desire.

A ridiculous thought, right? It must be her imagination. After fifty years of being gaga over the man, and him doing a big fat nothing, why would he be interested in her now? Just some girlish dreams that would never come true.

She sighed.

Ever since the big oaf helped renovate the project house, he'd been spending more time with the family at holiday dinners and get-togethers. It was hard for her to avoid him then. Harder still when she said careless words and had to eat crow and apologize to him.

Callie and James both ended up in the same checkout aisle. Her cheeks flamed hot. Her heart pounded out a staccato rhythm.

"Sorry." She glanced at him. "I didn't mean to snap at you back there."

"Rough day?" He pushed his glasses up the bridge of his nose and didn't look directly at her.

"Yeah. Something's on my mind. Has me on edge."

"Care to talk about it?"

"Not really." Why would he ask that? Like she wanted to discuss personal things with him? Namely, what the doctor told her? No thanks!

After she paid for her groceries, she shot Marcus a text letting him know she was ready to be picked up. Outside, she waited for him in front of the store, grocery bags in hand.

James strolled up to her, two grocery bags slung over his arms. "I've been wondering about something."

"What's that?"

His speaking to her felt odd, given their history of noncommunication.

"What's happening between us?" he asked softly.

She whirled around toward him so fast, she nearly gave herself whiplash. "What's happening between us?" She gawked at him, unable to move, shock holding her feet to the pavement. What in the world? If James thought something was happening between them, maybe it wasn't all her imagination!

Marcus pulled up in his navy Lexus. Saved by the Uber driver!

"Sorry. This is my ride."

"Oh, uh, sure." James's face turned that burgundy hue again, making him look like a boat captain with the wind blowing against his cheeks. He clasped her elbow gently. "Cal, I'd like us to talk about what I asked." He coughed like he felt nervous mentioning it again. "I've been thinking about, well, about us growing up. About your being Paul's sister—" He shrugged like that explained everything.

Why was he talking to her like this? When did he ever speak so forthrightly to her? And in front of the grocery store where anyone walking by might hear? Callie checked over her shoulder. Patty from the hardware store caught her gaze, her eyebrow pulsing up. Did her friend wonder what private conversation might be going on between her and James?

Just peachy.

"You ready, Miss Callie?" Marcus loaded up her groceries into the trunk of his car, then held the back passenger door open for her.

"Yes. Thanks, Marcus." She climbed into the transport vehicle and glanced up at James. "We'll talk later, I assume?"

"You can count on it." A warm smile crossed his mouth, heating up her emotional core.

She smiled back at him like a blooming teenager! Ninny.

Don't you dare go daydreaming about him! Don't think of him as handsome and the only man in the world for you, either.

Even with her disparaging thoughts, as the car pulled away from the curb, Callie kept her gaze fixed on James Weston until Marcus drove out of the parking lot. James really thought there was something going on between them? Even imagining such a possibility caused her heart to race for the moon. What if he liked her as she'd dreamed about him doing all these years?

Chapter Three

The next day Callie sat at the dining room table picking at two bland, saltless scrambled eggs and a hand-sized cluster of grapes. The scent of Kathleen's bacon, fried potatoes, and French toast from earlier hung in the air like a bouquet of deliciousness. Callie would have preferred a breakfast like that.

Instead, the nearly tasteless eggs and grapes mocked her. *You'll never get to have scrumptious food again! You're doomed to blandness! How will you survive without sugar?*

She put a bite of eggs into her mouth and chewed slowly. Then imagined herself gagging.

Why was she letting the doctor dictate how she ate? Callie shoved the fork tines back and forth over the surface of the eggs, her annoyance getting the better of her. She groaned loudly.

"Callie, dear, what's gotten into you?" Kathleen, her seventy-year-old housemate, shuffled into the room. Her long white hair almost glowed in the morning light coming through the bay window. "This doesn't look like your kind of breakfast. What's going on?"

Callie didn't want to explain. Didn't want anyone knowing about the crossroads she was at with her health. Being under doctor's orders to make better food choices was a private matter. However, the quartet of ladies—Bess, the mayor of Basalt Bay; Kathleen, the oldest of their group and a mosaic artist; Sarah, the youngest and a widow; and Callie—living in the project house had been through so much together, not telling them seemed too secretive. How could she even pull it off? She wasn't about to hide in her bedroom during meals. This dieting was already a pain in the neck, and she'd barely started!

"Are you okay?" Kathleen gave her a one arm hug. "You seem down in the dumps."

"Who wouldn't be?"

"Tell me. What's wrong?" Kathleen dropped her slender form into the chair next to Callie. Had she been on a diet a day in her life?

"Doc says I have to lose weight." There, she said the detestable words. "Change your lifestyle, or else!" She mimicked the doctor's tone of voice, exaggerating a little.

"Getting healthy is always a wise decision."

Callie eyed her eggs with distaste. "Not feeling it today."

"I suppose not. But it could be worse."

"How's that?"

"Remember the grapefruit fad? I tried that one." Kathleen chuckled. "And the diet where you don't eat fats? Did that too."

"Same here." Callie rocked her thumb toward herself, thankful for Kathleen's understanding. "And the milkshake breakfasts that tasted like cardboard?"

"Uh-huh. And the spinach and kale diet." Kathleen grimaced. "I had stringy green stuff dangling between my teeth for weeks."

Callie gazed at Kathleen with new appreciation. "Why did you participate in those weight-loss schemes when you are so slim?"

"Because I didn't like what I saw in the mirror. The imperfections." Kathleen shrugged then lowered her shoulders slowly. "Low self-esteem. Extremely low."

"You and me both. I gave up on diets."

"So did I." Kathleen smoothed her hands over the tabletop. "I threw my energy into art. Tried paint throwing, woodworking, small-sculpture welding, PVC pipe furniture, and rock art. Finally, I attempted mosaics. Fell head over heels in love with it."

"I didn't know you were into fads." Callie sipped her sugarless tea then pushed the glass away.

"I don't talk much about my years of being dissatisfied with myself." She clasped Callie's hand for a moment. "But the unhappy time was a part of my journey. Aren't we all on one?"

"I guess."

"What about your journey, my dear? Why are you doing this?" Kathleen swayed her delicate-looking hands toward Callie's plate. "Are you going to be a more conscientious eater so you can become strong and healthy? If so, good for you! Dive into it. Embrace it. Let your wholesome eating become the fabric of your journey."

"Embrace tasteless food?" Callie smirked. "All to appease a nosy doctor?"

"Not for the doctor. For you, my friend. To live your best life now and in the future." Kathleen clasped her hands together. "What do you love about your life already?"

"I don't know. I haven't thought about it."

"Think about it, my dear. Live your life so you love it!"

Interesting notion. What had she even enjoyed about her life up to this point? She knew what she hated. She was unmarried. Didn't have kids. Was overweight. Had a tired heart. Was lonely. Even Kathleen commented about her being down in the dumps.

"Callie, what do you want to do for the next thirty years?"

"Thirty years!" She'd be ninety-three. She took a long breath, fighting the tension that rose easily in her chest. Didn't the doctor warn her about keeping her stress levels low? "Try five. Maybe, ten years."

"All right. That's a good starting place. What do you want to do for the next ten years?"

"If I could choose—"

"You can if you start today!"

Kathleen's determined tone caught Callie by surprise. Usually her friend was soft-spoken and didn't make any waves. In fact, she seemed completely content with her life and her art.

"It isn't like you had a death warning, right?" Kathleen leaned closer. "Did you?"

"The doctor was frank about me needing to make changes in my diet and exercise routine, or else!"

Kathleen patted her hand. "Then you are blessed. You have time to prioritize. A lot of folks don't get a warning. Focus on what you love about you. On what you want to do with the energy and beauty of life you still get to live." She stood suddenly. "I think I'll have some tea like you're having."

"Without sugar, you mean?"

"That's right. I'm fixing mine that way too!"

"You don't have to do that."

"I want to be healthier also."

While Kathleen fixed her tea, Callie pondered her question. What did she love about herself? About her life?

She'd sold her house and moved to the project house with Kathleen and Bess—a huge step. The three of them agreed to use the spare bedrooms for women who might need some encouragement or help along life's way. So far, they'd welcomed Ruby, Callie's nephew's wife; Sarah, a widow who still lived with them; Alison, a newspaper reporter who later married into the family; and Teal, Forest's sister who was separated from her husband. Each time they opened their doors to someone, Callie enjoyed offering advice and trying to encourage the women. Serving others made her feel good about herself too, like she was being useful in the world.

What else did she want to do with her life?

An image of James standing in front of Lewis's Super yesterday came to mind. Sweet, handsome James. What *was* happening between them? Maybe if she got to the bottom of that, she'd discover what she wanted to do next in her life.

Chapter Four

Callie enjoyed not owning a car or having to worry about a car payment and insurance. She rarely traveled far from Basalt Bay anyway. When she lived in town, she was within walking range of most places. Since moving out to the project house farther south of town, she had to rely on friends with vehicles or else call Marcus to come get her. But she still preferred those options to the headache of vehicle upkeep.

After the Uber ride to her brother's house, she stood on the front porch of their childhood home, hand raised but not knocking. This was the same door she ran in and out of a million times when they were kids. The same one facing James's house on the other side of the street. How many times did she sit on this porch hoping for a glimpse of her brother's cute but annoying friend? She glanced over her shoulder now in case James might be outside in his front yard. He wasn't.

Probably for the best. She didn't need the distraction of watching him, wondering what he meant about something happening between them. Did he want something more to happen? Was that what he was asking her?

She gulped. Even in her wandering thoughts, James was a distraction. She must focus on what she came here to do. This visit was about her talking with Pauly. Getting some things aired between them.

She knocked firmly on the door. She didn't have a timid bone in her body, so she wouldn't cower before her older brother no matter how gruff he appeared today. She was struggling with abstaining from sugar. Abstaining from bitterness and long-held grudges might be harder.

Kathleen's question about how she wanted to spend the rest of her life had been churning in her thoughts. After some inner reflection, she decided on one thing. Making amends with Pauly topped her list. But thanks to his pigheaded stubbornness, resolving their issues might be tougher than drinking a gallon of unsweetened tea in one setting!

Finally, the door squawked open. Pauly's face blanched. "What on earth? Why are *you* here?" His shoulders bunched up to his ears. His scowl made deep creases around his eyes.

"I stopped by to talk with you. Are you going to let me in?" Speaking just as gruffly as he did, she nodded toward the two rocking chairs. "Or shall we sit here on the porch?"

Her brother rolled his eyes like he wanted to show her he didn't care a nickel about what she came by to say. Too bad. Let him stand there all day rolling his eyes, she wouldn't budge. She came to talk. They were going to talk!

She tapped her foot on the floorboards. The thick-soled shoes she wore made a thumping sound against the wood. "Well? I don't have all day."

"That's what I thought you did have. All day to sit around gabbing with your gossiping friends and talking about everyone who breathes in Basalt Bay." He itched the front of his stained holey T-shirt.

Oh, he was grumpy! And he looked as unkempt and unshaven as he was mean.

Callie clenched her jaw, feeling like her internal temperature was skyrocketing. "I didn't come here to fight with you, Pauly Cedars. But you make me want to fight with you, so help me!" She clenched her right fist next to her pants, not showing him the movement. Although, she'd like to wave her fist beneath his nose. Maybe give him a black eye. That would show him.

"I guess we'll keep our discussion outside, then." Huffing, Pauly exited the house and shut the door firmly behind him like he thought she might try sneaking in behind his back. Seeing him act that way, she was tempted to do that very thing. "What do you want this time?"

"I'll have a seat if we're going to chat out here." She dropped down onto one of the rockers, glad the one that broke beneath her last year was gone. "I'd ask for a glass of sweet tea, but I'm refraining, so don't bother."

"Refraining from sweet tea? Hard to believe," Pauly said in a growly tone. He crossed his arms and stared down at her like a judge might do to a criminal. "Why aren't you drinking sweet tea?"

"Are you going to take a seat? I came to talk with you. Not pinch my neck staring up at you like you're the lord of the castle." Not that she felt the least bit intimidated by him.

"Good grief, woman! Can't you be civil?"

"Not with you standing over me like I'm a serf, your lordship." She gnawed on her inner cheek, craving a large glass of sweet tea more and more by the second. Stress about her relationship with Pauly always made her thirsty for the sugary drink. "Well?" she said, hearing the harping tone in her voice but not subduing it.

Groaning, Pauly dropped into the other rocker. "Happy?" He stared hard in the direction of the sea as if looking at a scenic view. But she knew he was staring at James's house, since the seascape was blocked by his house on the other side of the street. Maybe Pauly wished his buddy were here chatting with him instead of his pesky sister. "So, what's this about? I have things to do."

"Missing your TV show? The latest commercials?" Callie glared at him, taking in his slouching posture. "Can't a sister want to spend time with her brother?"

Slapping his palms over his knees, he started to stand. "If that's all you came here to say—"

"Wait!" She clasped his wrist. At his glare, she quickly released it. "Please. I didn't mean to sound so rude. Honestly, you just make me so—"

"Fine. What is it?" He leaned back into his chair and crossed his arms. "Spit it out so I can get back to—"

"Your TV program. I know. I know." Tension rippled through her. "Pauly, earlier this year we worked together to keep the girls safe, didn't we?" She tried appealing to his fatherhood and sense of decency.

"So what? That's over and done with. Just a bad memory."

"Okay, then. We both have hurts from our past. Things I said and did offended you. Things you said and did bugged me to death. We need to face whatever—"

"No, we don't. The past is the past. Leave it where it belongs." He uncrossed his arms and clenched the rocker arms. "I didn't invite you here to dig up old wounds."

"You don't invite me here at all! I wish you would. We need to talk." She huffed out a loud breath. When did having a conversation with her sibling become so laborious? "I want to make things right between us, you big goon. That's why I'm here."

Pauly groaned. At least he didn't get up and go inside, slamming the door behind him like he usually did.

"I realize I've, uh, stepped on your toes a few times over the years." She hated admitting anything to her brother. But sometimes she was over-zealous, pounding out her wishes to him.

"Stepped on them?" His chest swelled. No doubt, with pride and arrogance. "Is that what you call your cruel behavior?"

She flinched. Cruel?

Leaning toward her, he punctuated the air with his index finger. "Ever hear of the bull in a china shop?"

"Now, see here—"

"You're a dragon in the china shop! Blowing out fire and meanness."

Callie gaped at her brother's hurtful words. She was no dragon hissing out fire! His blame casting broke her heart. But relief swept through her, too. He was talking. They were communicating at some grumpy level of siblinghood.

"Regardless of what you think of me, I'm sorry for hurting you. Penny too." She gulped, swallowing down the urge to lambaste his late wife. Penny had caused enough harm in their family to last decades. And Pauly allowed the dissension and hurt feelings to happen. Although Callie bringing up the touchy subject wouldn't help. "At the time, I may have overreached, but I did what I felt was right."

"Right for whom? You?" Pauly's rage blasted out in his tone.

Callie rocked her chair as fervently as he rocked his, her heart pounding hard beneath her breastbone. She wanted to defend herself. To shout out that her brother wrongly married a woman on the rebound. A shrew-like artist.

But he was right, too. All their misunderstandings and problems were a part of their past. If she stirred up any of it, he'd walk into the house, slam the door, and lock it! Past experiences taught her that.

Taking a deep breath, she subdued her urge to yell and make him listen to her viewpoint. She did enough shouting at him over the years. She wanted to try living more peacefully now. More lovingly, if possible. "Back then, I was looking out for your kids," she said in a quiet voice. "I loved them. And you!"

"Love," he spat. "How you behaved wasn't loving or kind."

A sword of regret pierced her heart.

"Oh, Pauly. I am your sister. I have a right to be with my nieces and nephew. You tried to stop me from being there for them. I couldn't accept that!"

"There we have it. Your wishes. Your demands. You should go. I've heard enough." He shoved away from his chair and strode heavily across the porch. "Like I said, the past is over. Never speak of it again."

"If it's so over, why can't you forget and forgive? How about if we act like brother and sister now? Friends. Pals like when we were young. Pauly, talk to me. Let's get the festering wound exposed to the air." If only he would open up. Even if it hurt, she wanted to be close to her brother again. This didn't have anything to do with her health crisis, either. This had to do with two siblings who'd grown too far apart. Two siblings who needed each other.

"We talked. We're done. Goodbye."

"You are so prideful, brother!"

"You have a big mouth spewing hateful things, sister!" The floorboards creaked with each footstep until he stopped in front of the door.

She hated what he said. Hated that he might be right. "Just so you know, I'm coming back tomorrow."

"Why? To torment me?"

"If tormenting you makes you talk to me, then yes." She waited for him to meet her gaze. "I love you, Pauly Cedars. You are my only sibling. Please, talk with me. Then we can be finished talking about it."

"We're done with it now." He strode inside and slammed the door.

Callie let out the longest sigh she ever sighed. She stayed on the porch chair for another fifteen minutes, muttering silent prayers, begging God to heal the gaping wound between her and Pauly before it was too late.

Chapter Five

After her meager dinner of a tiny portion of meat, a salad with reduced-calorie dressing, and a glass of water, Callie called a meeting of the three homeowners. It was time for her to have a talk with Kathleen and Bess.

"What's this about? Is there a problem?" Kathleen asked with concern in her tone as she sat down at the dining room table.

"I want us to have a planning session." Nursing a headache that was probably due to her lack of sugar, Callie settled into her usual spot at the head of the table.

"What are we planning?" Bess sipped from a cup of hot tea that smelled sweetly delicious.

A stark craving rushed through Callie. She took a drink of her sugarless brew. Cringed. Would she ever adjust to the mediocre flavor?

"I want us to have a chat and make some plans for the old girl." She squinted up at the ceiling. "We've been in the project house for almost a year. I think we should discuss some of the things we hope to do here."

"Some of our goals have come to fruition." Kathleen smoothed her hand over the tabletop like a caress. "Sarah has blossomed and grown since she's been with us."

"True." Sarah seemed happy and content with her life at the project house and in Basalt Bay. She was one of their success stories. But that wasn't enough. Otherwise, why was Callie feeling dissatisfied? Why did it seem like something was unfinished? "Shouldn't we be doing more?"

"More?" Bess exchanged a look with Kathleen. "Goodness, I've been so busy at the mayor's office, if I've neglected our purpose here, I apologize."

"It's not that." Callie didn't mean to guilt anyone. She rubbed her temples. "Would you be all right with us meeting once a month and brainstorming about our goals?"

"Do you think we aren't being helpful like we hoped to be? Four women have stayed with us for varying lengths of time over the last year. What are you thinking of doing that we haven't already done?" Kathleen asked softly.

"Ever since the trial ended and everything just went back—"

"To normal?"

"Got boring?"

Bess and Kathleen asked simultaneously.

"Yes." Callie sighed and clasped her hands in her lap. "Since then, I've had an unrest I don't even understand. It's like a toothache. Or a headache. A painful reminder that I have something unfinished in my life."

Perhaps her health crisis was at fault. Accepting she might not get to enjoy the long life she hoped for was possibly making her yearn for things to happen faster. Like her failure at communicating with Pauly. Even though she sincerely tried, more internal hurts were stirred up. She should have been more patient and waited for the right timing.

"You're distressed about something." Kathleen met her gaze with a kind expression. "Why don't you share with us what's bothering you, dear?"

What was bothering her right now was a throbbing headache. She took another sip of her herbal tea. "When we joined up to renovate this house, we agreed it would be a place of helping other women who were down on their luck, or in need of assistance or a refuge."

"Isn't that what we've been doing?" Bess linked her fingers together against the tabletop.

"With Sarah, yes. And a few others. But where do we go from here?" Callie met the other two women's gazes, hoping they felt the pull to do more like she did. "During the trouble in town at the beginning of the year, we banded together. We stood up for one another."

"Unity has continued in the town," Bess said confidently. "With the way the people voted me in with such a high percentage, our hometown is still pulling together."

"That's good. Real good." Callie heaved another sigh, trying to override her agitation and irritability. She had to do better at calming herself. "What are we doing to help others who are hurting or in a crisis now? What do we want to do better here?"

"Is this about what you want to do with the next ten years of your life?" Kathleen nodded slowly as if answering the question for her.

"Maybe. I feel an urge to get something meaningful accomplished. Or to feel useful." Callie swayed her hands toward the other ladies. "What do the three of us envision for the project house? Are we content with waiting for a person to knock on the door and say they need our help?" That wasn't what she wanted. She hated waiting!

"I'm working on my mosaics most of the time." Kathleen shrugged. "Selling my pieces in Paige's gallery gives me profound pleasure. But I still want to help others here too."

"I'm busy with my mayoral work," Bess said in a light tone of voice. "But I, too, agree with what we set out to do with this house. I admit I haven't thought much about it lately."

"So it's just me with this unrest." Callie swallowed the dryness in her throat with a slurp of tea. "I'm here. Doing n—"

"Don't you say 'nothing,'" Kathleen interjected. "You are of great value and immense importance to our family here."

Is that what this was about? Feeling undervalued? Unimportant? Surely, it was more than that.

"When we agreed to take in women, we felt like we were on a mission. I guess I don't want that feeling of meeting a need in someone's life to stop." Callie rotated her shoulders, trying to ease some tension.

"I agree." Kathleen nodded.

Bess smiled. "Me too."

"Where can we find someone else who needs our help enough to move in with us?" Kathleen patted Callie's hand. "The others found us. I thought God would send people our way in the same manner. In His time."

"Maybe that's what will happen again." Callie thought for a moment. "Or we might need to reach out to a person who's more aware of the needs in our community."

"Like whom?" Bess asked.

"Pastor Sagle, perhaps. He's acquainted with other ministers in neighboring towns, too."

"He'd be discreet." Bess nodded. "I'm glad you brought this to our attention, Callie."

"So, we agree that our mission to help ladies in need of a support system is still our goal?"

"Absolutely," Kathleen said.

"One hundred percent." Bess lifted her cup in a salute. "I'm all in."

"That's a relief to hear." Callie heaved a sigh. The burden on her spirit felt lifted. If not entirely gone, at least lighter.

Bess had her mayoral duties. Kathleen worked full time on her art. Getting the idea of extending hospitality and support to others off the ground would fall into Callie's lap. But that was okay. This would be her purpose. Her way of being a blessing to others with whatever time God gave her to live on this earth.

Chapter Six

"You haven't been in my office before, have you?" Pastor Sagle eyed Callie from across his messy desk. "What seems to be the problem?"

"Did I say there was a problem?" Why was he framing her visit in a negative light instead of a positive one?

"Well, no." Chuckling, the gray-haired pastor ran his hands over his thinning hair. "You said you had an important matter to discuss."

"So I do." Callie noticed the piles of papers on the pastor's desk, the slightly askew paintings on the wall, and the starkness of the dark bookshelves. The man needed a secretary. Or a housekeeper. "I've never been here before. It reminds me of a bear cave," she said with her usual bluntness. Then cringed. "Sorry. I'm trying not to be so abrasive."

Pastor Sagle laughed. "A cave sounds about right."

"I'll get right to the point." Callie took a quick breath, thankful last night's headache hadn't returned. "Bess, Kathleen, and I bought the old Peterson place with the intention of opening our doors to women in need of temporary housing or a refuge in life's storm."

"That sounds terrific." Pastor Sagle crossed his arms over the clutter on his desk. "Is there a problem with your plan?"

"I don't know what I expected. Maybe that God would shine a gigantic flashlight from women in dire circumstances right to our front door." She shrugged a couple of times. "That hasn't happened except for one person."

"Sarah." Pastor Sagle nodded. "She's been coming to our services with Kathleen."

"That's right. She's been with us about nine months. She works with Paige in the gallery. Is happier now than when we first met her."

"What you ladies have undertaken is admirable. Not everyone would open their home to a stranger the way you have." Pastor Sagle smiled as if he were proud of them.

Callie gnawed on her lower lip. "Thank you. However, we don't want accolades. What we need is your help."

"Help, how?"

"Are you in contact with anyone who might need a place of refuge? A woman, mind you, who might benefit"—Callie glanced toward the bookshelf, contemplating her next words—"by living with some ladies who'd encourage her and support her for a time. Maybe someone who's going through grief, a trauma, a divorce, or some other discouraging situation."

Pastor Sagle smoothed his palm over his chin that certainly needed a shave. "I'm not sure I—"

"I'm sorry to have wasted your time." *And mine.* Callie scooted forward in her chair, suddenly in a hurry to leave. "Maybe someone else would be better suited to assist us."

"Wait. Don't be so hasty."

"Then what?" If the pastor couldn't be of service, she'd try someone else. Maybe go to a homeless shelter in Florence or Coos Bay. Then she realized she was being impatient and irritable again. *Good night. Give the man a chance to put two thoughts together.*

"What you're suggesting sounds like a blessing to anyone in transition, recovery, or in need of help." Pastor Sagle linked his fingers together in a relaxed pose. "Someone did come to mind, but it's a private matter I recently learned about. It's complicated."

"Isn't it usually?" Callie clutched her purse strap.

"What would the sleeping arrangements be like?"

"What does that matter?" She squinted at him. "Second-floor guest room."

"I wondered about the stairs. Some folks might have difficulty climbing them."

"Oh. I understand. That's why I require the first-floor bedroom."

Pastor Sagle picked up a pen and tapped it on a notebook page. "Let me check in with another pastor, and I'll get back with you."

"All right. Thank you." Callie pushed up from her chair. "If you can help us reach out to someone, we'd appreciate it."

"Sure, sure." The pastor stood and shook her hand. "It's wonderful of you ladies to provide this kind of ministry. I admire you for it."

"Oh, well—" Heat rushed up her face. She wasn't used to such praise. "It's good for us to do meaningful things with our lives while we can."

"Absolutely. If everyone felt that way, imagine what the world might be like." He followed her to the door. "Thanks for stopping by. I'll be in touch."

"Thank you, Pastor."

If anyone had connections to other ministries along the western seaboard, Pastor Sagle did. But waiting was hard for Callie. It was a good thing she had another stop to make, or she might be tempted to go by the gallery for a pastry.

Pauly might not appreciate seeing her again so soon, but she warned him she'd be dropping by. She was determined to have an honest conversation with him, whether he liked it or not!

Chapter Seven

Fall meant two things to James Weston. One, get the plant beds ready for winter. Two, clean out the roof gutters. Neither were enjoyable chores. But like any other homeownership task, he did the work without complaining or thinking much about it. He enjoyed getting to work outdoors in the mild fall weather. He loved gardening. So the tasks didn't seem overly taxing.

As he stood on the ladder cleaning wet leaves out of the gutter at the front of the house, his gaze wandered across the street as it often did whenever there was activity at Paul's house. The lovely woman sitting on his friend's porch made him momentarily freeze, his hands extended midair. His throat went dry. He quickly adjusted his glasses so he could see her better.

Callie sat in the rocking chair on the front porch, rocking forcefully. Even from here, James saw that her grayish blue sweater brought out the silvery streaks in her short, multi-toned black and gray hair.

Was Paul avoiding her? Sometimes his buddy's head was as hard as a rock, especially where his sister was involved. James observed their lack of interaction enough times over the years—Callie coming by to visit Paul only to wind up sitting on the porch by herself.

Did she see him on the ladder? Should he wave? If he did, would he look like a fool, hoping for the attention of the girl next door?

Good grief! Of course he wanted to snag her attention. Why wouldn't he?

Back when he and Paul were kids, Callie was their shadow, always trailing them. They got pretty good at dodging her.

That wasn't the case now. James didn't want to avoid Callie Cedars. Lately, he was utterly captivated by her smile and sparkling eyes. The way she gnawed on her lower lip sometimes drew his attention to her mouth like a moth to a light. He was attracted to her in a way he had never been with any other woman before.

A couple of times he thought she might care for him too. That's why he mentioned it to her the other day at the grocery store. Not his wisest move. He should have stopped by the project house and had a discussion with her, instead of springing the question on her in a public place.

What was happening between them? He mulled the question over for a few moments. Were they falling for each other? Did he want Callie to notice him and be attracted to him?

In a heartbeat. In a nanosecond. In a breath when he had only one left.

He sighed.

Enough. He'd better finish the gutter and get off this ladder before he became distracted and slipped off. No need to make a spectacle of himself in front of Callie by freefalling through the air, especially with his bum knee.

Maybe after he was done with cleaning the gutter, he would saunter across the street as if he came over to talk with Paul. Then he'd sit down on the empty rocker and chat with Callie. That ought to surprise her.

Ten minutes later, he stood in his neighbor's yard. "Hey, Cal." He dipped his chin and stuffed his hands into his jacket pockets.

Her fervent chair rocking came to a halt. Face flushed, she smiled. "Why, hello, James."

He strode up the three stairs. Without waiting for an invitation, he plopped down on the other rocker. "Nice fall weather for this time of year, huh?"

"Sure is. I like our moderate weather by the coast. Always have."

"Yeah, me too. Can you imagine the heat folks have to endure in Arizona?"

"No, I can't."

Their chairs moved in a unified rhythm as if only one chair rocked on the porch instead of two. Ridiculously, his thoughts leaped to imagining their two hearts beating as one. Living their lives in sync with each other's.

Ah, Cal. If only you knew how much I like you.

"Where's Paul?"

"Oh, you know my brother." She shrugged deeply. "Stubborn. Mule headed. Determined to do things his way, and only his way."

"Sounds familiar." He chuckled.

The rockers made their dueling thumps against the floorboards, the sun shining down on them, the silence comfortable.

"Cal—"

"James—"

An awkward chuckling passed between them.

The door creaked open, and Paul trudged out of the house. "What's going on out here on my porch?"

"Your porch?" Callie's voice hit a high note. "You're living in Mama's house. This house is as much mine as yours. I'm certainly allowed to sit on the porch!"

"You always have to remind me about everything being yours, don't you?" Paul thrust his finger toward Callie. "If you wanted our parents' house so badly, you should have told me a lifetime ago. Then I would have moved out."

"I don't want the house, Pauly. You infuriate me to high heaven is all." Callie huffed. "Old habits die hard."

"Ain't that the truth?" Some of Paul's bluster seemed to evaporate.

Should James even be here? Maybe he was overstepping by hanging around during this brother-sister squabble. Although, he heard plenty of their arguments over the decades.

"What do you want?" Paul asked gruffly, not relenting on his grudge or his grumpy attitude. "And what are you doing here?" He glared at James as if he might be to blame for Callie's presence.

"Enjoying a respite and some good company. That against the law?" James felt a little riled himself. He didn't like Paul catching him with his sister and sneering at him. But he wasn't going to let the other man interfere with his romantic pursuits either.

Romantic pursuits? Was he finally admitting that he was pursuing Callie? Was he willing to be honest with her about it?

"Why would you want to sit out here with her? Come in the house and we'll shoot the breeze." Paul pivoted toward the door.

James didn't like Paul inviting only him inside. In fact, it seemed downright rude. "Fine as I am. Thank you."

Paul glared at him over his shoulder. "You're serious? You'd rather sit out here with her?"

Callie eyed James suspiciously too.

"I'm tired after climbing up and down the ladder cleaning the gutters. Thought I'd rest my knee. Chat a little. Then I might come inside." He felt a little stubborn about wanting to visit more with Callie. He could chat with Paul any ole time.

"Suit yourself." Paul pulled open the door.

"Oh, Paul. Aren't you forgetting someone?"

"Who's that?"

James tipped his head toward Callie.

"What about her?"

"She's your sister. Have a heart."

Scowling, Paul faced Callie. "You need some sweet tea before you leave?"

"Yes. Uh, no. A glass of cold water, please."

"Water? Since when do you drink water instead of sweet tea?"

"Since I'm changing a few things in my life. I told you I was abstaining!" She glared at him. "Do you have rude things to say about me drinking water now, too?"

"I might. You make me crazy." He tromped inside and slammed the door behind him.

"The feeling is mutual!" Callie called out.

James chuckled. "Nothing has changed between you two."

"I had my hopes up for about ten seconds there." A small smile crossed her mouth that he was finding himself more and more attracted to. "He's stubborn and set in his ways."

"He is?" James asked with a grin.

"Yes, he is. I might be too."

James enjoyed looking at her lips that spread evenly over her lovely teeth. What would it be like to kiss her? To hold her close? He felt like he swallowed a mouthful of cotton at the unexpected, yet welcome thoughts.

"Thanks for sticking up for me in front of Pauly. That was nice of you."

"He shouldn't treat you disrespectfully."

"Nothing new about that."

Their rocking duet resumed. Callie eyed him with something akin to admiration in her gaze. He liked the thought of her thinking fondly of him.

Paul returned and thrust out a glass of water toward Callie and handed one to James, even though he didn't ask for anything to drink. Dehydrated from his escapade with the ladder and cleaning the gutters, he drank down half the glass.

"So, why aren't you drinking sweet tea?" Paul asked, sounding less antagonistic than before.

"It's a private matter." Callie sipped her water, not guzzling hers like James did. "I won't be asking you to fix me any again."

"Never?" A dark expression crossed Paul's face. "Something wrong with you?"

James took a couple of glances at Callie. She looked normal to him. Same lovely face. Same sparkling eyes.

"If you must know, yes! My body is, well, never mind. It's none of your concern. Either of yours." Her face hued a deep pink.

"I'm your brother, so it is my concern!" Paul's voice rose.

"Like you care. Oh, you make me so mad."

"Likewise."

"Should I leave so you two can chat? Er, argue?" James dared to interject.

"No!"

"Of course not!"

"All righty then." He stared across the street toward his house. The old place could use a paint job. A porch swing would be nice.

"So, are you going to tell me what's going on with you or not?" Paul asked.

"Why do you care?"

"I just do!"

A groan rumbled from Callie. "Doc says to change my ways. Eat healthier. Walk more. So I'm trying. Not that I think eating better will work." Her chair rocking slowed down.

Concern filtered through James. If the doctor said she should change her ways, what was going on with her? He hoped Paul pushed for answers so he could hear her response, too.

"That's all I'm going to say about it, so don't pester me."

"Your business is your business," Paul said like he had a chip on his shoulder. "Just like my business has always been my business."

"Oh, here we go." Callie crossed her arms. "I've apologized about the past, so get over it. I'm your sister. We're both getting old. Let's start acting like siblings again before it's too late. Is that so hard?"

"Yes, it is." Paul clenched his teeth. Then he stomped into the house and slammed the door.

"That went well, don't you think?" Callie asked with a half-teasing tone.

James didn't answer. He continued rocking, speculating about her state of health.

"Sorry you heard our discussion," she said quietly.

"Nothing I haven't heard before. Other than what you said about the doctor's warning. Are you okay?"

"I just need to make some changes." After a pause, she said, "Paul's lucky to have a friend like you for all these years."

"Thanks." He felt the same way about Paul. Buddies for life.

They sat in companionable silence, both rockers making a rubbing noise on the wooden floor. James enjoyed sitting next to Callie as if they were already courting. But, of course, that wasn't the case, *yet.*

Chapter Eight

The next day, Paisley's unexpected visit to the project house brightened Callie's day immensely, especially since she brought one-month-old Tanner with her. But when her niece dropped onto the sofa and sighed, sounding exhausted, concern filled her.

"What's wrong, Paisley Rose?" She sat on the other side of the couch and shuffled sideways to see her niece and the baby.

"I'm fine, Auntie." Paisley yawned. "Not getting much sleep. Just life with a newborn. Now, I'm here to ask if you are all right. Are you okay?"

"Me?" Oh, brother. News traveled faster than lightning in Basalt Bay. "What have you heard?"

"A few people texted me about you."

"A few? Those gossiping—"

"Paige, for starters. And Dad."

"Pauly?" Callie clasped her hands to her chest. Her brother worrying even slightly about her touched her heart.

"What did the doctor tell you?" Paisley rocked Tanner back and forth.

Ignoring her question, Callie held out her hands toward the baby. "May I hold him?"

"Of course." Paisley scooted closer and gently handed the baby over to Callie. She rested her hand an extra moment on the sleep sack surrounding Tanner's legs.

"He's so precious. He favors Peter."

"Really? You think so?" Paisley smiled warmly at her son.

"Mmhmm." Callie stared at the sweet angelic face of the boy, imagining what Peter looked like as a baby. She smoothed the back of her fingers across the baby's soft skin. The closest she came to motherhood was watching her brother's three kids growing up. Then Paige's daughter, Piper. Now, she felt the same way about this guy.

With two more family members expecting, she would have more chances to cuddle and love on babies in the future. Even if they weren't her grandchildren, she couldn't love them more if they were hers. She wanted to be a real part of their growing-up years. A loving, doting great aunt. In that moment, her current health situation and the chance she wouldn't be around for these little ones hit her like a baseball bat against the side of her head.

So, what was she going to do about it?

When Tanner reached his teenage years, and even when he graduated from college, she wanted to be here observing his accomplishments, cheering for him, and giving him hugs. According to Doctor Isabel, that meant making radical eating and exercise changes. Wasn't it worth whatever struggle and sacrifice she must endure to improve her health so she could live longer?

Inwardly, she groaned.

If she was going to commit to the diet and eat less sugar, she'd have to be more self-disciplined. Earlier today she wanted a blueberry scone so badly she almost caved in and ate one. Fortunately, Paisley dropped by and distracted her.

"What are you thinking of with such a sober expression, Auntie?"

"About how I want to watch this baby grow up." She kissed his warm forehead.

"You will." Paisley set her palm on Callie's wrist. "You will, right?"

"If I take my medicine. Eat healthier and exercise more. Lose some weight."

"Sounds like a good plan." Paisley pressed her lips together. "Does this mean there's something seriously wrong with you?"

"The old ticker is tired. Just like me," she said lightly. "I'm overweight. Nothing new about that."

"Oh, Auntie." Paisley's face crumpled.

"I didn't say I was dying, Paisley Rose. There's time to make changes. But I have been disgruntled about it for the last few days. Not trying very hard."

"Not you!" Paisley teased.

"My being mad at the world has to stop too." Callie heaved a sigh. "Too much stress is bad for me."

"What are you mad about?" Paisley asked softly like she knew she was treading on thin ice.

The baby fussed, and Callie passed him back to his mama without answering her question. She'd shared enough personal stuff. She enjoyed watching Paisley settle Tanner into nursing. Enjoyed the contented look on her niece's face as she took care of her baby, even if she was tired.

Everything felt right with the world around Callie, yet unrest churned within her like an egg beater churning oatmeal. She didn't like change. Usually dug in her heels. But it seemed she was swimming in a bog of change.

Kathleen's suggestion about embracing her life flashed like a neon sign in her brain. Embrace the annoying parts of her life right alongside the good things? How in the world was she going to do that?

Chapter Nine

Later in the day, a strong knocking at the door tore Callie away from hunting through the cookbooks she'd spread out on the kitchen island. If she was going to throw herself into eating healthier, she must come up with some tasty, enticing recipes. Since every one of the options she found called for ingredients she didn't have, she was more frustrated than when she started looking. Why weren't these recipes simpler?

Opening the door, she found James standing there, wringing his hat between his hands.

"I didn't expect to see you here." Her irritation with the recipes was probably why she spoke so crankily to him. Or maybe it was the sweet cravings she struggled to subdue that made her irritable.

"No, I don't suppose you did." He glanced at the floor, out toward the trees, and at the sky before glancing back in her direction. "I have something I want to pass by you."

"Why not call?" Ugh. Why did she have to act so unfriendly to him? "Sorry. Come in." Huffing, she backed up. "You might as well tell me what brought you out here." She waved him toward the kitchen. "Want some coffee or tea?"

"Coffee would be nice." He still twisted the hat in his hands, obviously nervous about being here, or talking to her. "Just black."

"Okay." Callie's heart hammered slightly out of rhythm. Being around James caused that to happen more often. She piled up her cookbooks and then relocated them to the counter. She fixed a cup of coffee for him and poured hot water over her already used tea bag.

James didn't speak until they were settled on stools at the wooden island. "You're probably wondering why I'm here."

Of course, she was. But she didn't comment lest she sound unfriendly again. Sitting together like this, just as friends, was nice. Being near James was something she could get used to. Something she could embrace.

"I was thinking about your"—he cleared his throat—"decision to live healthier."

He came all this way to discuss *that* with her? Didn't she tell him and Pauly her health didn't fall under their purview? Her temperature rose like a fire burned beneath her feet. Her stress reaction went bonkers too easily. She forced herself to breathe deeply, then slower.

"Are you okay, Cal?" James's eyes glistened.

"Don't look at me like I'm dying. I'm not there yet."

"Did I say anything about you dying?" He sounded perturbed. "Why do you take offense with everything I say?"

"Me?" She didn't take offense. She took anger. Fury, sometimes. "Pauly's the one who takes offense at everything. Not me."

"Right." James sipped his coffee.

"What does that mean?" She felt the urge to kick his shin like she did when she was seven and he laughed at her. When he didn't answer, she gritted her teeth. "You were about to explain. Why did you stop by, other than to pester me?"

James chuckled, annoying her more.

Even with her exasperation, she noticed the way his smile fit his face perfectly. She appreciated that he still had enough white hair to comb stylishly. And even with glasses on, the way his gaze twinkled with sparks of light in her direction stirred up butterfly wings in her stomach. She still felt attracted to this man after all these years and all the times she felt rejected by him. Too bad things didn't turn out differently between them forty years ago.

What if things changed between them, now, like James implied? Like she imagined a few times over the last year? Hope spread through her like a warm blanket settling over her shoulders. Did he have romantic feelings toward her? Maybe that's what he meant when he asked what was happening between them.

Meeting his gaze, her heart beat harder. "You said you wanted to talk with me." She softened her tone. "What is it?"

"You want Paul to treat you nicer, right?"

Her brother wasn't the one she wanted treating her nicer right now. Nor was he the one she wanted to discuss.

"What's it to you?" she said more sharply than she intended.

James stared at her with an indulgent look.

"Fine." Callie huffed. "Yes. Of course, I'd like my brother to treat me like a sister who he cares about instead of someone he barely tolerates."

"Exactly as I thought." James took a swig of his coffee. "I've watched you two boxing around each other, emotional and psychological dukes raised, for decades." He set down his cup with a soft clunk. "I think I have a solution."

"You have a solution for Pauly and me?"

This ought to be good. She and Pauly were at each other's throats for forty years and suddenly James had the answer to their problems?

"My brother and I have hardly spoken to each other in decades. Now you have the remedy for us?"

"That's right. Let's get married!"

The air whooshed from her lungs. "W-what? What did you say?" She gripped the edge of the wooden island so she wouldn't fall off her stool. Her heart pounded chaotically.

"Let's get married! That's my solution."

"James Weston, are you off your rocker?"

"Took you by surprise, didn't I?" He chuckled.

Oh. He was teasing her. What a cruel joke!

"I'll say. Big joke. Ha ha." She stood and promptly whisked their cups to the sink. Enough foolish talk. Suggesting they get married? How absurd!

"I talk about marriage, and you load the dishwasher?" James stood too. "I mean it, Cal. What if we went ahead and married each other?"

"Are you drinking? Inhaling fumes?" She whirled around fast, hands clenched, ready to punch him in the gut. How dare he ridicule her like this! "Did you fall and hit your head?"

"You want Paul to let go of the past, right?"

"Why are you butting into our business? Why the marriage nonsense?"

"I'm his best friend. You're his sister. If you and I got married, he'd have to accept you as his friend's wife. Me as his brother-in-law." He splayed out his hands. "Makes sense, doesn't it?"

"No! It makes zero sense. You should leave, now." If he didn't go fast, she would throw a dirty dish at him.

For James to propose to her under false pretenses, he must not have a clue how she felt about him for fifty years. Was his proposing marriage a massive gag that he and Pauly could roar in laughter about later?

Anger and humiliation simmered to a boiling point within her. "I have no idea why you came here or why you asked me what you asked me, but please leave. Go before I say words we'll both regret!" She thrust her rigid finger toward the door. "I mean it. Go!"

Instead of leaving, James engulfed her hand between both of his, stroking her fingers gently. The movement mesmerized her. Heat pulsed through every spot where his finger pads brushed against her skin.

Please, stop, she silently begged him.

"We like each other, don't we?" His whispery voice wooed her. "We enjoy talking together. We're friends. We get along."

"So what?" She jerked her hand away from his.

He must be talking about a marriage of companionship, not love. Was he that lonely?

"Cal?"

"You've hardly noticed I existed for fifty years. Now you want to marry me? Goodbye, James."

"I like you. We're both lonely."

So she was right.

He dared to stroke her cheek. His index finger brushing against her skin made heat infuse her face. "If we were married, you'd live across the street from Paul. Interact with him daily. Hourly, if you want. It would be like old times. You, me, and Paul being pals. Playing cards. Watching TV. Eating meals together."

"When did we ever do those things together? You and Pauly were pals. You two! Not me." She exhaled a breath, her chest deflating from bruised pride.

"Promise me you'll think about it, okay?"

"You might be an old coot, James, but you aren't this daft!" She pointed toward the door again. "Go, before I give you a piece of my mind you'll wish you never heard."

"Why are you so angry with me?" He plopped his hat on his head. "I asked you to marry me. Not go to war."

"You have no idea what you've done." He must be clueless about her, about women in general, to make such a cavalier suggestion. Callie opened the door forcefully. "Leave before I kick you out on your backside!"

"Callie—"

"James, so help me—"

"I'm going. I'm going."

As soon as his shoes hit the porch, she slammed the door, making the whole thing rattle.

Men! How could he offer her a token wedding proposal? Like that would salvage her and Pauly's relationship? Preposterous!

Her chest heaved. Humiliation burned hot within her. James's proposal stripped her down to bare emotions, exposing every romantic and loving thought she carried for him for five decades. For the slightest instant, tears burned in her eyes. But she was too angry and mortified to let even one drip down her cheek.

James Weston had declared war. She'd never forgive him. Never forget his arrogant, haphazard mockery of a marriage proposal!

Chapter Ten

"What have I done?" Running his hand over his forehead, James moaned. "I asked Callie to marry me on a whim. I've ruined everything." Shoulders hunched, he clutched the steering wheel so tightly his fingers ached as he drove home. Embarrassment and regret heated up his face, ears, and neck. He felt like he might be sick before he reached his driveway.

For a few minutes, he'd thought his idea amounted to brilliance. Marrying Callie solved everything! She and Paul would be close enough to work out their differences. James was lonely and in need of companionship. They were both single. Why did Callie get so angry? Didn't she care for him at all?

Perhaps, he misinterpreted the glances they exchanged since she moved out to the project house. He thought the attraction went both ways. Maybe his romantic sensors were too dull after so many years of bachelorhood.

He blamed his inexperience at romance for his inept proposal. He rarely dated in his whole life. How was he supposed to know the right things to say to a woman?

With the warm feelings he had toward Callie, he assumed she felt the same way. He thought they could enjoy a marriage based on friendship and mutual companionship, at least in the beginning. Apparently, he thought wrong. He stunk up the proposal. Did he suggest that Callie marry him to work things out with her brother? Of course that was a revolting idea!

Groaning, he parked in his driveway and stared at his house. This place had always been home. But lately when he ate a solitary meal, watched TV alone, and occasionally talked to himself, the ache of loneliness made him want to change some things.

He wanted a wife. He wanted Callie. Although he didn't grasp the depth of his feelings for her yet, she was the one he wanted to live with for the rest of his days. If he had twenty years left, he wanted to spend them with her. If he had ten years to live out this adventure called life, he wanted her as his journey partner.

But he had his chance to explain his true feelings and blew it! He shouldn't have made the offhanded proposal. He didn't mean to sound disingenuous or disrespectful to her. He was being honest. Paul would have to accept Callie and be kinder to her if she and James were wed. Their daily interactions would force that to happen. But he hadn't been upfront with her about how he felt, either.

Good night! He barely knew how he felt himself.

James wiped his hand over his smooth face. Even though he was retired, he still shaved daily like he did for the job for so many years. Did Callie like guys with scruffier faces? On movies and TV shows, men wore more facial hair than he did. Maybe he should try it and find out if her eyes brightened, or if she smiled at him more.

But why bother? She rejected his offer! Offer? Is that all he gave her? An offer he thought she couldn't refuse? Talk about bland, unromantic, and stupid.

He should apologize. He started up the engine again. Then shut off the motor. He'd give her time to cool off. Time for him to think, too. Come up with a better plan.

What if he confessed to Paul about asking his sister to marry him? What if he asked for Paul's blessing? Callie would probably accuse him of interfering.

Yeah, she'd be right. James fought a grin. He might be getting himself into more hot water with her. But talking with his buddy sounded like the best next step, even if Paul was Callie's brother.

James and Paul spent most of their lives traipsing back and forth between their houses. Paul's place had been a second home to James, except when Penny lived there. Then he hadn't felt as welcome. During Paul's married years, he came over to James's house often, the two of them grilling on the back deck, or shooting the breeze away from Penny and the kids.

At Paul's front door, James knocked then walked in like he usually did.

"Hey, James." Paul sat draped over his chair, staring at the television.

"So, you're watching your favorite soap opera."

"How many times do I have to tell you it isn't a soap opera?" Paul clicked the remote pause button and the loud noise evaporated. The screen showed a doctor and nurse in a flirting pose. "Have a seat. What's going on?"

Settling onto a brightly colored chair, James crossed his knee over the other one and swung his foot as if he had all day to dawdle. "I came by to tell you something. I asked Callie to marry me."

"What?" Paul jerked forward in his chair, eyes bugging.

"I asked your sister to marry me," he announced boldly. "May I have your blessing?"

"My blessing? Of all the—" Paul leaped to his feet. He slapped both palms over his face like the movement might erase what James said.

James nearly guffawed at his friend's overreaction.

Paul must have seen the smirk on his face. He lowered his hands. "You're teasing me! This is a joke, right?"

"Not a joke." James stood too.

"You're standing here telling me you asked Callie, my sister, to marry you?" Paul shouted. "After all these years? After the way she's—"

"She's what? What are you saying?" James's throat felt tight. He wanted to unfasten the top button on his shirt, but he didn't move an inch. What was Paul implying?

"Are you in love with her?"

"I wouldn't say love, exactly." James coughed and bumbled over the words. "What? Don't you want me for a brother-in-law?"

Paul rubbed his hand over his chin that needed a good shave. "Better you than anyone else. But marrying Callie? Seriously?"

"Remember when the three of us used to pal around? Your little sister always trailed after us like we needed her. Those were the days."

"You asked her to marry you for old time's sake?" Paul snorted. "You and I ignored her most of the time. Talk about a nuisance! My sister is the poster girl for the Most Annoying Women in the World Club."

"Now, Paul." James didn't mean to stir up more trouble between siblings. But Paul's comment made him think. Did he ever talk to Callie during their growing up years? Did he interact with her in high school? After her graduation, she and Paul were in conflict most of the time. "You might be right. However, I'm noticing her now."

"Hard not to with her bossing everyone around. Sticking her nose in where it doesn't belong. Gossiping woman." Paul dropped down on his chair and stared at the TV.

"So"—James plopped back down on his chair, elbows on his knees—"are you going to give me your blessing to go after your sister?"

"Go after her? You said you didn't love her."

"Do you mind if I try to get her to marry me?"

"What's so wrong with your life that you have to chase after my sister?" Paul growled out.

"Sharing my life with someone sounds nice." A slow smile crossed James's mouth. "I never had the chance to marry like you did. Don't you think it's about time I did?"

"No! Without love, be thankful you never married. Minus the kids who came from our union, I regret marrying outside of love."

Paul and Penny didn't have a love match, James knew that much. Paul married on the rebound. Yet they had three great kids. Grandkids too. James didn't have any of that.

"So, you asked Callie to marry you." Paul made a tsk-tsk sound. "What did she do?"

"Got mad."

"Of course, she did!"

"But I'm not giving up." James straightened his coat, determination filling him. "I plan to try again. Would you mind if Cal and I got married?"

"Yes! No. Not if it's what you want. But I can't imagine you two together after all these years." Paul shuddered as if repulsed by the idea.

"What about you?" James pointed toward the silent television. "Are you going to spend the rest of your life sitting in front of a screen, caught up in other folks' romances?"

"What else would I do?"

"Don't we still have lives to live?"

"Do we? No one comes by unless they want something."

"I'm here, aren't I?"

"And you want something. So you've proven my point."

James groaned. "At least you have children and grandkids."

"I'm grateful for them."

"And you have a sister who you ignore. Maybe you should stop sitting around and fix that."

"Don't tell me what to do." Paul glared at him like he stepped over the line.

"You should do what's right." James didn't care whether he made Paul angry or not. "If I married your sister, I'd want us to have family dinners together. Spend time playing cornhole or cards. I'd want you and me to still be friends."

"We would be." Paul shuffled his backside deeper into his chair. "We'd grill in the backyard and watch TV over here, same as always."

"No. If I marry Callie, this unsettled garbage between you and her needs to be resolved." James clenched his teeth together. "Come on, Paul. Why not bury the hatchet?"

"Did she put you up to this?"

"No, she did not." James tapped his index finger against his open palm. "I've watched you and Callie fighting long enough. If I decide I love her—"

"If you decide?"

"I mean, if she and I give marriage a try, I want you to be my best man. I want you and your sister to be happy again, too."

"Like you could make all that happen."

"Why not?" James grinned.

"First, Callie wouldn't marry you if you were the last man in Basalt Bay!"

How dare he make James's proposal into a contest! But hadn't they always tried to one-up each other since they were in elementary school?

"I say she will." If he put his mind to it, he could convince Callie to marry him.

"You marrying my bullheaded sister? That's not happening!"

"Want to bet?" As soon as James said the words, he wished he hadn't.

Paul pushed to his feet. "You're wagering with me over my sister's response to your proposal?"

"Yes, I am. I don't want to hear one word against it. Or her!" James stood, his fists clenched. They hadn't fought since junior high, but for a second he was tempted to belt his pal. He slowly opened his hand and extended it toward Paul. "If I get Callie to agree to marry me, will you do your best to make amends with her?"

"I didn't agree—"

"That's the deal." James kept his hand steady. "If I marry her, then you're going to make up with your sister. Agreed?"

Fifteen seconds passed with both glaring at each other.

"What do I get?"

James gulped. "I, uh, won't bring it up again."

"Fine." Paul heaved a sigh then shook James's hand. "Deal."

"Good."

Now he had to convince Callie to marry him. Hopefully, his wager with Paul wouldn't bite him in the backside.

Chapter Eleven

For the next three days, Callie spent a half hour each morning puttering around the guest room, tidying up the space, dusting, and praying. Previously, she rarely came upstairs. Now, she used this time to get a few more footsteps into her walking regimen and praying for the newest member of the project house, whoever that might be.

This morning, when she climbed the stairs, she heard Kathleen and Sarah talking in the planning room. What art projects were they working on now? At the dinner table last night, they spoke of mosaic techniques and mistakes or wrong color choices they made. Of course, Callie saw Kathleen's work at Paige's gallery and admired her for pursuing her dream when she was in her seventies. But hearing the two women discussing their love for art, Callie almost wanted to ask for lessons.

She'd never been a doodler or a painter. A hobby might get her mind off gobbling up the next sweet treat, since she had a few lapses lately. An unfortunate mistake of gooey brownies at midnight. Ice cream in the middle of the night. What kind of hobby would it take to distract her from those? She liked talking and sharing advice. Those probably didn't count as hobbies.

She dusted the bookshelf and rearranged a few items, then sat down in the rocker. Sarah used to stay in this room before she moved up to the renovated attic. Callie loved this space. It felt like a room filled with possibilities, dreams, and healing. She liked imagining who might stay here next. Maybe someone who'd been in an accident and was in recovery. Maybe a divorcee needing encouragement. Or a young woman needing some direction in her life.

Lord, please send someone our way who needs us.

Callie thought of how Sarah came to them as a discouraged, homeless widow, needing a fresh start. Now she seemed so happy, was learning a new craft, and worked full time in the gallery. Maybe one day she'd fall in love with another man, have kids, and move to her own home—hopefully, in Basalt Bay. Callie and Kathleen could be pseudo grandmas to her children, too.

Rocking the chair slowly, she enjoyed the rhythmic sounds of the rails rolling over the laminate flooring. Her thoughts returned to prayer.

Help the woman You send to us to be strengthened in her spirit. Heal any emotional wounds. Help us to be a blessing to her. Be with her now, wherever she is.

She sat silently for a few minutes.

And help me to stay on track with getting healthier. Food is such a temptation. But You understand that, right?

Didn't Jesus fast for forty days? Callie couldn't imagine not eating for two days! Still, thinking of the Lord empathizing with her situation brought her some peace.

Later, she took a short walk down the road and returned winded, which made being out of shape even more annoying. As she entered the house, the landline rang.

"Hello," she said, slightly out of breath. "This is Callie."

"Pastor Sagle, here."

"Good afternoon, Pastor." She brought the cordless phone to the dining room table and sat down. "Do you have news for me?"

"I do. I've been in contact with a pastoral friend in Florence."

"Yes?"

"We were chatting about the church's need for a roof and—"

"Did you find someone who needs us?" Callie inserted impatiently.

Pastor Sagle chuckled. "Yes, in fact, I did."

"I'm so glad." And relieved. When he didn't speak up soon enough, she asked, "Well?"

"Oh, right. Pastor Lemone is looking for temporary housing for a young mother and her son."

"A child? Oh, um." Callie took a big swallow. "We didn't consider kids staying here."

"No? Is that a problem?"

"Not necessarily. Children just have different needs."

"Sure, sure." The sounds of paper shuffling reached her. "Let me tell you a little about the woman's situation. Her husband abandoned her and the boy," Pastor Sagle said sadly.

"He abandoned them?"

"Yes."

The rat fink!

"She doesn't have family here on the West Coast. No income. Little food or provisions."

"And the child?"

"He's one-and-a-half. Quiet. Thin. Possibly malnourished."

"Oh, my goodness." Compassion quickly warmed Callie to the idea of taking on a mom and toddler.

"They may be in rough condition. In need of some tender loving care."

"Can I call you right back?"

"Of course." The pastor drew in a long breath. "You're still reluctant because of the child?"

"Yes. I need to run this by Bess and Kathleen. We make these decisions together."

"I understand. However, this woman may be a good fit for your project house otherwise."

"Thank you for the recommendation, Pastor."

Ending the call, Callie pressed her hands against her cheeks, still warm from her walk. A mom and her son needed a place to stay. She gazed around the room with a critical eye. If they were to take in a child, what items and decorations would they have to rearrange? Glass figurines on the windowsill, a sculpture of a whale on a pedestal in the corner, and a breakable lamp would never do. They needed some childproofing. Putting a few things away in the closet ought to solve that.

A child would be an endearing addition to their household. A little human needing hugs and comforting. A peaceful feeling spread through her. Eagerness, too. She loved Piper and Tanner. She'd love this little one.

When she and the other ladies decided to open their home to women in need, they should have considered there might be moms with kiddos in need of housing. Yet, they envisioned taking in only single women.

Callie gazed out the large windows toward the sea in the distance. She had never lived in the same house with a toddler underfoot. Would this lad cry loudly? Possibly waking up the house-hold in the middle of the night?

Ah, well. That would be okay. Yes, she was set in her ways. She liked things orderly and quiet. But any interruption to their lives would be worth the effort if doing so helped someone. In this case, two people, including a child who might be malnourished. Was God directing this mom and boy to the project house? To Callie and the other ladies here?

Determination filled her. She headed up the stairs—her second trip of the day. She was walking more already. Maybe losing some weight.

At the planning room doorway, she paused to catch her breath and watched as Kathleen pointed to some blue tiles on the board that Sarah leaned over.

"Oh, Callie. Hello, dear." Kathleen smiled welcomingly.

Sarah waved. "Hey, Callie."

"Good morning." Moving into the room, she gazed at the glass pieces of varying oceanic colors. "Such beautiful hues."

"They sure are. Come over and look at Sarah's beach scene." Kathleen swayed her hand toward a twelve by sixteen inch board partially filled with cut pieces of blue and green porcelain.

"It's lovely. You both do amazing work."

"Thank you." Sarah beamed. "I'm thankful for Kathleen's guidance. She's opened a whole world of art to me."

"You are a natural at mosaic work." Kathleen smiled like a proud mama. Then she turned back to Callie. "What's happened?"

"Pastor Sagle called."

Kathleen clasped her hands together. "Did he hear about someone who needs us?"

"Yes." Callie struggled to get a full breath. "A young mom with a toddler. Not yet two. But we didn't discuss taking in kids. We don't have toys or diapers or a bed. The house isn't childproofed."

"It'll be all right. Everything will work out," Kathleen said in a calming tone of voice. "We can put up gates. And we'll keep the door closed to this room."

"True. Putting gates up at the stairs would help."

"I can pick some up at the hardware store," Sarah volunteered. "I'm about to head into town for my shift at the gallery."

"Thank you." Callie met Kathleen's gaze. "What's your vote?"

"Are we voting? Sweetie, someone needs us. Let's rise to the challenge. If we can be a blessing to this young woman, let's do it!"

"Thank you for understanding." Callie squeezed her friend's hand. "I'll call Bess."

"I'm sure she'll say the same thing."

Kathleen was right. After Callie spoke on the phone with Bess, she called Pastor Sagle. "We would love to invite this woman and her son to stay with us."

"Wonderful news! I'll call Pastor Lemone." Pastor Sagle sighed as if he were relieved of a burden. "I've been praying about them since our phone call. I'm so thankful you ladies are willing to invite them into your home."

"We hope to be a blessing to whoever needs us."

"You have a generous heart, Callie. If only more people had a similar outlook."

"Maybe it'll be contagious, Pastor."

As soon as she said the words, an idea popped into her thoughts. What if it was contagious? What if she could influence more people in town to open their doors to those in need?

With promises to inform her of their guests' arrival, Pastor Sagle ended the call.

Callie thanked God for this new opportunity. She prayed they would be a blessing to their two visitors. And the idea about helping others being contagious didn't leave her.

Chapter Twelve

Callie didn't possess the gentle personality Kathleen did. She was a no-nonsense gal like her mother. If someone was having a hard time, she thought they should pick themselves up and get on with living. She didn't mind telling them so, either. No wallowing in self-pity. But when it came to caring about women in dire circumstances, her heart went out to them. And while she still gave them advice—how could she not?—she tried to be understanding and speak softly. Perhaps, Kathleen's friendliness was rubbing off on her.

Pondering these things, she removed glass knickknacks from the dining area. Everything in the lower floor couldn't be extricated. But ridding the room of breakable items accessible to tiny fingers seemed the wise thing to do.

Paige called and said Sarah told her about their guests' impending arrival. She asked if they'd like to use Piper's old crib. Some bedding and toys? She said the new baby wouldn't need those things for a while. Callie thanked her for the generous offer and agreed. Forest, Paige's husband, would bring the items by later and set up the crib in the guest room.

Callie had other matters to tend to also. What supplies should they have on hand for the toddler? Did the mom have enough clothes or diapers? What if she thought they were too old and unrelatable here at the project house? Sarah might be the best one to interact with her, being the youngest of their quartet. Or maybe Kathleen's gentle, motherly caring might be the most comforting to the young mom. Yet Callie was the one with the burden on her heart.

They'd all pitch in to help their guests acclimate. The rest was in God's hands. His love was the power fueling Callie, Kathleen, and Bess to open their home to others in the first place. She needed to remember that more and worry less.

James's proposal came to mind for the umpteenth time. The way he twirled his hat in his hands and asked her to marry him as if simply asking her if she wanted to join him for a cup of tea was uncanny. Unbelievable. Almost sacrilegious. The remembrance still irritated her.

She'd better not think about his so-called proposal, or her pipes would be steaming up. She needed to focus on the mom and child arriving this afternoon. What she'd like to say to James would have to wait.

A few hours later, Pastor Sagle arrived with a young Latino woman who nestled a small child in her arms. The boy was hiding his face against his mom's neck.

"This is Lola Presley and her son Micah."

"Welcome." Callie shook Lola's small hand.

The woman acted so shy she barely lifted her eyes to meet their gazes. Mom and boy appeared gaunt. Nearly starving, by all accounts. Callie and Kathleen would take care of those needs immediately. Kathleen already had homemade soup simmering on the stove.

"Thank you for allowing us to stay in your home." Lola stole a quick peek at Callie.

"You're welcome."

Pastor Sagle shuffled back and forth in his black shoes. "Are you all right, Lola? Will you be comfortable enough here? We're all concerned for your well-being and safety."

"Yes. I'll be fine."

"Then I'll leave you to get settled. Call if you need anything."

Callie saw the pastor to the door while Kathleen showed Lola and Micah the spare bedroom upstairs. Taking a few minutes to catch her breath and fix hot water for tea, she waited for the trio to come back downstairs.

Kathleen entered the kitchen alone. "Aren't they the sweetest? Lola oohed and aahed over the room. She loved the crib and toys. Poor dear. She needs a little human kindness."

"I agree." Callie sipped her tea and leaned against the counter. "Makes me glad we're here for her."

"Me too. She'll be down in a few minutes. Says she'll drink some chamomile tea." Kathleen stirred her soup, then prepared two cups of hot tea.

In the dining room, Callie sat down at the long table facing the window. She enjoyed the beautiful fall view of the trees changing colors and sipped her drink. Thoughts of James, which were never far from her mind, taunted her. Marry the man to get Pauly's emotional walls concerning her to come down? Never!

What a foolish man he was to even think she'd agree to his fake proposal! Although, his dumbfounded expression when she yelled at him to go away was humorous. Why had he been surprised by her reaction?

"What tickled your funny bone just now?" Kathleen settled into a seat, clasping her cup between her hands.

"Nothing worth repeating." Or remembering.

"If you don't want to talk about it, I understand. I explained about the gates and our concern about the stairway to Lola." Kathleen nodded in the direction of the stairs. "She said she'll keep a close watch on the boy."

"I'm sure she will." Callie sighed. "I've done my share of walking the floors with Piper, but I'll let Lola chase the little tyke. And I'll help as the need arises."

"Me too. Was a time I chased kiddos as fast as they ran." Kathleen chuckled. "Not anymore."

A few moments of quiet passed between them.

"I'm so thankful for you, Callie," Kathleen said quietly.

"Me?"

"Your determination to do good for others is admirable. I would have stayed in my art corner, head buried in my own interests." She smiled and a peaceful expression crossed her face. "You stood up for someone who was abandoned and helpless. Good for you. God bless you for doing that."

"Well, thank you." Callie wasn't out to garner praise, but Kathleen's kind words meant a lot to her.

She prayed she'd be a good host to Lola and Micah. A good friend. That Lola would find healing and rest in their project house. For a moment, she thought about the home's nickname. After living here for nearly a year, they still called it their project house. But wasn't that appropriate? Weren't they all projects in one way or another, growing and changing, healing and facing new challenges? Callie included!

She sighed, thankful for this old house and the blessing it was going to be for women in many walks of life in the future.

Chapter Thirteen

None of the ladies thought to get a high chair, so dinner turned out to be a difficult affair with Lola wrestling the crying toddler on her lap. She attempted to feed him, but her efforts were useless. He cried heart-wrenching sobs, and his face was a wet mess of tears and runny nose.

Kathleen retrieved a box of tissues and set them on the table beside Lola. "Here, sweetie. Use these if they help."

"Thank you." Lola wiped her son's face with a tissue which caused him to howl louder. "I'm sorry. So sorry for the noise." Her face darkened with embarrassment.

"Don't worry about it. You're doing fine," Kathleen said reassuringly. "It takes time to settle in."

Callie couldn't finish the soup Kathleen made. Between the boy's squalls and the unrest she felt over forgetting a high chair and food a one-year-old might like, she had too much tension churning inside her. Maybe they should have put this meal off for another hour.

Bess tried talking over the racket, probably trying to bring normalcy to the situation. Finally, no one attempted any conversation over the boy's cries and outbursts.

Callie had enough. All the cooing in the world wasn't going to stop this boy from belting out shrieks and wails. Lola needed food in her own wilted body. Standing, Callie held her arms out toward the child. "May I walk with him? Distract him for a few minutes and give you time to eat your meal?"

"He isn't good with strangers."

Micah squalled again.

"Let me try, okay?"

Lola nodded. "All right. Go to Callie, Micah."

Callie scooped up the boy in one quick movement, apparently startling him so much he stopped crying and stared wide-eyed at her. He shuddered and drew in a noisy breath. Then she settled him on her hip like she usually did with Piper and grabbed a wad of tissues.

"There, there. It's not so bad as all that." She shuffled back and forth between the living room and the dining area, pointing things out to him. "See the dog sculpture on the shelf. There's a picture of the beach." She went to the window and pointed toward things outside. "There's the ocean. Isn't it beautiful? Look at the bird flying high! Oh, that's an eagle."

Micah sniffled and seemed to be listening as she pointed at things. Tomorrow, she'd get ahold of some books and toys for downstairs. And a high chair.

When the small body lay limp against her chest, Callie settled into a soft chair in the living room and rocked him gently. He rustled like he might be close to waking up, so she hummed a lullaby she sometimes sang to Piper.

A few minutes later, Lola crept into the room, eyes wide. "After such silence, I felt I should check on him." She smiled and her whole face lost its look of tension. "He fell asleep with you so quickly. That is amazing. He doesn't sleep well for anyone else."

"Guess I have the Midas touch. Plus, he was exhausted."

"I guess you do. And he was." Lola held out her small hands. "Do you want me to take him?"

"I'm fine. Go ahead and do something else."

"What do you mean?" She gawked at Callie like she was speaking another language.

"I don't know. Maybe take a shower. Put your clothes in the dresser. Read a book. Drink some coffee. Do whatever you'd like to do for a few minutes." Callie patted Micah's back. "He and I are fine. Go. Go."

"Thank you so much, Callie. I'll be just a minute." Lola scurried out of the room, heading toward the dining room. It sounded like she was helping Bess and Kathleen clear the table.

Sighing, Callie rocked and gently patted the boy's back. All the while, she prayed silently for his and Lola's well-being and transition to living here. How could she help this mama and child who were entrusted to her care?

Chapter Fourteen

After ten days of being on a healthy diet, avoiding sugar, and walking more, Callie didn't find any reduction on the scale. In fact, she gained a couple of pounds! She felt a horrible dip in her morale. Her hopes for something positive happening within her body plummeted. The scones Kathleen made last night tempted her to eat three. In her imagination, the honey jar sitting on the counter taunted her—*Don't you want lots of honey in your tea?* Of course, she did!

Someone unexpectedly knocked at the door, and her agitation over her weight-loss failures sank her into a dark, grumpy mood. She felt a headache coming on too. "What do you want?" she demanded when she yanked open the door and found James and Pauly standing there. "Is the house on fire? Is there a tsunami warning? Why else would you two be at my door this early in the morning?" She pelted both with a stern glare.

Mouths dropped open, eyes wide, the men stared back at her, apparently, speechless.

"What's this about?" Couldn't they tell she was anxious and ill-prepared to see anyone? Especially them!

"Let us in and we'll tell you," Pauly said in an equally grumpy tone. "Or do we have to stand on the porch all day?"

Like he had room to talk! She was the one who usually stood on Pauly's porch trying to get him to let her into his house.

"I told you we shouldn't have come here. I'm leaving." Pauly whirled around.

"Wait. Wait." James grabbed his arm and gave Callie a woebegone look. "Have a heart, Cal. Can we come in and chat for a few minutes? We're sorry to disturb you."

"Fine. But don't expect sugar in your coffee!" She stormed back into the kitchen, not sure if the men would follow her or not. Wasn't she in a foul mood?

Their arrival better not have anything to do with James's phony marriage proposal. If it did, she might bite both their heads off!

Behind her, James coaxed Pauly to come inside. Her brother muttered a rude word.

She shouldn't have spoken so sharply to them. Goodness gracious. Pauly put her on edge. And James was just as bad.

"Are you coming in or not?" She grabbed two mugs out of the cupboard and plunked them down on the butcher-block island. After pouring the coffee, she grabbed a carton of creamer from the fridge and set the container firmly by the cups. They could fix the rest themselves. She didn't trust herself to come within smelling range of sugar-tainted creamer!

Hands clutching the edge of the island, she watched her brother guardedly enter the kitchen, glancing at her like she might throw a plate at him. If she did, that would serve him right! James shut the door and followed him into the kitchen. Both looked like naughty boys caught with frogs in their jacket pockets at school. What were they up to, anyway?

"There's coffee if you want it." She pointed at the cups. "Kathleen made scones yesterday." Maybe some delicious food would make amends for her tart behavior. She took down a plate and, using salad tongs, set a couple of pastries on it. She pushed the plate toward the men's side of the island, wanting to stuff one or two of the desserts in her mouth. "I'm sure they're good."

Pauly and James glanced awkwardly at each other, then at Callie.

"Are you going to stand there all day and make me guess why you two are here?" The chip on her shoulder grew larger. "What have you done? You might as well spit it out."

Pauly picked up one of the cups of coffee and slurped the liquid. "I gave him my blessing. Happy?"

"Blessing for what? And why should I be happy about it?"

Groaning, James slapped his forehead with his palm.

"For you to marry him. What else?"

"Marry James?" All the crabby emotions she'd fought and failed at subduing pummeled through her system like an emotionally-charged rocket blast. "I need your blessing to marry him"—she jabbed her index finger at James—"like I need a clogged heart valve! Get out of here, the both of you!" Why were they even having this conversation?

"I can't go until I eat one of these." James picked up a scone and leisurely took a bite. "Mm-mmm," he said while chewing, which bothered Callie even more. "Try one, Paul."

"Don't mind if I do." Pauly picked up the other scone and munched noisily.

Nuisance men! Maybe they'd choke on the dry scones.

"Great scones, Cal." James added extra creamer to his mug. "Tell Kathleen she's the best baker in the world."

"Yeah, yeah." Each thing they said caused more irritation. Why couldn't they just leave?

"Tell her thanks a million." Pauly took another swig of his coffee then set the mug down forcefully. "So, what's it going to be?"

"Going to be about what?" Callie dropped her right fist onto her hip. "Say what you came to say, then leave. Unlike you, I have things to do."

"Sure, you do. Twiddling your thumbs. Reading some magazine about how to gossip more."

Oh, he was asking for it. Anger surged through her afresh.

"Paul." James shook his head, warning him to be quiet. He met Callie's gaze and mouthed, "Sorry."

"I do more in a day than you do sitting around watching your soap operas!"

Pauly flinched. She'd hit her mark.

"I don't watch soap operas," he bit out in defined syllables. "Dr. Phil is educational."

"Right." She heard that excuse before. "So is counting raindrops and making mud pies."

"Why are you mad at me? What did I do?" Pauly demanded. "I came here to give you my blessing to marry my best friend. You should be grateful."

"Grateful? Papa died years ago. You aren't him. I don't need your blessing!" She gulped in a few unsteady breaths, barely getting the oxygen she needed. "When James asked me to marry him, he wasn't serious. So stop talking foolishly." She glanced at James. His eyes were moist. Teary, even. Why was he acting emotional? "He made a joke of asking me to marry him. Nothing else. So take your blessing and go!"

"Fine!"

"Double fine!" Callie heaved strong breaths.

If anything, she felt like a pawn in James's scheme to get her and Pauly to make amends. Like she was nothing. A convenient means to an end. Well, she wasn't having any part of their conniving and plotting, or whatever.

"Just go!" she reiterated since neither man had left yet.

"See if I ever come back here and talk with you again." Pauly stomped out of the house.

"Good!"

Groaning, James followed him to the door. He turned back slowly, twirling his derby hat in his hands. "Cal, you're wrong. I butchered the proposal, but I meant it. Honestly, I did. I would marry you in a heartbeat." He put his hat on, stepped onto the porch, and closed the door softly.

Sagging against the island, Callie let her hip support her weight. Her heart pounded furiously. James was jesting. He'd marry her in a heartbeat? The way he proposed wasn't something anyone on God's green earth would take seriously, right?

Chapter Fifteen

James clenched his jaw for most of the ride back to Paul's house, contemplating his pitiful discussion with Callie. Trying to make sense of it.

Paul remained silent until he brought his '68 Volkswagen Beetle to a fast stop in his grassy driveway. "You said talk to my sister, so I did!" He jabbed his index finger toward James. "Look how that turned out. Ever since we were kids, she's butted her nose into my life. She's to blame for us not talking. Not me."

James figured it took two people to give up talking. Two to communicate again. "I'm sorry the conversation didn't go better." Weren't their exchanges usually like this? Paul getting angry at Callie. Her storming off mad. Both fussing with each other and getting on each other's nerves.

"Now, do you see why a marriage to her would never work?"

"No, I don't see that."

"You mean to tell me you still want to marry that loud-mouthed bag of wind who doesn't have a civil word to say to either of us?" Paul adjusted his glasses that he usually wore when he was driving.

"Yep." James didn't care to discuss the way he felt about Callie. "Talk with her again. Try to make things right."

"Are you crazy?" Paul shut off the engine and grabbed the key. "I might never talk to her again! I'd rather nail a banner over the door of my house that says, 'Callie Cedars, stay out!'" He opened the car door. "Why you care about her is beyond my comprehension. When did you two ever have feelings for each other?"

"When did we not?"

Paul gave him a drop-jawed look again. Huffily, he climbed out of the knee-cruncher car.

James crawled out and marched to the other side of the vehicle. "Why is it so hard for you to conceive that I might have feelings for your sister?"

"You never acted like you did."

"You're right." He sighed, and his chest ached. "Until last year."

"What changed then?"

"I started to—" James groaned. "Nothing."

Paul wouldn't understand the way he felt about Callie, anyway. James had put off having romantic feelings toward any woman for most of his life. Figured he'd never marry. But then, his heart changed. Rather, someone changed his outlook on romance and marriage. *Callie.*

He guessed they were at the caring stage. At least, he was. Not love. Yet, how did a couple know if they were in love? Did a heart-shaped red light flash over their heads?

"Coming in?" Paul lifted his chin toward his house.

"Might as well." James tromped up the stairs, imagining Paul, Callie, and him doing the same thing back when they were kids. Running up these stairs after a game of Annie Over or baseball with the other kids in the neighborhood. Even when Paul yelled at his sister to get lost, she didn't. James chuckled at the memory.

In the living room, Paul threw his coat over the back of his chair and plopped down. Instantly, the TV blared.

Callie was right about Paul's television addiction. He spent far too much time in front of the screen. James preferred yard work and tinkering outside to being glued to the tube. After Paul's diabetic health scare last year, he seemed to have lost all interest in keeping up his house and grounds. Maybe he needed a nudge toward being productive with his time again.

James's nine-to-five job was over, but his life wasn't. Even the possibility of him and Callie getting married put a bounce in his step. Would Paul understand if he tried to explain?

"So, Paul—"

His buddy stared at the television with a dazed look.

"Are you going to sit there, peering at the screen for the rest of the day?"

"Huh? Did you say something?"

James chuckled, some of his previous tension easing. "Let's talk."

"What's to talk about?" Paul faced the screen again, slouching deeper into his chair. Probably ready for a long snooze.

James snagged the remote and punched OFF.

"Hey! Why'd you do that?"

"Sorry, pal." James tucked the controller between his leg and the chair arm. "I want to discuss what happened with Callie."

"Are you kidding me? Maybe you should head home. Leave me to my own devices." Paul pointed toward the hidden remote.

"After we talk, I'll vamoose. Then you can sit here moping in your chair, staring at Dr. Phil, or whatever, all day if you want."

"Maybe you are more like Callie than I thought."

"Maybe I am." James felt unsettled about what he still needed to say. Over the years they had their share of squabbles, but they never argued about Callie before. "I want to marry your sister."

"So you said. Try convincing her of that!" Paul made a face. "The idea of you marrying her puts a bad taste in my mouth. Nothing but trouble awaits you."

James ignored Paul's doom and gloom outlook. "What if we make each other happy?"

Paul belted out a sarcastic sounding laugh.

"It's possible," James said calmly. "If I married Cal and you put the sign you mentioned over your door, you'd be keeping me out too."

"You're serious?"

"I am. This cancerous thing between the two of you needs to end. Hate between siblings for so many years? That's wrong."

"Says you!" Paul yanked the glasses off his face and tossed them on the end table.

"I plan to pursue your sister."

"What do you know about pursuing a woman?"

"Not much. That's why I muffed up the proposal so badly." James didn't want to mentally rehash what he did. But he still had to try fixing things between him and Callie.

"What do you want from me? Hurry up, so I can get back to my show."

"I want you to have a life. Why are you sitting here like there isn't anything left to live for?" James pointed at the television. "Is this all you care about? You're still breathing. Why not do what Callie's doing and try to get healthier? Reach out to, I don't know, a woman!"

"A woman?" Paul bellowed. "At my age?"

"Why not? Why don't you contact Sue Anne?"

"Leave her out of this. I'm warning you." Paul's eyelids squinted to small slits.

"You're my age. We might still have thirty good years left. Why not have some companionship on the journey?"

"You've got to be kidding me." Paul slapped his palm over his forehead. "If this is what you wanted to talk to me about, and this is why you're going after my sister, you're more of a fool than I realized." He slumped back against his chair and closed his eyes. "Just go, will you?"

So much for getting Paul to understand. James braced his elbows against his knees. "What would you say to us double dating?"

"Are you nuts?" Paul opened one eye, glaring like a pirate with a patch over his eye.

"You've sat in your chair long enough. Why not have a woman in your life?"

"Get out of here!"

"I'm serious. Penny's been gone for four years. Why not go out and have another romance? A fling, if nothing else."

"A fling?" Paul let out an indignant bellow. "We were never the 'fling' sort of guys. Edward dominated at that!"

"So he did. Still gets your goat, doesn't it?"

"What does?"

"The way he stole Sue Anne from you."

"Don't bring up old garbage," Paul said through gritted teeth. "Edward is not to be mentioned here."

"All right. All right." James held up both hands, palms out.

After a few minutes of silence, Paul spoke quietly, his gaze homed in on the window, not on the television. "I never knew where she went. Then I found out the situation was exactly as I thought. He was a cad!"

"A dirty unapologetic cad."

A few moments of silence passed.

"There is one thing you might try," James said as a thought came to mind. "In the absence of Sarah's cloddish father, why not try to be a dad to her? Make amends with Callie and be a friend to her too. And go on a date with someone."

Paul groaned and thrust his hands over his thinning gray hair.

"Any of these suggestions would give you something to do other than watching that noisy contraption!" James tossed the remote to

Paul and stood. "I'm not going to sit on my backside doing nothing. I'm going to keep living, starting with trying to get Callie to marry me."

"I'm still betting on you failing!"

"I'm still counting on succeeding!"

James marched across the living room and left the house. All the way across the street and into his house, a fire of determination pumped through his veins, his lungs, and into his heart. His thoughts repeated the reason.

Callie, Callie, Callie.

Chapter Sixteen

Callie didn't consider herself wealthy, but she had some savings left over from the sale of her house to contribute to the needs of the household. And enough to help Lola and Micah, and others, as personal needs arose. She'd taken care of buying a high chair, books, toys, and snacks that were appropriate for a toddler. Was there anything she overlooked?

Lola had been staying with them for a couple of days now. Today seemed like a good time for Callie to have a discussion with her and find out if she needed anything from the store.

As soon as Lola reached the foot of the stairs, Callie asked, "If you've put Micah down for his nap, can we talk?"

"Oh, uh, sure." Lola paused in the center of the room. "I'm going to get some tea. Would you like some?"

"Sounds wonderful. But first let's have a chat." If they didn't get started, Micah might wake up, and Callie would lose her opportunity to visit with Lola.

"Okay." The younger woman sat down on one of the easy chairs and clutched her hands together in a nervous gesture.

"I'm going to get right to the point. Do you or Micah need anything?"

"Excuse me?"

"Do you need clothes or diapers? Shampoo? Medical supplies? Counseling?"

Lola's face hued red, so Callie let silence fill the space for a few moments. Was she being too pushy?

"I don't mean to pry. But if you need any supplies, we will help you get them."

"I'm not familiar with anyone else caring about my needs." Lola's almost black eyes filled with unshed tears. "You ladies have already been so kind to me and Micah. Thank you. I will forever be grateful."

"Of course. I hope I'm not making you feel uncomfortable with this talk." Callie tilted her head one way then the other, weighing her words. "I truly hope you feel welcome and at home here for as long as you want to stay."

"Yes, I do. And thank you."

"Kathleen, Bess, and I are older. Perhaps, not as aware of the needs of a younger woman and a child as we could be." Callie swayed out her hands. "But while you and Micah are with us, you are cared for and loved as if we are family. If there's anything you need, anything at all, please tell us. We want to help."

"You are much too kind."

"Is there something you need?" Callie persisted.

Lola averted her gaze like the conversation was an invasion of her privacy.

"Sarah's busy with work lately, but she's younger. She's someone you might relate to a little more," Callie suggested. "If you'd rather talk with her about this, that's okay."

Lola didn't comment.

"I'm heading into town in a while, so I can pick up something for you. It's no trouble."

After a long silence, Lola whispered, "I don't have money. Benny took our cash. For weeks, I had nothing. Not even basic supplies for our baby. Or me. So what you've already provided for us feels like a luxury."

Callie wanted to call Benjamin several rude names—unfit father, negligent husband, rotten provider, pathetic man. She remained silent. However, she called on every ounce of self-control and fortitude she possessed to keep her mouth shut and her thoughts to herself.

"I cried out to God to save my child." Lola sniffled, then stiffened her shoulders as if determining she wouldn't cry. "He answered my prayer when Pastor Lemone suggested Micah and I come and stay here." She met Callie's gaze with a somber look. "What more could I want than the friendship and kindness you ladies have shown me? A warm room for me and my son. Tea when I want it. Food and shelter."

"I'm glad we are here for you and Micah. You're going to be okay." Callie brought the subject back around to her needs. "If I were to pick up a few items at the store, what would be helpful?"

Lola inhaled slowly as if speaking of personal needs was too difficult a subject for her. "Feminine products would be nice."

"Of course." Why hadn't she thought of that? "Anything else?"

Lola met her gaze with a smile. "I have everything else I need."

Callie asked about brands and preferences.

"You mentioned counseling," Lola said offhandedly.

"That's right."

"Who do you recommend for my situation?"

"Pastor Sagle, perhaps. Or he'll know someone who might be available."

Lola nodded. "I'll keep it in mind. I want to be a good mom."

"You are a great mom." If Callie were sitting closer to Lola, she would have clasped her hand like she did with her nieces sometimes.

"I mean it. You love your boy. You are putting his needs before your own. You're doing your very best for him, even in coming here. I admire you for that."

"Thank you for your kind words. But with the sadness and the anger I feel toward Benny"—Lola patted her chest above her heart—"I fear I'm not the mom I should be."

Such wisdom was beautiful and ageless. If only Callie and Pauly had pursued counseling during their difficult years, their family dynamics might be far different today.

"Would you like me to set up an appointment with the pastor?"

"Let me think it over. Thank you for having this talk with me."

"Of course. I'm not an expert on parenting, nor about being a wife, but if you ever want to talk to someone, I'm here. The other ladies too."

"Thank you. Now, I'm going to fix that tea for us." Lola gave her a quick hug then left the room.

Callie remained seated, praying for the other woman's inner healing. She prayed about the anger she felt about Lola's louse of a husband too. If he ever dared to step foot on this property, Callie would have some heated, possibly explosive words to say to him!

Chapter Seventeen

"Oh, Callie!" Kathleen called in a singsong voice from the other room. "Someone's here for you. He's looking good too."

He? James Weston, no doubt. Why was he here? Wasn't his and Pauly's disastrous visit yesterday bad enough?

Callie glanced into the bedroom mirror, double-checking that no broccoli or spinach pieces were stuck between her front teeth. Patting her hand over her short-cropped hair, she made sure no rebellious strands were sticking up. There wasn't anything she could do about the fine wrinkle lines around her eyes. She blinked slowly. She'd always thought her eyes were her best feature. Dark brown irises that glistened like chocolate in certain lighting. Had James ever noticed them?

She sighed, wishing she'd lost some weight by now. Instead, the extra twenty-five pounds she was trying to shed seemed stuck to her middle with super glue.

"He's come bearing gifts," Kathleen said in an exaggerated tone. "Hard to resist a handsome man with presents in his hands."

Presents? Callie groaned. Then smoothed her hands down her loose-fitting blouse and pants. Should she put on a little lipstick? She rarely wore the stuff. No reason to make a fuss. It was just James. The guy who fake-proposed to her!

Still, her silly heart raced. She forced herself to breathe calmly and act dignified as she strode into the dining area.

James stood inside the doorway, clutching a dozen red roses. "Cal." He smiled apprehensively as if worried about how she might react to seeing him again so soon.

"What's this?" She lifted her chin toward the flowers.

"They're for you." He held out the roses to her.

Her first flowers from a boy. For a second, she got choked up before subduing the feeling.

Their fingers touched, hers tingling in the exchange of the bouquet. Here was a man who she'd admired for so long giving her flowers. Butterflies danced in her stomach. Maybe those long-ago dreams were stirring to life again.

If only James was being sincere. But after his phony proposal, how could she be certain of anything he said or did?

"Thank you. I don't know why you—"

"Yes, you do." He clasped her hand briefly. "Would you go for a stroll down the lane with me?"

"A stroll?" Flowers and a walk on the same day? Her face flushing hot, she stammered, "Y-yeah. I g-guess so. Let me put these in a vase. I'll grab my jacket."

She needed a minute to catch her breath and pull herself together. Slowly, she placed the flowers one by one into Kathleen's mosaic vase. Later, she'd clip them properly. She inhaled deeply, savoring the sweet floral scent. James brought her roses. Red roses that were symbolic of love.

Silly goose. This was probably still about him wanting to fix things between her and Pauly. These flowers didn't mean he was madly in love with her. But for a moment, imagining he brought them because he cared for her, because he loved her, was thrilling. And romantic! Like a fairytale coming true.

If only.

They strolled down the road a ways before James brought up the subject he obviously came to discuss. "After our visit yesterday, I spoke with Paul about us again."

"About us?" She stopped her forward motion. "What 'us' are you talking about, James?"

"You and me, of course."

She wanted to laugh. They weren't a couple. Sure, they flirted a little during the last year. Nothing came of it. No dates. No phone calls. Then out of the blue he asked her to marry him! That didn't make them anymore an "us" than they had been for the last half-century.

James set his hand on the small of her back, causing tingling sensations to charge up her spine. She continued walking beside him, although she felt uncomfortable with this line of discussion and the warmth of his hand at her back.

"He doesn't believe you and I have, well, true feelings for each other."

They didn't! Rather, he didn't.

Her shoe caught on a rock, and she stumbled slightly. James clutched the crook of her elbow, helping balance her, as if she couldn't do so without him.

"Stop interfering!" She pulled her arm away from his grasp, moving away from his touch and his possibly insincere attention. "I don't need you meddling into this lifelong argument I have with my brother."

Instead of responding to her demand, he asked, "What's wrong, Cal? I understand you don't want to marry me. I mean, why would you want that?" He grinned flirtatiously, disarming her annoyance with him.

Her heart thumped an irregular beat. Her face must be ten shades of red by now. A sixty-three-year-old woman blushing to the roots of her short hair because a man teased her? What happened to her usual bite and bluster? Maybe she enjoyed the private talk with James too much to be blunt or rude. But he still needed to hear the truth.

"Let's get one thing straight. I would never marry you to fix the abyss between Pauly and me. It would never work, anyway. He'd sniff out such a charade in an instant and be angrier than ever at me."

"Okay. So I have a new proposal."

Propose again? No way! Her heart couldn't bear the stress. She picked up the stride, hoping to outpace him.

"This time let's show him we mean it. We'll convince him that we're crazy about each other."

"Are you kidding me?" Callie stopped walking and flattened her hand over her chest, trying to calm her internal reaction. "You mean fake that we like each other?" This idea was worse than his last one!

"Wait. Cal, are you okay?" He clasped her free hand. "Your hand is shaking. Your breathing is—"

"Erratic?" No wonder! She jerked her hand from his. He had no right to be holding her hand. Toying with her emotions. "Are you suggesting we play along like we're in love for my brother's sake?"

"It might work." His shoulders shuffled up and down.

"And crabs on the beach might dance the polka!" She felt the urge to sock him in the gut like she did once when she was ten and he called her a tomboy. "You keep coming up with terrible ideas and I'll never speak to you again." She whirled around and walked faster toward the project house than she probably should have been walking. This conversation was over!

Whatever she wished was happening between her and James wasn't. He could flush his big ideas down the toilet right alongside the flowers he gave her!

Insincere scoundrel! How dare he bring her red roses! Clasp her hand tenderly. Act like he cared. Then have the audacity to propose a fake romance? She groaned loudly.

"Cal, wait! What did I say that's so wrong?" James caught up to her, limping slightly. "It wouldn't all be pretending. I meant—"

She stopped suddenly. "You meant what?"

"That we should convince him we're, uh, courting." He floundered on the last word.

"Courting? It's called dating. That's after two people are attracted to each other. Not when they're faking a relationship for a brother to notice his sister before she dies!" Her volume escalated with each word. She stomped the rest of the way back to the house, keeping ahead of James.

Inside the project house, she slammed the door. "Men! I'm finished with the lot of them." She went right to the roses she'd set on the center of the butcher-block island. "I'll decide your fate later."

James entered the house without knocking. She whirled around and glared at him as he walked over to her. How dare he—

"I'm sorry." He set his hands on her shoulders. "I'm not good at romance stuff, okay? I've never had a girlfriend. But I will do better. I promise."

She gulped, letting his tender tone soothe some of her hurt and fury.

"I'm sorry I said it wrong and messed up our romantic moment again."

He thought they had a romantic moment? When?

She gazed into his dark gray eyes. Speckles of black dotted his irises. She'd never noticed them before.

Without meaning to, she wet her lips. She wasn't imagining what his lips would feel like touching hers. Nor was she wondering what his breath tasted like. Nothing romantic because James didn't think of her like that! Still, curiously, her gaze dropped to his lips that looked soft and slightly damp.

James smoothed the back of his knuckles down her cheek, startling her with his gentleness. "You have the prettiest eyes, Cal."

"Oh, uh, thanks." She gulped. Fearing for her heart, for her sanity, she shuffled backwards. Confused by her reaction to him, she needed space, yet she longed for more of the invisible bond she felt developing between them.

If this was all fake to him—that possibility cooled her right down—she didn't want to encourage him in any way that would end with her having a broken heart. Finding out his kindnesses were a ruse would be pure torture.

"Thank you for the roses." Maybe she wouldn't throw them out, after all.

"First time I ever gave a girl flowers, other than to my mom." He shrugged and seemed embarrassed by the admission.

"Really?"

"The absolute truth. Before I go, I have a question for you." His eyes moistened, those flecks sparkling in the light. A smile spread across his soft-looking lips. "This time my request doesn't have anything to do with your brother, okay?"

"All right." She gnawed on her lower lip, and James's gaze homed in on her nervous action. She forced her mouth to relax. "What's your question?"

"Will you go out on a real date with me?" He blinked rapidly. "Have dinner with me? Just the two of us."

The guy she dreamed of since she was twelve was asking her out on a date? Fearing she might collapse at his feet, she clutched her hands together for balance. "Yes. I'll go out with you."

Even if this might not be real to him, how could she refuse the first date invitation she'd ever received? Of course, she'd go out with James Weston!

Chapter Eighteen

Throughout the day, Callie fretted. What should she wear on a date? Should she buy a new outfit? Have her hair done? What about her nails? She never wore coloring on her fingernails. Never dyed her hair. What was the protocol for dating at her age?

Ugh. Age shouldn't sneak into the equation. But what on earth did a mature woman wear on a first date? Worrying about clothes and makeup wasn't like her. Yet she'd never been on a date before!

She put on a light coating of rosy lipstick and blush that complemented the burgundy-hued dress she chose. Some black mascara might accentuate her dark brown eyes. She stood back and looked at herself in her full-length mirror, critiquing herself. Then sighed.

James looked so sweet yesterday when he asked her out. Surely this date didn't have anything to do with his ridiculous idea about pulling the wool over Pauly's eyes. It better not have anything to do with that!

She wanted to trust James. He said he didn't know how to be romantic. Well, she didn't have any experience in the amorous department either. What if he toyed with her feelings? Going on a date with her, then laughing about their time together with Pauly? Even the possibility of him being dishonest about his reason for dating her made her emotions ignite with fury.

Breathe. Stop fretting.

It's one date. One outing with her brother's best friend. Maybe something more would come of it. Maybe this night out would be a fond memory and nothing else.

A knock on the door signaled James's arrival. As if this were prom night back in high school, Kathleen snapped photos with her cell phone of Callie strolling toward the door. "You look beautiful, my dear. I'm so happy for you. Have so much fun!" She kept taking snapshots.

"Stop that." Callie fanned her hands at Kathleen. "Don't make more of this than it is."

"Any time a man gives you roses and takes you out for dinner is worth making a fuss over."

Callie probably should have had her nails done. Or curled her hair. She groaned.

Kathleen hugged her. "Have fun, sweetie. Relax and enjoy it."

"I'll try." If she didn't get sick first. Taking another deep breath, she opened the door.

James twirled his derby hat between his hands. He shuffled back and forth in his shiny black shoes. Tugged on a navy tie. Adjusted his glasses. His uneasy mannerisms made her feel less anxious.

"Callie. You look fabulous!"

"Thank you. You clean up nicely too." She liked his cream-colored cardigan, navy tie, and dark slacks.

He held out his arm chivalrously. "Ready to go?"

"Certainly." Heart pounding, she met Kathleen's merry gaze then followed James into the night.

At the oceanside restaurant about ten miles north of Basalt Bay, Callie twisted a maroon cloth napkin between her hands as she waited for the food they ordered to arrive. What should she do with her hands? If she settled them on the table, she'd reveal the plain state of her fingernails. Wringing them in her lap would make her appear overly nervous.

"Are you all right?" James leaned forward, eyes sparkling.

Rats. He noticed her fidgeting.

"I'm fine. Unaccustomed to dolling up and going out is all."

"Me too." He stuck his index finger between the knot of his tie and his throat and tugged on the fabric. "Don't like wearing ties, either."

"Then take it off." She smiled, relaxing a little. "If it's as uncomfortable as these nylons I put on, you're miserable. Haven't worn them in nearly a decade."

They both chuckled. They had spent a lifetime as acquaintances. However, in this setting of an intimate table for two with a candle glowing on the table between them, tension simmered as if they were unfamiliar with each other. Back on Pauly's porch, Callie wouldn't have the slightest jitters around James. Why now?

"So"—she took control of some of the awkwardness—"what do you like to do when you're not shooting the breeze with my brother?"

"Gardening. Puttering with wood in the shop behind my house." He played with the condensation on his water glass. "I take more walks these days."

"Me too." Callie drummed her fingernails on the cloth-covered table. "Less being inactive. Doing some weight-bearing exercises."

"We could take walks together." His eyes glistened in the candlelight. "I enjoy walking and talking with you, Cal. Would you care to go on a walk with me tomorrow?"

It didn't sound as if he thought of this outing as a one-time event. If they continued walking and talking, would she get her hopes up, only to have them dashed? On the other hand, maybe their dating would become a regular thing. Highly improbable. Still, she couldn't let go of the idea of a closer friendship and romance building between them.

"Sounds lovely, James. Thank you."

She wanted to spend more time with him. However, if his purpose was to make Pauly and her work out their problems, none of his romantic overtures mattered. That concern made her keep her guard up.

"It's been three-quarters of a year, but I never told you how proud I was of you for picking up that cast iron pan and defending your nieces during the standoff." James tipped his head and met her gaze with a shining look of appreciation.

"Thanks. Everyone helped." She picked up her water glass and took a couple of gulps. "You were brave too. Heroic, even."

James's cheeks hued burgundy. "Nice of you to say."

She enjoyed seeing him blush. Her humble hero.

Their food arrived—grilled salmon for her, fried chicken for him—turning their conversation to favorite dishes, backyard barbecues, and some topics from a recent community meeting. They even made plans for a fall picnic before colder weather settled in.

In some ways, they were already acting like a couple, making plans to spend time together, chatting and laughing. Did James think of her in a romantic way? How could she be certain he was being genuine when she still had so many doubts?

Chapter Nineteen

Ever since James dropped off Callie last night, he looked forward to walking and talking with her again. He felt drawn to her. Intrigued. Fascinated. When did he ever think so much about one woman before?

He called himself all kinds of a fool for his utter lack of romantic experience. Didn't he ask Callie to marry him to get her to make amends with her brother? How anti-romantic was that? And last night, he didn't make a single attempt to hold her hand or kiss her.

As they stood on her porch, he felt awkward and clumsy. Sweaty hands, dry lips, his feet shuffling back and forth like standing still was impossible. He told her goodbye and left. Idiot!

Trying to guess what a woman might want when it came to affection and romance left him baffled. The few dates he went on in the past turned out okay. Although, he never understood why the ladies didn't want to continue going out with him. And the ones he never called back didn't seem to mind. Other than the movies he'd seen, he knew diddly-squat about courting a woman.

"You're awfully quiet," Callie commented as they walked down the road near the project house.

"Just thinking."

"I'm a say-it-and-be-done-with-it sort of gal. If you've got something on your mind, say it."

She nailed that difference between them.

"I, uh, don't know how to do this."

"Do what?" She tipped her head, staring at him.

"Court. Date. Be romantic." Heat infused his face. Did he look like a blushing schoolboy?

"Go on."

"I'm struggling here." He paused and lightly clasped her hand. "I care about you, Cal."

Her jaw dropped. Her face hued a pretty shade of pink.

"I enjoyed our outing last night so much," he said.

Any second, she'd surely yank her fingers away from his.

"What are you saying, James?" She frowned. As he imagined, she pulled her hand back and messed with the edge of her sweater.

"I asked you to marry me, and you scoffed."

"You weren't serious!"

"What if I was?"

"You weren't, so it doesn't matter."

Callie walked again, slower this time. He gauged his steps to hers.

What could he say or do to convince her of his honesty and honor? "I enjoy talking with you. I enjoy spending time together. I thought we might, uh, have something going."

"Like what? What are you talking about beyond your meddling with Pauly and me?"

He gulped at her strong tone of voice. "I'm talking about caring for you, Callie. Wanting more to happen between us." He shrugged, wishing he were brave enough to kiss her. "Romance. Commitment. That sort of stuff."

"Are you saying what I think you're saying?"

"What do you think I'm saying?"

"Wait." She stopped and glared at him. "Does this have anything to do with your phony proposal?"

"No!"

"Because I'd rather live my whole life alone than marry someone for a reason other than love." She wagged her index finger at him. "Even to make peace with my brother isn't reason enough to marry you!"

"Thanks for the vote of confidence."

"You know what I mean."

James sighed. Did he care for Callie as more than a friend? Love would come in time. But how did she feel about him? "What I'm saying isn't anything about the other proposal. And maybe, it sort of is," he added sheepishly.

"I don't want anything to do with that one!"

"I'm sorry." He ran his palms lightly down both of her arms, taking a risk of her rejecting him. "Did you like going out on a date with me?"

She pressed her lips together.

"Did you?"

"Yes! No mystery about that."

"On the contrary. You are a complete mystery to me, Callie Cedars." He tried keeping his voice softer than he usually spoke. "I want to discover more about you. You intrigue me. It's like I've known you forever, yet I don't know you at all."

She gulped like his comments took her by surprise.

"I already care about you. Honest, I do."

"As your friend's punk sister?" She pointed down the road. "Are we going to walk, or not?"

Despite her gruff tone, he held his hand out to her. "Shall we walk together, Cal? Learn about each other? Find out if there's more between us?"

She stared at his hand for about fifteen seconds. Then, slowly, she rested her palm against his. Their fingers linked and fit perfectly together.

"I like holding your hand and walking with you, too," she said.

A surge of energy and hope made him feel twenty years younger.

Was this the beginning of love? Or was it possible he'd loved Callie Cedars for a long time and never recognized it?

Hand in hand, admiring the fall colors and the sounds of the bay beyond the trees, they walked and talked like old friends. She pointed out a flock of geese heading south. He picked up a light blue stone and turned it over and over in his hand, wiping the surface clean. When he held the rock out to her, she tucked it into her sweater pocket. A keepsake of their time together?

By the time they returned to the project house, James's question from earlier twirled in his brain. What would kissing Callie be like? If he took her in his arms and pressed his mouth to hers, warmly and passionately, what would she say?

Chapter Twenty

Callie paused in front of the project house door without opening it. Should she ask James to come inside for coffee? They went out on a date last night. Now, they'd taken a walk and held hands. That seemed like enough togetherness for twenty-four hours. She didn't know what the next step should be in a situation like this.

Meeting his gaze, she noticed again how lovely his dark eyes were. A few freckles peppered his cheeks reminding her of him as a kid. She'd never been this close to him, other than when she stood as a runner on first base and James waited next to her, their tennis shoes nearly touching on the square of dirt marking the base.

If only he looked at her then like he gazed at her now, their whole lives might have been different. They might have loved each other. Been high school sweethearts. Married. Had kids. Sigh.

He said he cared for her. Caring was a far cry from loving. Two people might care for each other for years without their friendship ever turning into romantic love. However, James acted more tender toward her now. What if he had romantic feelings for her after all this time? Could her heart handle that?

"Talk to you later," she said.

"Wait." He cleared his throat, his gaze dropping to his shoes.

"What is it?"

"I have a question to ask you."

"All right." Familiar with the way he pondered his thoughts before sharing them with her, she waited.

He lifted his gaze gradually to hers. "Cal, what would you have done if I kissed you last night after our date?"

Her pounding heart beat faster. She swallowed a couple of times. "What would I have done? Why, kissed you back, of course!"

The widest smile crossed James's mouth. "Good to hear. Real good." He nearly skipped down the steps, even with his slight limp.

"That's it? Good to hear?"

On the gravel driveway, he paused. "Next time, let's try it." He winked at her then moved out of sight.

Next time? So he planned to ask her out again!

She walked into the house, but in her thoughts she was dancing. Closing the door, she leaned against it, her knees feeling weak. What would kissing James Weston be like? Would it be a light brushing of their lips? Butterfly soft. Or something much more? She sighed dreamily.

Later, James called her cell phone. "I have an idea I want to run by you."

She liked his light rumbly tones that tickled her ear as he spoke. "Okay."

"Tide's low. A late afternoon beach walk sounds inviting, doesn't it?" He cleared his throat like he felt awkward with the inquiry. "Do you still like to look for shells? I remember you doing that when you were a girl."

"Haven't gone shell hunting in a couple of decades."

"No time like the present. Want to walk and look for shells with me?"

His promise about them kissing next time fluttered through her thoughts. Would he kiss her on their beach walk?

"I wouldn't mind getting some more steps in. My doctor would approve." As soon as she said the unemotional words, she wished she'd been more sincere. "Yes, James. I'd love to take a beach walk with you."

"Excellent. Can you be ready in a half hour?"

"I'll be ready."

While she donned loose-fitting jeans and rarely worn hiking boots, she pondered James's comment from earlier. She imagined their lips touching softly, their bodies close together. Where would she put her hands during a romantic embrace? Over his shoulders? Around his back?

What if his suggestion of them kissing was based on his plan to intervene in Pauly's and her battle? What if he was faking an affection for her that he didn't feel? What if someone saw them kissing and spread rumors?

Ugh. Why couldn't she enjoy his company and accept that he might care for her?

Maybe her doubts were based on her years of feeling rejected by him. Fifty years of him ignoring her girlish crush might have ruined their chances of anything meaningful happening now. So what if he took her on one date, held her hand and walked with her? Was she supposed to jump up and down because he finally noticed her?

Along with her misgivings, a chip grew on her shoulder. What if his talk of kissing her was a joke? Would James tell her brother about it? Anger infused her as these questions raced around in her mind. Her heart pounding in her temples sounded like a hammer thudding against a metal gong.

Calm down. James is a nice man. He says he cares for me.

Drawing in a deep breath, she put on her jacket. She didn't have experience kissing a man. Holding hands might be deceptive, but a kiss didn't lie. If James Weston kissed her today, then she'd know the truth.

Chapter Twenty-one

As soon as they reached the beach, James clasped Callie's cool hand. The ease of taking her hand in his, and the way she linked her fingers with his, amazed him. Why hadn't he done this when they were younger? How did he let so many years pass without making a move on Callie? She lived across the street all those years. Talk about blind! Talk about not seeing what was directly in front of him.

Their gazes met and his footsteps felt lighter. Ever since he left her this morning, he hadn't gotten kissing her off his mind. Callie said she would have kissed him back. He should have just smooched with her then!

Before he drove out to the project house, he contemplated bringing her another gift. Maybe chocolates. Until he recalled her avoidance of sweets. Maybe he'd get a knickknack. Or a piece of fruit. Anything to put a smile on her face.

Instead, he came empty-handed, but not empty-hearted. He felt so many things about Callie. So many emotions he suppressed over the years bubbled up within him now. How long had he felt this way toward his neighbor's sister, perhaps, without even realizing it?

Strolling across the mudflats holding Callie's hand in his, he suddenly felt tongue-tied. Not sure what to say to bring their conversation toward romance, or their possible future together, he simply walked beside her. Holding her hand and crossing the sandy beach felt like they were on an adventure. No pressure to make plans or to do anything. Just being with her pleased him. He hoped she felt the same way.

When their gazes met and she glanced away, he wanted to help her be more comfortable with him. He hoped she wanted him to be more than just her brother's friend. He wouldn't mind if she called him her boyfriend. His cheeks warmed at the thought.

"Do you want to hunt for shells?"

"Sure. If we find any whole ones, I'll keep them."

He let go of her hand and withdrew a plastic grocery bag from his pocket. "I brought this. If we find any treasures, we can save them."

"How nice of you," Callie said in a soft tone. "I didn't think of bringing one. My thoughts were all in a dither." She blushed like she wished she hadn't mentioned that part.

He got a kick out of hearing she was flustered or distracted by something, or someone. Dare he hope that distraction might be him? Maybe she was picturing the kiss he mentioned. Hoping for that? Feeling ten feet tall, he ambled along beside Callie, both staring at the ground, searching for shells or rocks.

"Here's a pretty one." She squatted down and picked up a muddy rock. "An agate." She wiped off the mud and stood, fingering the light-blue rock. "I used to love finding these."

"It's beautiful like you." The words, while sincerely meant, were foreign to him. Still, he grinned and winked at her, hoping to flirt with her a little.

Her drop-jawed expression was priceless. She wasn't used to hearing such things from him!

She resumed walking. "Those comments are unnecessary, James."

"Why is that?" He measured his stride to hers, allowing for his gimpy knee.

"I'm not the beautiful, pampered type. I don't need words of affirmation." She lifted her chin, giving him one of her haughty looks.

He almost chuckled. Not wanting to be insensitive, he didn't. "Why, Callie Cedars." He clasped his hand around the crook of her elbow, bringing her to a halt. "Are you telling me no man has called you beautiful lately?"

She snorted, then glared at him so strongly he thought she might stomp away. "No. And don't make anything of it!"

With her glaring at him, kissing her on the mouth for the first time might not be a smart move. But the moment called for action. She might not need words of affirmation, but the two of them needed a connection. He wanted to assure her of his sincerity. He already considered her beautiful and smart and witty. Even if they weren't in love yet, he cared about her as a dear friend. Maybe more.

He brushed his mouth against her cheek. Her skin felt cool against his warm lips. "You are beautiful, Cal. You are a special person to me."

Her gaze fixed on him, moisture pooled in her eyes. "Oh, the wind is making me teary." She brushed her hand over her eyes.

Unsure what to do next, he clasped her hand again, and they walked farther down the beach. Callie might not be used to him saying she was beautiful. But he planned to say the words again and again until she believed them.

Chapter Twenty-two

Tired of her usual vegetable entrees, Callie hunted online for a new sweet potato recipe without finding much success. She read the ingredients list for a couple of options, frustrated with her absence of essential items. While she perused the Web via her phone, Micah's crying in the living room grated on her nerves. She flipped to another recipe, and the toddler's high-pitched wail set her teeth on edge.

Goodness. How could anyone concentrate?

Lola shushed the boy and walked the floors between the living room and dining room, her voice fading and then drawing closer again. The poor woman sounded exhausted. Had she even had a break this morning? She probably needed a few minutes to herself.

Leaving the sweet potato slices on the island, Callie crossed into the dining room. "Is there anything I can do to help?"

"Sorry for all the noise. I think he might be sick."

"Don't worry about his crying. It must be hard having to stay in the house so much." Callie tucked the dish towel into her apron pocket, then thrust out her hands toward the little guy who was wrenching and twisting in Lola's arms. "Shall I try? I might be able to distract him or calm him down while you call a doctor."

Lola's mouth fell open as if she were surprised by the request, which made Callie frustrated with herself for not offering to help sooner.

"Please. Let me help."

"All right. Thank you. I'll use the bathroom if that's okay."

"Of course."

Callie paced with Micah as Lola had been doing, shushing him and trying to cuddle him. "There, there." Her body type was cushier than Lola's thin one. As if she were a pillow, Micah gave a whimpering sigh of exhaustion, pressed his cheek against her, and fell asleep. "Well, now. Aren't you the tired one?" She shuffled back and forth, humming a lullaby.

Lola strode back into the room, then let out a little huff. "How did you get him to sleep so quickly?"

"I have no idea. I did what I do with Piper, shushing, singing, and moving around."

"Which I've been doing for over an hour." Lola rocked her thumb toward the kitchen. "Do you mind if I get some coffee?"

"Help yourself. Do whatever you need to do."

"Thank you, Callie. So much." Lola scurried from the room.

Callie continued swaying the limp toddler in her arms and walked into the living room. Eventually, she sat down in one of the soft chairs with Micah crumpled against her chest. She closed her eyes and enjoyed the maternal sensations of holding and rocking a small child, feeling as if she were already a part of Lola and Micah's family.

"He was so tired," Lola said from the doorway.

"If you need to get anything done, throw a load of wash in, take a shower, whatever, go right ahead." Callie smoothed her hand over the boy's back. She'd return to hunting for a new recipe later. "Your little one is quite content for now."

"I may take you up on that."

"Did you want to call the clinic?" Callie felt the warmth emanating from Micah's body as she moved slightly. He must have a temperature.

"Maybe I should." Lola pulled her cell phone out of her back pocket and returned to the kitchen.

Callie heard her muffled conversation.

"Kid meds, rest, and lots of fluids," Lola said when she returned. "I'll keep a watch on his temp." She strode over and touched the back of her fingers against his temple. "Still warm." She settled onto the couch. "I've been meaning to say thank you."

"For what?"

"For giving us a place to stay. For welcoming us here. All this." She swayed her hands toward the living room space, then at Callie holding her son.

"You're welcome. And you are welcome to stay here for as long as you want. I mean that. You are part of our project house family now."

"Thank you. He likes you. You're like his Abuela." Lola nodded toward the toddler.

"What's that?"

"Grandmother."

Callie smiled. Grandmother. She liked that.

"I didn't have any family to help me. It's been hard being a single mom since my husband left us alone."

"Must have been tough."

"This house and your friendship, and Kathleen's, is more than I ever imagined. Beyond anything I hoped for."

"Are you feeling more rested? Strengthened in your spirit?" Callie floundered with what to ask the other woman that wouldn't be too personal. "Are you doing okay?"

"Today I'm such a mess!" Lola raked her fingers through her long dark hair in frantic motions. "I didn't get much sleep. I should take a shower. But I don't want to leave Micah even for a minute."

"He's fine. I'll call if there's the slightest change."

Lola's eyes blinked slowly as if she could barely keep them open. "This is so nice. I'll just—" She leaned her head against the back cushion and was snoring quietly a couple of minutes later.

The poor dear.

Callie prayed for Lola and Micah. These two were precious to her already. Watching them leave one day would be so hard. Hopefully, that wouldn't happen for a long time. In the meantime, she'd enjoy all the pseudo grandma hugs and baby holding she could get.

Thank You, Lord, for letting me be a part of Lola and Micah's journey. Please protect them. Let them feel completely loved and cared for while they are here.

Chapter Twenty-three

Two weeks after her last appointment with Doctor Isabel, Callie returned to the doctor's office. She hated getting on the scale in front of the nurse. Hated going through the motions of being scrutinized and questioned about her efforts to control her weight. Was she eating per the doctor's orders? Taking her medicine? Exercising regularly? What did she eat this morning?

She didn't want to answer the nurse's prying questions. But the thirty-something woman was just doing her job. Treating her like one more task in her day, too.

Finally, Doctor Isabel entered the small exam room that reminded Callie of a jail cell.

"Good morning, Callie! How are you doing?" she said a little too brightly.

"Wishing I was anywhere but here."

Doctor Isabel chuckled. "You and me both. I'd rather be out walking on the beach on this gorgeous fall day. What would you like to be doing?" She sat down in a chair in front of where Callie sat on the uncomfortable examination table.

"I'd like to be walking too." With James. She glanced at the ceiling as the doctor checked her pulse. Then she felt the stethoscope pressing against her chest. "I've been doing more walking. Much more than I used to, anyway."

"That's good to hear."

Even if the scale didn't reveal her efforts, she wanted the doctor to know she'd taken her get-healthy speech to heart.

"Your numbers are a smidge better."

She had to say, "a smidge."

"Does this mean I can eat pastries again?"

"Hardly." Doctor Isabel smirked.

After listening to her heart and lungs, then writing furiously on a chart, the doctor met Callie's gaze somberly. "What steps have you taken to get healthier in the last month?"

"I've mostly stopped eating sugar."

"Mostly?"

Callie puckered her lips. "Eating salads. Lean meat and veggies. Whole foods, per your suggestion. No sugar in my tea, which is a downright travesty."

"Do you have more energy?"

"Not really."

"You will. Now, tell me about exercising. What have you done differently since I last saw you?"

"As I said, walking. Beach walking. Trudging through the sand takes more effort. Burns more calories." No need to mention she went on a date with James to do so.

"Let's increase your steps."

"Increase?" Giving up sweet tea and pastries weren't enough?

"I want you to lose weight, Callie. Your heart is still working too hard."

Callie groaned.

"Let's consider your walking times as medicine." Doctor Isabel gave her one of her perceptive looks. "I'm upping the dosage. If you're walking one mile a day, try one-and-a-quarter for the next week. Then up that a little." She set the chart on the counter. "It's nice to have a buddy."

"What do you mean?" Did she hear about James and her walking together? People in Basalt Bay were such gossips, she might have.

"It's nice to have a walking partner." Doctor Isabel's eyebrows rose. "What did you think I meant?"

"Nothing." Callie pressed her lips together.

"You are staying with other ladies, right? One of them might enjoy walking with you."

"Maybe." But she preferred walking with James.

Doctor Isabel stood. "Sometimes when we're talking with someone, the time flies by and we wind up walking farther than we planned."

Talking with someone. Holding his hand. *Kissing him.*

"Callie?"

"Oh, huh? What?"

"See you next month."

"Yeah, sure. Why not?"

By then, she'd surely have lost some weight and given her heart the rest it needed. Maybe in a month's time, she'd know whether she and James stood a chance of being more than friends, too.

Chapter Twenty-four

James had been daydreaming about Callie all morning, so when she called him on his cell, their conversation felt like an extension of his thoughts and dreams.

"Would you like to take another walk with me, James?"

He gulped at hearing his name said in such a throaty tone in his ear. Perhaps her tonal shift signaled a change from friendship to a deeper relationship. Or was that his wishful thinking?

"Walking with you sounds great! Whatever you want, Cal, I'm here for you."

She chuckled softly and the sound washed over him like a fine rain, refreshing and peaceful.

"I meant another beach walk. Not a date."

"I'd go anywhere with you." He tried matching his tone to her previous husky vibe. "Walking on the beach counts as a date too."

"It might," she whispered.

He liked this flirting between them. The back and forth innuendos made him eager to spend more time with her.

"So, you'll drive out and walk with me in an hour or so?"

"Will do. Can't wait."

After the call ended, he walked around his house whistling tunes from the sixties. When had his heart felt so light? So filled with hope for the future?

Even with his lighthearted feelings, he and Callie strolled a ways down the beach before he built up the courage to reach for her hand again. As soon as his palm touched hers, warmth and awareness passed through him. Their gazes met. Her hand was cool. His, warm. Startling coolness meeting warmth intrigued him, making him imagine the feel of cool lips against the heat of his own.

He smiled at her. She smiled too, soft and inviting.

"What's on your mind, Cal?"

Kissing her was on his mind!

"Why do you think I have something on my mind?" She shook her head, the wind fluttering her short hair with the movement.

"Your dark eyes shimmered and you leaned forward like you were moving in for a discussion." He winked. "Or a kiss."

"You are a rapscallion, James Weston!"

"Maybe I am." He chuckled and tugged on her hand playfully.

"What do you want to do with the rest of your time on this earth?"

Her serious question surprised him and veered his thoughts away from romance and flirting.

"I suppose I want to be happy and content with my life."

"That's it?" Her eyes lost some of their luster. Tension flowed from her hands into his in the way she tightened her grip.

"What answer were you hoping for? I don't have any big aspirations."

Their pace slowed. Drawing in a long breath, she pulled her hand away. He felt the loss immediately.

"I'm not hoping for a certain answer." She stuffed both fists into her coat pockets, and her shoulders lifted. "We should still have plans and dreams. Those didn't die when we started looking into Medicare!"

He chuckled at her vehemence.

"I suppose some of my youthful dreams wilted with age and loneliness." He was being as honest and transparent as he could be.

Callie must have understood. She gently linked their fingers together again and nodded, encouraging him to continue.

"I'm looking forward to planting a garden next spring. I'd like to expand my small vegetable plot. Maybe go on a camping trip."

"I've never grown vegetables."

At least she didn't mock his minimal dreams.

The waves rolled up the shoreline, making their stride angle toward drier land.

"We could try gardening together. Camping might be fun, too." He didn't have much to contribute to a conversation about dreams and goals.

"Does anything else excite you about the future?"

What was she getting at? Was she hinting about marriage?

"Like?"

"I don't know." She rubbed her free hand over the back of her neck. "I've only recently pondered my part in making a difference in someone else's life."

So, this wasn't a marriage discussion. He wished she wanted to be with him and live their lives together.

Callie's walking speed slowed down even more. "I want to help other women by giving them a place to rest and recuperate. Doing something positive with whatever time I have left is important to me." She linked her hand into the crook of his arm.

"Like what you've done with Sarah and Lola at the project house?"

"Yes, that's right." Her gaze met his with a softer look. "I've had my disagreements with Pauly over the years, but I've always known he was there if I needed him. I've tried to assure my nieces I'm here for them too. Especially in the absence of their mom." She stopped walking. "I want to continue helping women who might not have a support system. Do you understand what I'm saying?"

"Uh-huh. Sure." It dawned on him that she had her life's work in front of her. Did that preclude her from wanting to form a lasting attachment with him? From wanting to marry him?

Disheartened, he felt like a fifty pound weight rested on his shoulders as they strode through the sand back toward the project house. He'd entertained so many hopes about what marriage to Callie would be like. So many thoughts about their future together. Was she subtly telling him she didn't feel the same way?

After a while, Callie tugged on his arm. "Why did you go silent? Do you find my dreams absurd at my age?"

"Not at all! Your dreams about serving others are admirable." He let out a long sigh that burned up his chest. "It's just … I've had some notions recently."

"What kind of notions?"

Facing her, he held his hands out, palms up. After a hesitancy, she clasped her hands in both of his, staring at him with wide-open eyes.

"These kinds of notions, Cal." He squeezed her hands gently. "I asked you to marry me."

"Not seriously."

"Maybe not as serious as I should have been." But he had asked the question. He never did that with anyone else. "You have dreams of helping other ladies, but where does that leave us?"

"Is there an 'us?' Are you invested in there being an 'us?'"

"Yes, I am. I want to see where this leads to between us."

"Then why did you go silent when I shared my dreams with you? I don't like being made to feel as if my thoughts are of no consequence."

"It's not that. Your thoughts are deeply important to me." A gust of wind blew against them from off the ocean. He turned them slightly to avoid getting sand in their eyes. "It's just that my vegetable patch and your lofty goals don't line up together so well."

"Maybe not. But talking about them, even arguing about them, is better than you going silent and me not knowing what you're thinking."

Talking honestly with a woman was unfamiliar territory to James. "I've lived alone with my thoughts for a lot of years, Cal. Sometimes I'm going to be quiet. You've always been freer with expressing your thoughts." He eyed her uncertainly. Would she be offended by his assessment?

A flirtatious smile crossed her mouth. "True. However, I've kept a few secrets of my own."

"Oh?" Did she mean secrets about him? Now that was an intriguing idea!

Chapter Twenty-five

Callie answered the door and found a dark-haired, mid-thirties, bearded man standing on her porch. A wary yet stern expression lined his face. His gaze shifted from Callie's face to somewhere beyond her, inside the house. She closed the door slightly behind her.

"May I help you?"

"Is Lola here?"

Was this man Lola's husband?

"Who are you?" She made her voice sound stern.

"Ben." He cleared his throat. "Benjamin Presley. I'm—"

"I know who you are." She thrust her finger toward the driveway. "You should leave now, before I call the deputy!"

"Please. I need to speak with my wife. I want to see my son. Where is Lola? Is she here?"

He sounded desperate, but Callie wasn't falling for any of his nonsense.

"I'm not telling you anything, other than to say, get off my property! You're trespassing!"

He backed up a couple of feet and palmed the air, his hat still clutched in one hand. "I don't want to cause any trouble. That's not why I'm here."

"Then leave. Get back in your vehicle and drive out of town."

"I can't do that."

"Callie?" Lola's quiet voice called from the dining room. "Are you okay?"

"I'm fine. Stay back." Callie kept her gaze on the man, ready to rush back into the house and slam the door in Benjamin's face. "If you want to talk with Lola, make an appointment with the deputy or a lawyer to accompany you." She pointed outward again. "Don't come here like this again, or I will make a formal complaint."

The man's eyes flooded with tears. "I want to talk with my wife. I need to see her. That's all." He gulped. "Lola? I've made mistakes. I just want to—"

"Don't speak to her! I'm warning you!"

Benjamin peered over Callie's shoulder as if trying to see through the crack in the door. "Lola, baby, I miss you. I'm sorry for getting angry and leaving you. It will never happen again. I swear I'm finished with alcohol!"

"Leave!"

Scowling, he stared hard at Callie for several seconds. "I'll go. But I'll be back." He strode off the porch.

Callie marched back inside, slammed the door, and bolted it.

"How did he find me?" Lola's panicked-looking gaze met Callie's. She gripped her hands together, the whites of her knuckles showing.

"I don't know, but he did." Callie gave the younger woman a brief hug. "Are you okay?"

"It scared me to hear his voice. I'm trembling all through my body." Lola wrapped her arms around herself. "What should I do? He said he'll come back. Should I go and hide somewhere else?"

"No. You'll stay right here. We've fended off worse than him." Callie pictured the attackers who invaded their house a year ago. "Let's call and talk to Pastor Sagle." She walked into the kitchen and grabbed her cell phone. "I'll give Deputy Brian a heads-up too."

Lola followed her. "He said he was sorry. He's finished with drinking. That's good, right?"

"If he means it, that's good. But what is he willing to do to prove he's sorry and ready to change his ways? I don't trust him."

Lola's dark eyes filled with tears. "He's always sorry after a fight. After he slugged the wall and made a hole in it, he was so ashamed. He's never hit me."

"But?" Callie clenched her teeth.

"I fear him when he gets crazy with drinking."

"Yelling and acting aggressively can be mentally and emotionally abusive, even without physical contact. He must change before you are with him alone." Callie met Lola's gaze and tried maintaining a nonjudgmental attitude. Still, she felt compelled to say what was on her mind. "You deserve better than a man who yells at you or belittles you because he's drinking and angry. Your son deserves to be safe and well cared for, too."

"I agree in here." Lola patted her head. "But in here I think I should forgive him." She patted her chest. "Love him no matter what he's done. Especially if he is sorry as he says."

Callie sighed. "What about him abandoning you?"

"Even so, I must try to make my marriage work."

"You're sweet for being so forgiving. Please, don't make any rash decisions. And don't leave the house. Stay put and we'll talk with the pastor."

"I'm weak. If I were here alone, I would give in to his soft voice. I always give in. Now, I will go and check on Micah." Lola jogged across the room and hurried up the stairs, sniffling.

Scrolling through her contact list, Callie searched for Pastor Sagle's number. Then Lola's words registered. *"I would give in to his soft voice.* "Would she go back with her louse of a husband in a moment of weakness? Before there was any real change?

Callie felt the anguish of those questions breaking her heart. If it were up to her, Lola would never see Benjamin again, let alone try to make her marriage work. But despite her internal grief, the decision wasn't hers to make.

An hour later, Pastor Sagle sat in a chair opposite Lola and Callie, who sat side by side on the couch. Lola twisted a baby toy in her hand while she answered the pastor's questions.

"What do you hope will happen in the future, Lola?" Pastor Sagle held his coffee cup and gazed at her with a caring expression.

"I want my baby to be healthy and safe. I also love my husband." She took a noisy breath. "I feel guilty for leaving him. Not telling him where I was going. When we married, I vowed to stay with him. To be faithful."

"Oh, Lola," Callie mumbled.

Lola clasped her hand. Callie gently squeezed back.

"Did he hurt you? Previously, I mean," Pastor Sagle said.

"Not physically. When he's drinking, he yells and says threatening things. I am terrified of him, then." She shuddered. "But I won't file any complaints. I know he loves me."

Callie wanted to say, "You should never go back to the clod!" But she held her tongue. Her frustration with Benjamin's unannounced arrival at her door still thudded through her. She'd do anything to protect Lola and Micah. But what if Benjamin showed up here while she was away? Would he convince Lola to forget about his selfish, cad-like behavior and leave with him?

The thought nearly made her sick to her stomach.

"There's the matter of his leaving you and the baby alone without provisions," Pastor Sagle said. "Not telling you where he went, being gone for days. While it wasn't legal abandonment, I consider it morally inexcusable."

"Me too," Callie said, glad the pastor used such strong wording and emotion.

"But he is my husband. I am to respect him. Believe the best in him." Lola's lips trembled. "That's what my father expects of me. The example my mama gave to me while she lived."

"Did your father ever mistreat your mother?" the pastor asked quietly.

"Yelling. Lots of anger on both sides."

Callie let the air in her lungs out slowly.

"My mama was devoted to him." Lola lifted her chin. "I will do no less." Then she wilted onto the couch, curling up against the pillows like a child. "But there's Micah to consider."

"Of course, you must think about his welfare. And your own." Callie scooted over and took the young woman in her arms and held her as she sobbed for about five minutes.

Pastor Sagle closed his eyes, obviously praying.

"I'm sorry for my outburst." Lola pushed away from Callie. "It's childish of me."

"It's okay to cry. Nothing to be sorry about."

"You are kind. Both of you." She sniffed and wiped the sleeve of her blue hoodie over her face. "What should I do? Stay. Leave. Go back to him?"

"Please, stay," Callie said softly. "I want you to get healthy and strong."

"Benjamin realizes where we are now. Despite my brave talk of my mama and papa, I am not my mama." She clenched both of her fists. "I will not allow Benjamin to make my son afraid again!"

"I know you won't." Callie's heart burned with anger.

Lola leaned against her as if all her previous bravado fled. "What should I do? Tell me."

"Stay, dear one. You are safe here. Micah is safe and well. You both can live in peace." Callie met Pastor Sagle's gaze. An understanding passed between them.

How could they protect Lola if she wouldn't take steps to protect herself?

Chapter Twenty-six

Callie sat across from Deputy Brian in his cluttered office. His desk was littered with stacks of papers, an assortment of dirty coffee cups, and take-out containers. It wasn't much of an office for a public servant. A small town like theirs couldn't afford a fancy space for the lawman, but he should keep the room clean!

Callie didn't even want to come here today, since she'd never respected the deputy much. But he represented the law in Basalt Bay. He was cleared of all charges concerning the attack on the town. And she had Lola's well-being to consider.

"I have a woman in my care who needs protection from a verbally abusive spouse who abandoned her." She rapped her knuckles against the edge of his messy desk, emphasizing her point. "What can you do to provide assistance?"

"Tell her to come in and file a complaint." Deputy Brian lifted his hands in a shrug. "If she doesn't, my hands are tied."

"Can't you follow the guy? Park your car outside our house. Act threatening if he comes back!" Callie glared at the deputy who sometimes came across as lazy and more interested in his computer screen and coffee mug than in helping anyone.

"As I said, I—"

"I don't want to hear your excuses!"

"Excuse me?" His chest puffed up. "Why don't you and those ladies beef up your security? Put in an alarm system. Or video surveillance."

"That's your idea of helping? Some help." Callie didn't try to hide the derision in her tone. "My friend needs protection today!"

Deputy Brian took a long slurp of his coffee. "If there's immediate danger, or if the woman decides to file the paperwork, give me a call."

"This was a wasted trip." Callie pushed up from her chair. "Why did I even bother?"

"Sorry, ma'am. I'd like to do more." He stood but didn't move away from the desk and his computer.

"If you wanted to do something, you would."

"I can make a couple of passes by your house later. I still recommend the security equipment."

Groaning, Callie left the deputy's office in a bad mood. All the way to Lewis's Super, she stewed. An alarm system. Outdoor surveillance cameras. What good would those do? She doubted they'd detour Benjamin Presley from approaching the project house the next time he got it in his mind to speak with Lola. Or, heaven forbid, trying to enter their house when Callie and Kathleen weren't present to protect Lola and Micah.

As she picked out fruit and vegetables for tonight's dinner, her thoughts churned. Maybe Judah would help with installing a video camera. She could call one of those alarm installation companies. Probably should have already done that so her guests would feel safer at the project house. What she wanted to do was shut down Benjamin's ability to return to the house. To have someone, namely the town's sorry excuse of a deputy, slap a restraining order across his face. That would satisfy her.

Forest was a private investigator. Maybe she'd hire him to investigate Benjamin and dig up some dirt on him. A sleaze like him must be up to no good.

If she found out Lola's husband was involved in something illegal—selling drugs, cheating on his taxes, or evading the law— she'd do something! She'd pound on Deputy Brian's door until he did his job the way she thought he should.

What did other women in similar predicaments do? To whom did they turn? When Bess left her abusive husband, she lived with her son, Judah. What about women in Basalt Bay and the other coastal towns nearby who didn't have anyone to turn to in a crisis? Did they feel stuck, unable to depend on anyone? The thought of women who felt alone, neglected, and forgotten when they were already going through a harsh situation made Callie feel terribly sad.

She, Bess, and Kathleen had two spare rooms in the project house, three in a pinch if they converted their planning room into a bedroom. Sarah was already staying in the attic conversion. That left one guest room on the second floor for Lola and Micah.

How could they serve other women in need when they were nearly out of space? Even if she knew of another person going through a difficult time right this second, she didn't have a bedroom to offer her.

Her burden to help and her means of helping weren't matching up. Their house was big, yet not big enough. The urgency to reach out to those who might be as desperate as Lola wouldn't leave Callie. In fact, Benjamin daring to stand belligerently on her porch and make his demands known made her more determined than ever to open their door to those who might not be able to open a door for themselves.

Lord, help us figure out what to do. You've put this desire on my heart to help others. I want to follow Your leading. Please, show me what to do next.

Chapter Twenty-seven

"I can't thank you enough!" Callie said to Judah the next afternoon. "You installed the video cameras faster than a serviceman would have done."

"You're welcome. I'm glad I could take a couple hours off work." Her nephew-in-law held up a blueberry scone. "I appreciate the homemade goodies too."

"I'll tell Kathleen you enjoyed it. I've sworn off baking. Grudgingly, so."

"Are you feeling any better?" He gave her a one arm hug.

"'Better' is debatable. I'm tolerant of my situation. I enjoy walking again. So that's something." Callie heaved a sigh. "I'm waiting for a zap of good ole energy to hit me. Otherwise, I mostly complain about my lack of sugary treats." Although she wasn't feeling as irritable and jittery as she had over the last two weeks. That had to be a good sign.

Judah, the chivalrous man he was, didn't say anything else about her weight-loss efforts. He took another bite of his scone. "Anything else I can repair or check while I'm here?" It was nice of him to ask since he had been the supervisor in charge of the project house renovation.

"No, thanks. Just the surveillance equipment. I spoke with an alarm estimator briefly. The ladies and I will discuss his spendy recommendations."

"Okay. I'll be on my way then."

"Thanks again. Give Tanner a kiss for me."

"Will do."

After Judah left, Lola slipped into the kitchen. "Will it help?"

"The cameras facing the porch and driveway? Since the suggestion came from Deputy Brian, I hope so." Callie filled a glass full of water. "If Benjamin lurks around the property, we'll have proof of his trespassing."

"Was the deputy angry that I wouldn't file a complaint?" Lola sighed as if exhausted by the topic.

"Not angry. But there's not much he can do with the way things stand, or so he said. If Benjamin is caught doing something wrong, then things would be different." Callie took a long drink. "What would you say about me having him followed?"

"Followed?"

"Trailed. Secretly watched." Callie should talk with Forest about it.

"That would make him crazy!" Lola leaned against the wall leading into the kitchen. "What good will it do anyway?"

"I have an acquaintance who will watch him and see if he's doing anything questionable." Callie set down her glass in the sink. "At the least, see if he's staying sober like he said he was."

"I should talk with him first."

"No! That might not be safe for you."

Lola stood straighter and stared at Callie with a bold look. "I can't hide from my husband forever. I must face him. As long as he stays away from strong drink, I'll be fine." She slumped against the wall again. "But I still don't want to put Micah in a harmful situation."

"Please, stay away from Benjamin for now."

Lola didn't comment. Her dark eyes stared at the floor, not meeting Callie's gaze.

"If you must speak to him, take Pastor Sagle or Deputy Brian along. Okay?"

"I appreciate all you've done for me." Lola scuffed the heel of her shoe against the floor. "I don't mean to sound ungrateful."

"You don't. I'm glad we have a room available for you. We'll do everything in our power to make sure you and Micah are safe while you're with us." If she left, there wasn't anything Callie could do. She prayed it wouldn't come to that.

"Thank you." Lola crossed the space between them and hugged Callie. "Thank you for the video cameras too. You've done a lot for Micah and me already."

Lola left the room, and Callie felt a deep ache of worry. If only she could guarantee Lola's safety and keep her from making a dreadful mistake in going back to her husband too soon. But if she spoke forcefully in her argument against Benjamin, in her distaste of him as a husband and father, Lola might run right back to him. Didn't she say she felt weak about him?

They couldn't keep Lola locked up in her room. She must want to stay. She must want their help, or someone's help like Pastor Sagle's.

The saying about a village being needed to help raise a child came to mind. Wasn't that true about helping others in need, too? It took more than one person's desire to help. More than one person's resources.

Ohhh.

Callie was having an epiphany! Lola needed more than Callie and the other ladies at the project house had to give. She needed God. And she needed help from others.

Ideas flooded Callie, coming at her so fast she needed to write them down to remember them all. What if they started a coalition of women who were willing to help others in times of need and crisis? Not to take the place of counselors, medical personnel, or law enforcement. But for the women in town to band together and come alongside other women who were hurting or going through a struggle in life. To be like caring family members—sisters, moms, aunts, grandmothers.

This idea of Callie's went beyond her abilities. Bigger than Kathleen, Bess, and her, combined. However, it could be a city-wide mission! They were a small town. They should have the heart of a small town.

Even though Callie couldn't help all the women she wanted to help, maybe sharing her ideas, stirring them up in others, was exactly the thing she needed to do to make her feel like her life counted. Goosebumps raced up and down her arms.

She had the strongest urge to call James and tell him about her burgeoning ideas. Would he understand?

Chapter Twenty-eight

For two days, Callie's question about what his hopes and dreams might be for the future churned in James's mind. He told her about his goal to increase the garden. It was a practical goal. Certainly not a dream. Did she think that made him the most boring man in Basalt Bay?

He raked the leaves in his backyard and pondered her question some more. What goals did he have beyond gardening? Sometimes, he and Paul talked about driving down the coast and camping. Checking out sea lion caves. Visiting aquariums. Unfortunately, his camper got ruined during Hurricane Blaine.

Callie's dreams were more noble than his. She wanted to help women out of jams. Make a difference in someone's life. James had volunteered his time when he did carpentry work for the project house renovation. In a sermon he heard, Pastor Sagle said no good deed went unnoticed by heaven. James glanced heavenward, hoping it was true.

The next time he and Callie were together, he'd talk with her more about their goals. Then he would give her a better answer about what he'd like to do with his life. But first, he had to figure it out himself. With his limited energy and finances, what could he do?

He continued his chore of raking up leaves.

"What are you doing?" Paul's gruff voice reached him. "I texted you twice without a response."

"Sorry." James turned and watched his friend crossing the yard. "I'm taking care of the leaves. Didn't hear the phone."

"At least your not answering forced me out of my chair." Paul grumbled. "Looks nicer here than my backyard does."

"Thanks. I enjoy keeping the place tidy. Always did."

"I used to do that, too, before—" Paul left the sentence unfinished.

James raked a few more leaves into the pile, figuring he knew what Paul almost said. Before his health scare. Before Penny died. Before Hurricanes Addy and Blaine hit.

"What has you so preoccupied you didn't hear your phone?"

"Just thinking. I've been chewing on a question Callie asked me."

"Good grief. What's she stirring up now?"

"She asked me what I want to do with the rest of my life." James snorted, recalling his previous conversation with Paul. "Sort of like I asked you the other day."

"And? Did you come up with anything?" Paul scratched his whiskered chin. "Funny thing is, I've been pondering the same thing since you asked me."

"That right?" James eyed his buddy. "Are the two of us having an old-life crisis?"

"Maybe. It would explain a lot." Paul chuckled, his cranky tone disappearing. "If we are, let's debate it over pizza. We can drown our sorrows in cheese and pepperoni! Just put a frozen pizza in the oven. What do you say?"

"Sounds good to me." James pointed at the leaf pile. "I'll finish this and be right over."

A half-hour later the two of them were gobbling up pizza slices and potato chips. Shooting the breeze about Sunday night's football game. Laughing about a ridiculous call made by one of the refs. Commenting on the mild fall weather.

"Making headway with my bullheaded sister?"

The off-topic question surprised James.

"Oh, uh, some." No way would he tell Paul personal stuff about him and Callie. Not about them holding hands. Not about him daydreaming about kissing her.

"I knew it wouldn't work. Didn't I tell you so?" Paul swatted the air with his palm. "Don't worry. You'll find someone else."

"Hold on. I didn't say I'm giving up."

"No? What are you going to do then?" Paul stood, grabbed a cookie bag with a Lewis's Super label off the counter, and took two out in his hand before dropping back into his chair.

"I'm figuring things out." James grabbed a couple of cookies from the bag also. "The question she asked got me chewing on it. What have I done to help anyone?"

"Lots of things. You helped fix up the house Callie's living in. Don't get worked up over anything she says." Paul took a bite of his chocolate chip cookie then waved the remaining part toward James like a pointer. "She asks questions, states her opinions, and then leaves me more frustrated than I was in the first place."

"Her question keeps circling around in my brain," James said mostly to himself. He had wanted to do something creative with wood for a long time. But he'd never given it a go. What if he were brave enough to try now? To give an old dream a shot? "I like to tinker with wood in my shed. I used to want to make furniture."

"I can picture that." Paul took a bite of another cookie. "You'd be good at making picnic tables and such."

"So would you. You did those odd jobs at the hardware store. Including some carpentry."

"That's the truth." Paul nodded slowly. "I did more than my share of remodeling tasks."

"I did carpentry work for years but never made a single thing for myself." James recalled the wooden tables, rocking chairs, and Adirondack chairs he used to envision making. Once upon a time, he thought of owning his own shop in town. Never took the leap. Why didn't he ever try?

Was taking such a large step now ludicrous? Why? Because of his age? Who decided when age inhibited new efforts? He wasn't going to let his retired status stop him from doing anything. "What would you say if I used my shop in back to make a few pieces of furniture? As an experiment, you understand. Then tried selling them."

"I'd say go for it. You've got the time. Maybe I could help."

"You would do that?"

"Sure. I did woodworking in shop class back in high school." Paul's eyes took on a glow. "I've sanded a few boards in my time. Stained some wood."

Excitement pulsed through James. He felt like he was standing on the precipice of a new adventure. A brand new chapter in life, if he was willing to take the plunge. What if his experiment failed? What if he lost more money than he made? Ugh. He wasn't going to entertain thoughts of failure when he hadn't even started.

He and Paul would get a kick out of working together and making some furniture. If nothing turned out good enough to sell, they'd use the pieces themselves. Or give them away. See there. That would be doing something good for someone else.

Even with some doubts spinning in his brain, hope surged through him, too. He felt inspired! This was how he felt when he pitched in at the project house. A sense of working for a common cause hit him then. The same feeling struck him now as he pondered him and Paul doing woodworking projects.

"I'm going to clear out a space right away. If you want to help, I'd appreciate the assistance." It would get Paul away from the television too. "We could be partners in the business."

"Is that right? Well, well. Who would have thought we'd try anything like this?"

"Callie did."

"What?" Paul blasted out.

"Callie's question got me thinking positively about my future, our future, and what we might accomplish."

"My sister has her hand in everything! She'll rule the world if we let her." Groaning, Paul smacked his palm against his forehead. "If we succeed, she'll never let me live it down."

James chuckled. "Especially if she were my wife!"

"Hey, now. I think I already won our bet."

"No, you did not!"

Paul cast a glare in his direction as if he were going to keep arguing about it. Instead, he asked, "Is there money in the homemade furniture business?"

"Might be." James tried ignoring the irritation Paul's previous comment caused. "We don't know if our experiment will turn a profit. But how will we find out unless we try?" Just like he didn't know if he could persuade Callie to marry him unless he gave their budding romance his best effort.

"Sounds exciting though, doesn't it?" Paul smoothed his palms across the table. "I'll make a few sketches."

"That would be great!"

Paul being enthusiastic about anything again seemed miraculous.

"If we sold a few items and donated some of the funds to a good cause, we'd be doing a noble act too, like Callie."

"Do you have to keep bringing up my sister?"

"You bet I do!"

James couldn't wait to tell Callie the news about him and Paul going into the furniture-making business. She wouldn't believe it! He had her to thank for stirring up all these ideas in him, and in Paul, too.

Chapter Twenty-nine

"I've asked to meet with you in our planning room for a couple of reasons." Callie smiled at Bess and Kathleen who were sitting at the table in the upstairs room Kathleen used for her art projects. At the other end of the table, an array of blue and green glass pieces were spread out, grouped together by hues. "This room holds special memories for me because of our planning sessions for Bess's mayoral campaign."

"For me too." Bess sighed. "How is Lola doing? Is she okay?"

"She's doing better. This thing with her husband—I wish I could say ex-husband—troubles me immensely. It seems he's a loose cannon ready to explode."

"If there's anything I can do, tell me," Bess said. "Your security upgrades should help."

"I hope so."

They had already discussed the alarm system installment, and each agreed to contribute to the cause.

"What's your concern about today?" Tipping her head, Kathleen gazed intently at Callie.

"I like speaking my mind, so I'm going to share my thoughts, then both of you can put in your two cents. I'm not trying to be bossy about what we should do with this house." Although that's probably how she acted in the past. "What would you think about converting this space into another guest room?"

"Ohhh." Kathleen clasped her hands together in front of her chest. "Then we'd have room for someone else to stay with us, right?"

"Yes."

"That sounds wonderful!"

"I'm okay with us doing that." Bess glanced around the room. "Where would Kathleen do her artwork?"

"Don't mind me!" Kathleen said. "I'll move my table into my bedroom. Using this space has been a blessing. But I'm fine with relocating my art studio into my room. Even Sarah can work on her mosaic in there."

"You're sure?" Bess asked.

"Absolutely."

"I don't mean to run you off." Callie felt the tightness in her chest easing. Because of Kathleen's use of the room, she hated to push her idea. That her housemate didn't mind giving up the area to help someone who might need the space was a relief.

"Now, tell us." Kathleen patted Callie's hand. "What do you have in mind?"

Callie was thankful for her friend's gentle, loving spirit. And for Bess's generous nature. She had nothing to fear from these two possibly rejecting her ideas.

"As you know, I've felt some unrest and an urgency to do something meaningful. I'd like us to assist more women like we've done with Sarah and Lola." She sagged against the back of the folding chair. "I need to get off my backside and move more. I must get my mind off wanting to eat all the wrong foods. Doing something that warms my heart and gives me hope for a healthier future seems sensible." Was she explaining herself well enough?

"Do you want to invite someone else to stay with us soon?" Bess asked, gazing around the room as if picturing it set up as a bedroom. "We'll have to buy more furniture."

"Yes. But I don't have anyone lined up yet." Callie rubbed her thumb over the edge of the table. "If we converted this room into a bedroom, we'd have another usable space."

"I agree we need another room in case the Lord leads another wounded soul to us." Kathleen smiled in her peaceful manner.

"Otherwise, the inn is full," Callie said.

"You have my blessing. I'll move my boxes of glass pieces out of here."

"You have my blessing also." Teary-eyed, Bess stroked the tabletop. "This old house has been a refuge for me. Not just as a place to get away from my ex. But a place of renewal. Sharing this experience with others is meaningful to me also."

"There is one other thing I want to run by you." Callie tapped her fingers together. "I'd like to have a meeting here to see if there might be others who are interested in helping women like we're doing."

"Oh?" Kathleen's eyes brightened.

"If more ladies were involved, more women would find shelter and support in a timely manner."

"Sounds like a worthy ambition. Will you invite just a few?" Bess held eye contact with Callie. "Make a general invitation. Or what?"

"Just a casual gathering."

"What if we held a meeting in the community hall?" Bess offered.

"I'd like to start small." Callie sighed. "I may be off base in assuming others want to get involved, but I hope to convince a few. Maybe God is already speaking to some hearts about this as He's been nudging me."

"What do you need us to do?" Bess asked.

"Help with baked goods for refreshments would be nice." Callie patted her stomach. "Since I'm avoiding sweets, I think baking would be too great a temptation. I'll pick up some things at Lewis's if you're both busy."

"Count me in!" Kathleen raised her right hand. "I'll make cookies and scones."

"I'll pick up fruit and veggie trays," Bess said.

"Great. You two are the best."

Kathleen clasped Callie's and Bess's hands. "I love that we can make a difference right here in our own house with the resources the Lord has given us."

"I think so too. Now, if we convince a few other women to do the same thing, that will be even better."

"Why, Callie Cedars!" Kathleen said with a grin. "You have changed. You're glowing with enthusiasm!"

"Maybe, I have." Callie laughed, and the lighthearted feeling of hope delighted her.

Chapter Thirty

Three days without seeing Callie, and James was beside himself with a desire to talk with her and share his ideas about making furniture. He thought of calling her a bunch of times this morning but didn't want to talk about his plans over the phone. That was his reasoning for dropping in on her unannounced. Surely, she'd be as eager to see him as he was to see her.

However, by her frantic look of exasperation when she opened the door and saw him standing there, he was mistaken. This wasn't a good time to tell her how he cleared out his shed and set up his planer to smooth out old boards. How he and Paul emptied one of the first-floor bedrooms in the house and would use the room as a holding area for their creations. Their discussion about a business plan probably wouldn't impress her, either.

"What are you doing here?" Callie's hair puffed out like she'd been raking her fingers through her short gray and black strands. The scent emanating from the house was a mix of delicious-smelling freshly baked cookies and some sort of citrus cleaner.

James's stomach growled as he inhaled the cookie scent. He'd been so preoccupied, he neglected lunch. "Are you busy?"

"Busier than I've been in a month of Sundays! Did I forget about an outing?"

"No. I wanted to stop by and talk with you. I'd like to share an idea. But if this is a bad time—" He gulped back his explanation. "I, uh, miss you, Cal."

"Well, there's this—" She pulsed her hand toward the kitchen. Then she sighed and opened the door. "I'm sorry for being abrupt. I'm frazzled, but I have a few minutes. Please, come in."

"All right." He strode inside and went straight for the dining room table spread with a myriad of delicacies—cookies, scones, tiny bread squares rolled and held together with toothpicks, a bowl of mixed nuts, and loads of veggies and fruit on platters. Enough snack food to feed an army!

"What's all this?" His mouth watered as he imagined eating some of the goodies.

"We're having a little gathering this afternoon."

"Gathering?" She was hosting a party and didn't invite him? "Is it someone's birthday?"

"No. It's a women's meeting."

"Oh." That made sense.

"Hello, James!" Kathleen bustled into the dining area from the kitchen wearing a bright blue apron. "Help yourself to a cookie. There are plenty!"

"Don't mind if I do." He reached for a sugar cookie, taking one off the top of the pile. He loved sugar cookies.

Callie tapped her foot in an impatient gesture and stared longingly at his cookie. Was she upset about him taking a sugar cookie when she was avoiding them?

"Was there something you needed?"

"Not needed. Let's talk later, hmm?" He bit into the cookie. "These are great!"

"As I said, we have an event happening here shortly." Callie's shoulders sagged. "Things are hectic. The ladies will be here in less than an hour."

"I get the picture." He sauntered back to the door. "I'll call another time."

"Okay. Thanks for stopping by, James."

Callie seemed busier than ever. He thought their budding relationship would be more relaxed. He didn't think he needed to call before checking in with her. He and Paul popped in to talk with each other all the time. Maybe that wouldn't work with him and Callie.

But he didn't want to leave things unsettled, either. "Have a nice meeting. I hope everything works out how you'd like it to."

"Thank you." A softer smile crossed her lips.

"Would you like to go out to dinner with me tomorrow?" he asked spontaneously.

"Oh, sure. I guess that would be fine."

"Good. I'll look forward to it. Then we can share about every-thing that's happening in our lives."

He left her smiling, glad he made a date with her. He'd have to make reservations somewhere nice. Then he'd get the chance to tell her about the dreams he was conjuring up to make furniture and start a business. And he could hear all about the meeting she was having. Hopefully, they could find a way to have a relationship that went beyond their individual hopes and desires for the future.

Because the way James saw it, his future included Callie as his wife.

Chapter Thirty-one

Public speaking wasn't her thing, but Callie felt excited about the opportunity to address the ten ladies who gathered in the living room. Only slightly out of breath, she inhaled slowly before beginning her persuasive speech.

A small group of women with a unified purpose could surely make a difference in a town of eleven-hundred residents! It was up to her to inspire these women to catch her vision. If she failed— No, she would not throw a spoon down the drain by dooming her aspirations with negative thoughts.

She sent a silent prayer heavenward for guidance. Then she met the gazes of her friends. Bess, Kathleen, and Sarah smiled back at her. Longtime friends, Maggie, owner of the Beachside Inn, and Patty, owner of the local hardware store, gazed back at her with questions in their eyes. Did they wonder if she was trying to hoodwink them into buying something?

Alison Masters, a journalist for the local paper who spent a short time at the project house, held a pen and notepad, ready to take notes. The other four women—Deb Johnson, co-owner of Lewis's Super,

Mattie Hays, librarian, Casey Clemons, previous flower shop owner before Hurricane Addy hit, and Sue Taylor, City Council member—sipped tea and faced Callie with curious expressions. She had only told them she wanted to share an idea with them.

"I've asked you ladies to meet with me this afternoon because I have a Good Samaritan project to discuss with you. I hope you will hear me out and consider getting involved."

"What kind of project?" Maggie scowled.

"What's this about, Callie?" Patty asked. "Looks like mostly businesswomen here."

"I hope to inspire you with an idea. From there, it's up to each of you to choose what you'll do with it, if anything." She took a deep breath. "I'm so glad you all came today."

"We're all ears," Sue Taylor said.

"As you know, Bess, Kathleen, and I took on the Peterson place as a renovation project."

"It turned out lovely." Deb nodded toward the stairwell. "I remember being in this room years ago."

"It was my grandmother's house," Sarah said.

"That's right. Then it fell into disrepair." Callie cleared her throat, determined to keep the topic on track. "When we took on such a big house, the three of us decided to do something special with the extra rooms. We wanted to share them with women who might be going through a rough patch in their lives, providing safety and a place of rest."

"That's admirable, Callie," Mattie said. "But what does that have to do with us?"

Callie took a sip of her tea and then set her cup back down on the coffee table. "How many of us have gone through a difficult time in life? Perhaps, a season when we felt alone. Wounded emotionally. Grieving. Or hurt by life's storms. Yet, if someone had come alongside us and shown kindness and friendship, our discouragement might not have been as severe."

A few of the ladies nodded. Several glanced downward or focused on their teacups.

Sarah lifted her hand. "I was homeless. Wandering up the coast. Sleeping on beaches." She squeezed her eyes shut for a moment. "I thought I'd stop and look at my grandmother's old house before I moseyed up north. But then, these lovely ladies invited me to stay with them." She smiled at Bess and Kathleen, sitting on the couch. "Here I am a year later, doing much better. I have a job I love. I'm learning mosaic art from Kathleen. This place has become my home. Being here reminds me that God has been watching over me, even in my lowest times." She cleared her throat as if to control her emotions. "I'm more prepared to live my life again, thanks to Callie and the others."

"Thank you for sharing that, Sarah." Callie met her gaze and nodded. "Others have come through our doors, too. We hope we have made a difference in their lives and encouraged them in their journey." She thought of Lola and Micah.

"Callie, are you implying that all of us should bring strangers in off the streets?" Maggie asked in a high voice. "Invite them into our homes? Not me!"

"I'm with Maggie," Patty said staunchly. "What you've done here is admirable, but dangerous. Look at the attack you suffered, what, ten months ago?"

"The uprising in Basalt Bay didn't have anything to do with the people who were staying with us." Bess patted the air as if attempting to calm the agitation in the room.

"Still," Patty said, "strangers are, well, strangers! You can't be too careful these days."

"That's for sure!" Maggie pulsed her index finger.

"Some have merely landed in a difficult place in life. I wasn't dangerous or on drugs. My husband died. I was grieving and alone."

Sarah clenched her hands together, her shoulders hunched. "I lost my purpose for living. But here in Basalt Bay, and in this house, I found it again."

"Ahh, sweetie." Kathleen hugged her.

"What do you do now?" Alison asked as if she didn't already know. "For my readers."

"I work in the art gallery." Sarah smoothed her hands over her denim jumper. "I've made new friends and found family because Kathleen, Bess, and Callie took me in."

"May I quote you?" Alison asked.

"I guess."

"What I have in mind"—Callie brought the conversation back to her idea—"is a society of like-minded women who want to help others. We'll band together for a good cause."

"You mean giving free room and board?" Maggie asked, sounding appalled.

"Not just that. Maybe providing a meal, a bus ticket, or a place for someone to get out of the rain." Callie made eye contact with a few of the more supportive ladies. "I don't mean to pressure any of you into doing something you don't want to do. I'd like us to discuss suggestions about how to help more women in our community. All of us making a positive impact in people's lives will reach more than if only a few of us were doing so."

"Are you considering fundraising?" Sue asked. "Because if you are, you'll want to go through the proper steps to start a nonprofit."

"What would that involve?" Callie wanted to stir up a heart of service in these women, but she hadn't considered the responsibilities that might entail.

"I've set up a nonprofit before, so I have some experience with it." Sue met Callie's gaze, then shifted toward Bess. "It involves things like naming your organization, choosing directors, filing articles of incorporation, establishing governing policies, and a host of other things."

"Oh, my goodness," Callie said as the enormity of it hit her.

"But don't worry." Sue chuckled. "I can guide the board through it."

"The board?" Callie asked.

"Yes. Also, we would need to choose a president, treasurer, and secretary. Someone needs to keep minutes."

Callie felt overwhelmed.

"Callie, dear, are you all right?" Kathleen fanned her face like she looked close to fainting.

"I'll be all right in a moment. Thank you. What should we do next?" Callie looked toward Sue for advice, thankful someone in the group knew the requirements for starting up a nonprofit organization.

"Let me do some research about the steps, and I'll get back to you." Sue swayed her hands toward the others. "This meeting is a preliminary meeting to gauge interest, right?"

"That's right," Callie said.

"If we were to start up a nonprofit group, we might want to host a benefit or a large fundraiser to get the ball rolling."

"We could have bake sales," Mattie suggested. "Or rummage sales."

"Maybe a car wash," Casey said.

"Or an art event," Sarah added.

"Certainly! Everyone's ideas are appreciated." However, to Callie, it felt like they were jumping the gun. This meeting was to find out if any of these women were interested in her thoughts about providing support. "If you feel the heart to be involved in this group, I want to invite you to be a part of a movement in Basalt Bay."

"A movement?" Maggie scoffed. "What's this about, Callie?"

"I want us to start a group with the purpose of providing a refuge for women in need and for garnering funds to help them." Callie felt a fluttering of excitement.

"What would this nonprofit group entail?" Sue asked in a diplomatic way. "We all lead busy lives. What do you envision?"

Everyone turned toward Callie.

"I hope we would encourage other women by supplying lodging, food, and supplies during times of difficulty. Meeting those needs might come in a variety of ways."

"Would this be a church group?" Patty asked.

"Not a church group. Compassionate, yes. But we want any woman in Basalt Bay to feel welcomed and encouraged to participate." Callie hoped the ladies heard in her voice the passion she had for this project. "I'd like to call it the Women's Caring Society or the Basalt Bay Caring Society. Something like that."

"I love it!" Kathleen clasped her hands together.

"Has a nice ring to it," Sarah said.

"There's a state database where we can find out if the name has been taken." Sue nodded toward Bess. "I'm certain the title including Basalt Bay is available."

"That's right," Bess agreed. "That one probably hasn't been used."

"What else?" Alison asked as she wrote on her pad.

"In the past, we've incurred some trouble with gossip in our hometown," Callie said, hoping to broach the topic delicately. "I admit to my share of idle chatter. But I'm changing my ways. Where my mouth previously got me into trouble, I want my heart to lead me to help others."

"Why Callie Cedars!" Maggie said emphatically. "Are you accusing us of gossiping?"

Callie nearly chortled. She considered Maggie Thomas the queen of gossip in Basalt Bay. But Callie was far from innocent.

"Haven't you done enough by taking in the women you already have?" Maggie asked in an irked tone.

"I don't feel as if I've done nearly enough. We've only begun to make a difference."

"What's gotten into you? Why this sudden need to"—Maggie fluttered her hands in the air—"help everyone?"

Callie took a step forward, facing her. "Because we can. And if we can, we should. A women's society with the purpose of helping others would encourage us to act kinder to our neighbors who might be hurting and alone."

"'Love your neighbor as yourself,'" Sarah quoted softly.

"Amen," Kathleen said.

A silence settled over the room.

Callie decided to make a call to action. "Who is interested in being a part of the Basalt Bay Caring Society?"

Kathleen thrust her hand up. "I'll be the first to join!"

"Count me in," Bess said.

The guests gazed at each other as if trying to figure out what the other women thought.

Sue lifted her hand. "I am one-hundred percent behind us gathering to talk about how to help others in our community. It's compassionate and caring. But what's our real mission? What are we agreeing to do?"

"Our group will be about sharing our hearts, and sometimes our homes. Mostly it's about working together, women helping women. Making a difference with what we have," Callie said, recalling Kathleen's words in their meeting at the project house. "That might mean writing an encouraging text to someone. Taking another woman out for coffee. Being a friend. Making sure the widow down the street has food for dinner." Callie took a deep breath and sighed. She'd said enough.

"I'm moved, Callie. Really, I am." Sue brushed her fingers beneath her eyes. "I became a member of the City Council after my dad died. I inherited the position. But this idea of reaching out to women who are hurting or in need of friendship touches me. Thank you for sharing about it. I'm all in. And I'm willing to help with setting up the nonprofit."

"Thank you." Callie pressed her palm over her heart.

"At the library, some women enter our doors who look bedraggled and weary of life," Mattie said. "Others appear homeless. I'd be proud to participate in a group that wants to help them. I have a spare room at my house, too."

"That's wonderful. Thank you." Callie smiled at her.

"Sounds to me like a quilting bee with everyone clustering around doing what we do—talking about people! Not making any difference." Maggie crossed her arms over her chest. "Then we go home as lonely as before. What's the use?"

Sadness filtered through Callie. She'd never considered Maggie as being lonely or bitter. Outspoken, yes. She was her gossiping pal for eons. Now Callie recognized her as a woman who needed encouragement and to feel included. Why didn't she see the needs of others right in front of her before?

"I hope more will be accomplished in our group than chatting over a sewing project." Callie kept her voice soft, trying not to bully Maggie into participating. "We could all use more friends. I sure could." She reached her hand toward Maggie. "I think we should all do better at looking out for each other and being better neighbors, don't you?"

With some obvious reluctance, Maggie gave Callie's hand a slight squeeze.

Nods and affirming smiles spread around the group.

After the meeting ended, where all but Maggie and Patty signed up for the Caring Society, Callie was both pleased and concerned. While she was thankful for those who agreed to be a part of their group, she'd hoped for unanimous involvement. If she couldn't convince her own friends to jump in and volunteer, she had a lot more work to do.

Chapter Thirty-two

At Bert's diner the next day, Callie sat across from Forest, waiting to hear his news. A few days ago, she asked him to investigate Lola's husband. This morning, Forest texted her to meet him here.

"Well? Did you find him?" she asked as soon as the server poured their coffees.

"I found him." Forest sipped his hot drink.

"And?" Callie felt impatience rising within her. "Is he still in town?"

"Yes. He's staying with a friend."

"Benjamin Presley has a friend in Basalt Bay? Who in their right mind would be his friend?"

Forest leaned closer to her and said quietly, "A woman."

"A woman!" Callie caught the glances of a few people and lowered her voice. "Explain, please, before I have an arrhythmia right here."

"Relax. He's staying with a previous girlfriend."

"The rat fink! You expect me to relax after hearing that?" Callie clutched her mug tightly. "I knew he was trouble. But this, this makes me furious!" She gulped down a long swallow of black coffee, burning her tongue in the process.

"Is there anything else you need from me?"

"Other than dropping Benjamin Presley off in Timbuktu?"

"Other than that." Forest cracked a grin.

"Keep watching him, will you?"

"Sure. I can do that. What are you hoping to find out about him?" He fingered the rim of his cup and glanced at the door.

"If he's up to no good, and that's what it sounds like he is up to, I want to know." She huffed. "Should I tell Lola about this? Keeping it a secret seems wrong."

Forest shrugged, his gray-green eyes darkening. "If you do, all you can tell her are the facts. He's at his ex's house. We don't know that they are in a relationship. Or if he's just crashing on her couch."

"He's staying there with her. Isn't it obvious he's up to no good?"

"Not really." He set down his mug with a soft thud. "I'll keep my eyes open, if that's what you want me to do."

"Of course, it is." Callie rubbed the back of her neck, trying to relieve some tension. "This guy shows up acting humble, wooing Lola to get her to talk with him. Then he goes back to his girlfriend? Unbelievable! What is he after?"

"You'd make a good detective, Callie. You're passionate and determined to find out the truth." He squinted at her. "Remember the curious cat analogy? Watch out."

"That's why I hired you!"

He snickered. "All righty, then. I'd better get back to work."

After Forest left, Callie dug out change to pay the bill for their coffee and a tip. Before she stood up, Maggie entered the diner. Maybe this would give Callie an opportunity to talk with her. However, Maggie glanced briefly in her direction, then strode to the other side of the room. Was she avoiding her?

Callie paid her bill then crossed the room to Maggie's table. Maggie clutched her menu, holding it high, and didn't glance up.

"Hello, Maggie."

"Callie? Oh, hello." Maggie slowly lowered the menu a couple inches. "I didn't notice you."

That seemed unlikely.

"Do you mind if I sit down for a minute?"

"Not really. I'm about to order brunch."

"That's fine." Callie settled into the chair across from her. "This will give us a chance to clear the air."

"Does the air need clearing?" Maggie peered at her over the top of her maroon reading glasses.

"Don't you think so? I thought you might be feeling out of sorts after our meeting."

"Really, Callie, I don't have to explain myself to you. So what if I don't wish to participate in your goodwill club? You're the one who's changed. Not me." Maggie sighed melodramatically. "While you may be bored with your life, I have a full plate without providing free room and board to vagrants."

Callie gritted her teeth. "I'm not starting the Caring Society because I'm bored with my life."

"No? Then why?"

Callie groaned. Maggie obviously didn't see the heart behind her idea. She must not have understood anything about yesterday's meeting.

Lucy Carmichael, the redheaded server who seemed to flirt with all the men who entered the establishment, rushed up to the table. "Sorry, ladies. The place is busier than usual. Are you ready to order?"

"Nothing for me, thank you," Callie said.

"I'll have the brunch special. Eggs over easy." Maggie passed Lucy the menu. "No burned toast this time, either."

"Certainly not, Ms. Thomas." Lucy scurried away from their table and then paused by a booth with four men who appeared to be having a business meeting. Leaning down, she flashed smiles around at all of them.

Callie rolled her eyes. Maggie might not get her order as quickly as she wished. But she didn't mention the woman's flirty behavior like she would have done in the past. Instead, she focused on what she came over to Maggie's table to say.

"I hope you'll continue coming to our meetings."

"Why would I?"

"Because you have something to offer the women in our town. Your knowledge, your affable personality"—Callie winked, bringing some levity to the tense conversation—"would go a long way in helping other women feel at home in our group."

"My personality isn't one speck affable, and you know it."

"Honestly, Maggie, I'm not trying to corner you." Callie leaned forward, not wanting others to hear their conversation. "I reached out to my friends about this idea because I was comfortable doing so. I thought they'd understand my intentions. If you are against participating, I respect that. I won't ask you to our meetings again."

"What have you done with the Callie Cedars I've known for all these years?" Maggie's voice rose. "Where's the woman who wouldn't back down or take a hint of guff from anyone?"

"I may be softening in my older age." A health scare and a man in her life might be the reasons, but she didn't say so.

"Older age? You're younger than I am."

Callie didn't want to explain her health situation, but she wanted to insert some honesty. "I'd like to look beyond myself and care for my fellow human beings. Do you ever ponder what this world might be like with more people caring for each other instead of quarreling and demanding attention for themselves?"

Maggie opened and closed her mouth several times.

"Yes, I'm changing. I'm sorry if that is off-putting. I'm sorry for gossiping so much in the past, too. I just want to do some good while I can."

"Now, I've heard everything." In a surprising move, Maggie gripped Callie's hand. "You still have a lot of years ahead. A lot of time to do good. Look at all you did to get Bess into office. Look at how you held a frying pan over that assailant's head. According to Sarah's testimony, you've done plenty to help her, too." As quickly as she clasped Callie's hand, she released it.

"Thank you, Maggie." Callie got a little choked up. "That means a lot to me."

Maggie stared at her hands, not meeting Callie's gaze.

"What you did just then is a way you could help other women in town."

"Pshaw."

"I mean it. Some women have never experienced another lady standing up for her." Callie chuckled dryly. "Even I have rarely heard kindnesses exchanged between us. But after living in the project house with Kathleen, a natural encourager, and with the Lord whispering in my heart lately, I want to be the person who offers kindness instead of meanly-spoken words. I want to be a better person. Don't you?"

"None of us have had kindnesses spoken to us, other than our mother's words when we were girls," Maggie muttered. "Does anyone know what encouragement feels like? I certainly don't."

"I'm so sorry, Maggie." Despite the din in the restaurant, Callie patted Maggie's arm and said quietly, almost in a whisper, "I haven't been the friend I should have been to you. I want to do better. That's why the concept of the Caring Society touches my heart. Let's do some good with whatever time we have left. Heaven knows we've done some harm with our wagging tongues."

Maggie's jaw dropped.

"Well, I have, anyway. I'd like the chance to be a blessing to others now."

"All right. All right!" Maggie said in a begrudging tone, "So, when is your next meeting? And what do you expect me to do about it?"

Chapter Thirty-three

Callie returned from her outing at Bert's and found Kathleen pacing across the dining room, her face pasty and wrinkled with worry lines.

"What's wrong?"

"Oh, Callie." Kathleen rushed to her and clasped her hands. "Lola left us!"

"What?" Wasn't this what she feared might happen? That Lola's husband would come looking for her and coax her away while Callie was gone. "Left where?"

"No idea. Her bedroom door was ajar. I came downstairs. She and Micah were already gone. I didn't hear a car or anything." She twisted her hands together. "It happened on my watch. I'm so sorry. I should have been more aware."

"What could you have done?" Callie gritted her teeth. "Although saying this makes me sick, if she wanted to go back to her husband so badly, there's nothing any of us could have done to stop her."

"Maybe she went for a walk. Needed time to think."

"Are her things in her room?"

"No." Kathleen shook her head, her expression crumpling with sorrow. "But she didn't come here with much, so it's hard to tell for sure."

Gripping the edge of the dining room table, Callie said a silent prayer for their young charge whom she feared had returned to her husband. Her two-timing, no-good, deadbeat husband.

Callie snapped her fingers. "Let's take a look at the video footage." She dropped into a chair at the table. Now, what were the steps Judah showed her to access the video on her mobile device? She clicked on the icon.

"Find anything?" Kathleen sat in the chair next to her, leaning toward her to see the screen too.

"Not yet."

A couple of taps later, Callie played a video of Lola carrying Micah and walking beside Benjamin out to a dark pickup truck. Callie held her breath as the trio strolled down the path.

"How do we know she went of her own volition?" Kathleen asked.

On the screen, Lola turned and smiled at Benjamin.

"That's how." Callie sighed. She didn't even get the chance to tell Lola about Benjamin staying with his old flame.

"What should we do now?" Kathleen asked.

"Pray. Rant. Grieve. Not much else we can do unless she calls and asks for our help."

"If she does"—a hopeful look crossed Kathleen's face—"we'll take her back with loving arms, won't we?"

"In a heartbeat." An ache filled the pit of Callie's stomach.

Sometimes loving arms and friendship weren't enough. The woman must want a better life than being with a mean-mouthed, angry man. A cad like Benjamin didn't deserve a warmhearted person like Lola as a spouse. What if he started drinking again? What if he was cruel to Micah during his next binge?

Callie wanted to weep.

"Let's pray for her right now." Kathleen clasped Callie's hand again.

"Yes, let's do that."

Both women prayed earnestly for the young mother they cared about so much. As Callie prayed and cried quietly, she imagined she felt like a mama aching for her daughter and grandson who might be in harm's way. If anyone could help Lola and Micah, God could. His love surrounded them. He would protect them. Callie had to believe that.

After their prayer ended, Kathleen went into the kitchen. A few minutes later, she returned with two cups of hot peppermint tea. "This is my remedy for what ails our broken hearts."

Callie's tea didn't have honey in hers, but she was getting used to the unsweetened flavor. Even her cravings were changing. She thanked God for that.

"Since we both need an honest-to-goodness distraction, why don't you tell me about what's going on between you and James." Kathleen's eyes twinkled. "That'll get our minds off worrying about Lola for a few minutes anyway. If I'm prying, I'm sorry."

"There's not much to report. Two foolish sixty-somethings trying to figure out if there's anything between them."

"And is there?" Kathleen sipped her tea. "Do you care for him?"

"I like James. Have for a long time." Admitting that much felt like too much of a revelation. "He asked me to marry him. Teasingly, that is."

"What on earth?" Kathleen set her teacup down with a clunk. "He proposed? Why didn't you tell me?"

"Because it didn't mean anything. His proposal was a joke."

"But he asked you!"

"Only because of a foolhardy plan to convince my brother to let bygones be bygones."

"By marrying you?"

"Uh-huh. A loony idea if I ever heard one!" Callie took a drink of her tea. "But even with his phony proposal, I enjoy being with him. Holding his hand. Walking and talking. And when he peers into my eyes … I can hardly breathe."

"Oh, my dear. Has he kissed you?"

"Kathleen!" Callie's face turned hot.

"Sorry." Kathleen nudged her elbow. "Did he?"

"No, he did not! He, um, asked about it, though." Callie bit her lip to stop a grin. "Later, I thought a kiss might have been the answer."

"To what?"

"Everything. Mainly, does he care for me as I care for him?"

"Oh, Callie," Kathleen practically cooed. "You do like him."

"I said I did, didn't I?"

"Tell me more."

Callie felt like a junior high girl tittering with her best friend about the boys in their physical education class. If only it were that simple. With the way her feelings simmered for James for fifty years, what was she supposed to do with such strong emotions now?

Besides, she needed to focus her attention and her prayers on Lola. She dearly wished she had been here when the younger woman decided to leave. Maybe she wouldn't have been able to change her mind, but she would have tried.

Chapter Thirty-four

Later that afternoon, with the unsettled way Callie was feeling about Lola's departure, she desperately needed a distraction. When James called and asked, "Cal, would you be interested in going on a boat ride for our date tonight?" his invitation seemed like a perfect diversion, other than the boating part. "Sounds romantic, doesn't it?" James chuckled lightly.

The sound of his happiness washed over her like a shower of refreshing water, soothing her anxiety and stimulating her heartbeat. No matter what he asked her to do today, she wanted to spend time with him. Maybe doing something away from the project house was a good idea, too.

"I guess it does."

She briefly explained about Lola leaving, warning him that she might not be in the best of moods.

"Do you want to postpone our date? I'd understand if you did."

She appreciated his thoughtfulness.

"No. I'd rather go out with you. Maybe you can distract me."

"Hmmm. I like the sound of that," he said warmly.

That evening they boarded a yacht south of Basalt Bay. James booked a dinner and cruise on the *Pacific Hannah*, a thirty-five-foot event vessel. Four other couples were on board also.

Callie liked sitting on a bench on the deck beside James, their arms pressed against each other's, watching the setting sun send a cascade of color across the semi-still waters of the bay. "This is lovely, James. Thank you for inviting me."

"Sure. I wanted to do something special with you."

"Special?" Her heart throbbed in her ears. She wet her lips. What a silly reaction! Then again, she desired affection between them. Thought about it often enough. Would this outing be the right moment for them to kiss for the first time? If so, she couldn't think of a better diversion.

"Everything we do together is special to me, Cal." James clasped her hand between both of his warm ones. "You mean something to me." He seemed to be baring his heart.

"I like being with you too." She took a deep breath and let it out slowly. She was attracted to James, no doubt about it. "Thank you for planning this time for us to be together. Especially after the day I had."

"Of course. I hope we'll have lots of adventures like this in the future."

"You do?"

"Definitely!"

She sighed, letting thoughts of her and James spending more time together simmer in her mind.

"I've been eager to tell you about a new project Paul and I are doing." His eyes sparkled with enthusiasm. "We're going into the woodworking business!"

"You are? When did this happen?"

For a few minutes, James told her about the dream he had of building furniture ever since he was a young man. How her words— *her words*—encouraged him to look inside himself for purpose and drive in his senior years. Since he already had a planer, a shed to work in, and space in the house to store furniture, he was going to start by making a bench. Then moving on to other pieces like garden chairs and tables.

"What a fabulous idea! And Pauly is okay with this? He wants to help?"

"Help? We're going to be partners in this venture!"

"I can hardly believe it." Callie sat quietly for a few minutes, taking it all in. James and Pauly were starting a small business? Her brother was doing something other than sitting around watching television all day? Wonder of wonders!

Maybe it was due to the excitement of James's news, or because Callie was so eager to experience romance with him, when they turned toward each other, knees bumping, she knew this was the moment she'd been waiting for. His Adam's apple bobbed up and down. A tic pulsed in his lower eyelid. A sign of nervousness?

Heart pounding in her chest like a runaway locomotive, she moved an inch closer to him, hoping he'd meet her halfway. His gaze seemed fixated on her eyes, her lips, and her eyes again. He leaned a little closer, too. Her eyelids slid closed. Their lips met in a soft, tender kiss. Fireworks exploded in her thoughts like that moment at the end of the old TV show, "Love American Style," when the couple finally kissed. Nothing else in the world mattered other than James's mouth caressing hers.

They broke apart, momentarily breathing in each other's breaths. Then his lips touched hers again like ultra-soft butterfly wings brushing against her skin. His mouth explored hers with tenderness and a sweet passion she never knew existed. Everything she ever dreamed of in a first kiss came true in his arms.

Oh, James.

The cool sea breeze reached her warm lips as he pulled back from their embrace. They smiled timidly at each other. His cheeks were flushed. Hers probably were too. His eyes twinkled at her like shooting stars. Every soft wrinkled line around his gray eyes drew her back to him. She wanted to touch his face and trace a wrinkle or two. For her fingers to memorize each dip of his cheeks and the multi-textured feel of his five o'clock shadow.

"Thank you, Cal. That was a lovely kiss."

"Perfection. Better than sugar."

Kissing him was like eating one cookie and thinking that would satisfy her. But it only made her want another one. And another.

James settled his arm over her shoulders, aligning her side with his. "Isn't the view amazing?" Sighing, he leaned the side of his head against hers and gazed out toward the water.

He stared at the sea, but she wanted him to turn back toward her and kiss her again. Would he consider her too forward if she initiated another kiss? She had a lot of years to make up for when it came to smooching with James Weston!

But the dinner bell gonged, so she didn't get the chance to try.

Chapter Thirty-five

For two days, one of them being a quick trip to Eugene, James couldn't get his and Callie's kissing off his brain. Romancing with her like that surely sealed the deal that they were meant to be together. If she still questioned his authenticity and earnestness, their kisses and embraces must have shown her he was serious about her. Would she marry him if he asked her again?

He'd already stuck his foot in his mouth by claiming their marriage might fix things between her and Paul. But that hadn't been the only reason he wanted to marry her. He cared for Callie. They had a history together. Things were warming up between them over the last year, culminating in those passionate kisses on the boat. He let out a long sigh, his heart aching from wanting to be with her again.

He tapped her name on his phone.

"Good morning, James."

"Hey, Cal. Want to go out with me today?"

"Isn't that too soon?"

"Is it? It's been two days!"

Maybe she wasn't as interested in dating him as he felt about going out with her again. That must mean his kisses hadn't been convincing enough. He'd better remedy that ASAP.

"I have some things to do." She coughed. "It's not because I don't want to spend time with you. But why the rush?"

"No rush." That wasn't exactly true. Wasn't he in a rush to move things toward romance and marriage? They didn't have decades to let love simmer on a back burner.

"Maybe we should take this slowly." By her tone, she didn't believe it any more than he did.

"Slowly? Why?"

"Not what you want to hear, huh?" Suddenly, she sounded playful.

"Oh. You're teasing me."

"Maybe I am." When she chuckled, his world felt brighter.

"I like hearing your laugh, Cal."

"I like yours, too."

"We should have more laughter today. You should go out with me again."

"I have a meeting to plan."

"Meeting, shhmeeting."

"James—"

"I'm serious about wanting to be with you. I care about you, Cal. Let's see where this thing is going. I'd like to go out with you. Kiss you again," he said boldly, exposing his thoughts.

"James, why are you so impatient?"

She scoffed like she recalled those fifty years of negligence she accused him of and didn't like the remembrance. He didn't blame her.

"Maybe because of how much I liked kissing you the other night," he admitted in a husky tone. "What did you think about it?"

"I'd say it's right up there next to a double-layer chocolate cake." He heard the smile in her tone. "It's a good thing kissing doesn't have any calories."

"See there. It's a win-win! So, will you take the time to meet me later?"

"Okay. I guess I can squeeze you into my busy schedule." She chuckled in a way he found adorable.

"All right. Is four okay?"

"That will work." She paused. "James?"

He liked hearing her say his name. "Hmm?"

"My Caring Society is important to me." She released a breath like she'd been holding it, and it took a supreme effort to let it out slowly. "So is the project house."

"I understand."

Wait. Did she mean she didn't want to pursue a relationship or marry him because the project house and the women's group were more important to her? Like he was, what, second or third place in her life? The thought of being shoved aside because of her causes gnawed at his middle.

Weren't her projects and their relationship of equal value? He sure hoped so, especially since he planned on asking her to marry him again.

Chapter Thirty-six

Callie sat across from Forest at the gallery coffee shop, emotionally bracing herself for whatever he was about to tell her. She'd asked him to check on Lola. He sent her a text about meeting him this afternoon, so he must have news.

Sarah set a cup of tea on the table in front of Callie, and one filled with black coffee in front of Forest. "Is that all?"

"Yes. Thank you." Callie waited until she went back into the coffee preparation area before asking, "So, what's the verdict?"

"You were right." Forest took a sip of his coffee. "I tracked Lola and Benjamin back to Florence. She's with him. Sharing the same apartment."

Callie swallowed hard. "Is she well?"

"Hard to judge that. Benjamin opened the truck door for her, carried Micah inside the building, that sort of thing."

"All right. I guess there's nothing more I can do." She fingered the handle of her cup.

With her desire to provide shelter to women in need, Callie had to accept that she couldn't control the outcome of everyone's lives. Her part was to love the people God sent her way and try encouraging them. Not to force them to make the choices she wanted them to make. Still, the pain of Lola's leaving hurt terribly.

Why didn't she wait for Benjamin to go to counseling or rehab? Instead, she succumbed to his wishes. His demands. Didn't she say she was weak where he was concerned?

"I suppose there's nothing to be done about it now," Callie said glumly.

"Wait and pray. If she comes back, welcome her and love her again."

"Like a mama with her daughter. Kathleen and I have discussed our reaction if she returns." She sniffed back some tender emotion. "It's difficult to accept. I want much more for Lola and Micah."

"I'm sure."

"Anything else I can get for you two?" Sarah held up a coffee decanter.

"No, thank you." Callie hadn't even taken a sip of her tea yet.

"I'm fine." Forest nodded at Sarah.

"Tell Kathleen two of her mosaics sold this morning. I'm so excited for her."

"I will. She'll be glad to hear that."

Sarah one arm hugged Callie as if sensing her inner turmoil, or maybe she'd overheard snippets of the conversation. "I love you. I'm inspired by what you tried to do for Lola, what you've done for me, and what you're hoping to do for others. It won't always work out as you wish, but I'm proud of you for trying."

"Thanks. Love you too." Callie patted Sarah's hand before the younger woman went to talk with a customer. In many ways, Sarah seemed like the daughter she never had. Or at least, like one of her nieces. She was so thankful God put these women in her life to be a part of her family.

Alone at the table with Forest, Callie dug through her purse for the check she prepared. "Thank you for the work you did on this case.

I'm thankful to be able to call on you when I need help with investigating a situation." She slid the check that included a bonus across the table facedown. "For now, this concludes my need for your services."

"I don't like taking money from you. You're my wife's aunt. I shouldn't—"

"Don't even think about refusing it. I may call on you for help again."

"Okay." Forest sighed then tucked the check into his shirt pocket. "Do you want me to keep my radar on alert for any missteps by Benjamin Presley?"

"Would you? I'd appreciate it."

"I will." He stood and hugged Callie. "Or I'll ask Deputy Brian to mention it to one of his buddies in the Florence precinct."

"Thank you. I'll be grateful for the reassurance."

After Forest left, Callie sat at the table a while longer, drinking her tea and pondering their discussion. In a few minutes, she'd text James and tell him she was ready to be picked up. He said he wanted to be with her again because he liked kissing her. Well, she liked kissing him too!

The gigantic crush she had for him all those years was growing and building exponentially. But how was she going to proceed with a relationship with him and stay focused on the project house and the women's group?

"Are you okay, Callie?" Sarah asked, picking up Forest's empty mug.

"I'm all right. Just contemplating some things."

"You couldn't have done anything better for Lola," she said as if trying to second-guess what was troubling her. "You know that, right?"

"Thanks. It's hard not to wonder what else I might have done for her."

"You and the other ladies provided a stable home for Lola and Micah." A sympathetic expression crossed Sarah's face. "She still loves her husband. She's taking a risk by going back to him, but it's her risk to take."

"You're right." Callie nodded, but the pain of wishing things had gone differently didn't ease.

Chapter Thirty-seven

James drove toward Baker's Point, a landmark along the coastal road, with Callie sitting in the passenger seat staring out the side window. Ever since he picked her up at the coffee shop, she was quiet. Did she hate that he was pushing them into a deeper relationship, perhaps before she was ready? She'd warned him that her causes were important to her. But surely at their age, they knew how to juggle the important things in their lives.

He had to admit that ring shopping in Eugene yesterday might have been premature. He heard Callie's hesitancy in her tone when she told him about prioritizing her women's group. If she flat out refused him again, what then?

James and Paul's need for wood and supplies was why they went to Eugene in the first place. They hunted through lumber supply stores and purchased the tools they needed, along with enough cedar and oak boards for a few projects. Afterward, James slipped away to a jewelry store while Paul went in search of snacks for the drive home.

Then at Bert's Fish Shack last evening, James ran into an old pal who said he'd sell him some reclaimed barn wood for cheap. The lumber companies would deliver the wood they purchased tomorrow. Everything was coming together for their business. He couldn't wait to begin their venture!

Asking Callie to marry him again? He wasn't as certain about that.

Nearing Baker's Point, he wanted to reach into his jacket pocket and touch the ring box just to make sure it was still there. But Callie might notice and ask what he was hiding.

He stole a couple of sideways glances at her. She shook her head and sighed. Was her tense behavior about Lola leaving the project house? Callie obviously still felt the loss greatly.

Maybe now wasn't the time for him to bring up a conversation about marriage. She probably needed a listening ear more than a proposal from him. Yet he had the ring. The proposal burned in his thoughts. What would it hurt to ask Callie what she thought about them getting married?

"Got something on your mind?" she asked.

"Oh, uh. Yeah." He chuckled nervously which made him sound ten years old. "I've got some things on my mind."

"Will you marry me?" "Will you live all the days of your life with me?"

"Where are you taking me?"

"Baker's Point."

"Why there?" Her voice rose.

"You'll see."

He hadn't prepared anything fancy at the gazebo at Baker's Point. No bells and whistles. Callie wasn't into fanfare anyway. He imagined her wanting a heartfelt interaction between them when he proposed. Nothing frivolous. That suited him just fine too.

The gazebo had been rebuilt last Christmas after the old one was demolished by Hurricane Addy. He and Callie witnessed her niece and nephew-in-law's renewing of their vows there, so he knew this place would be special to her for a proposal.

James pulled into the parking lot, shut off the engine, then got out and hurried around the car before Callie asked him any other questions. He opened her door and extended his hand. "Will you walk with me, sweetheart?"

"Okay." Squinting at him, she held his hand while she exited the vehicle. He didn't let go of her hand as they walked down the sandy trail toward the gazebo on the beach.

Callie glanced at him a few more times. She must be wondering what was going on since he brought her all the way out here. Baker's Point had a reputation around Basalt Bay for being the perfect proposal location.

"This brings back fond memories," she said when they reached the wooden structure that Judah and Forest built in December.

James appreciated the simple but sturdy structure the younger fellows had made.

"Sure does." He fumbled with the ring box in his jacket pocket. "How about if you and I stand in the gazebo?"

"Why would we do that?"

"Humor me, okay?" He tugged on her hand.

"James—"

"Please, Cal?"

If she wouldn't come with him, he'd drop to his knee right here in the sand. However, proposing inside the gazebo seemed more romantic. Plus, he'd have the wooden railing to hold onto if he got stuck on his knee or fell over. Why did he have to picture himself making an abominable disaster of this proposal?

"All right," she finally said, sighing like stepping into the gazebo was the last thing in the world she wanted to do.

James led her inside the structure, still holding her hand.

The wind blew Callie's hair. She stared toward the waves pounding the shoreline below them and inhaled deeply. "This is nice. It's been many years since I stood inside the gazebo like this."

"Me too. I'm glad we're here together."

Her gaze met his with questions she didn't speak.

"Callie?" He clasped both her hands. "I have no idea why I was an absent-minded clod for so long."

"What do you mean?"

"I don't know why I didn't see you, or us, for the couple we could have been all these years."

"James. We had only one evening of kissing." Yet her soft smile said that what they shared was more than that.

"It made me want more. Lots more." Letting go of one of her hands, he stroked her cheek. "I like kissing you, Cal. I like imagining us taking our relationship further."

"James." Her eyes widened like his frankness surprised her. Or maybe his fingers playing with her earlobe distracted her. Her skin was so soft. He wanted to kiss her. To hold her for hours with the wind blowing off the sea toward them.

"Is that why you brought me all the way out to Baker's Point? To steal kisses?"

"Is that what a fellow has to do?" He played along with her teasing. "Steal kisses?"

"No." She set her hands on the chest of his coat. "I give them freely to only one man."

"One man" meant him. His heart pounded like a bass drum. He'd pictured himself dropping on his knee the instant they reached the gazebo. Especially with the engagement ring singeing a hole through his coat.

Instead, they gazed into each other's eyes, their arms around each other. She moved her hand and stroked her fingers along his chin, her eyes moist as she peered at him. With kissing her on his brain, the question he planned to ask her fled from his thoughts.

He closed the gap between them, brushing his lips warmly against hers. They moved with the sway of the wind, almost as if they were dancing to the music of the sea. This kiss was as sweet, if not sweeter than the ones on the boat.

Aww, Callie. His sweet, sweet Callie.

He didn't want to wait for another second to ask her to marry him. He enjoyed kissing and holding her, and even though he didn't say he loved her yet, he had to find out if she felt the same way about him. Did she love him too?

"Callie." He backed up slightly, reclaiming her hands with his. "You've been the kid sister next door for most of my life."

"That's not very flattering, James."

"Sorry. I just feel so—" Slowly, he lowered himself to his knee, their gazes locked.

"James?"

"I'm sorry our romantic paths didn't cross sooner. I'm sorry I was a thick-skulled ninny about romance. But I see you now. I want you now."

She uttered a soft sound of awe.

"I love you, Cal. More than anything or anyone on this planet. More than my life." As he said the words, he knew they were true. Paul was his best pal. But Callie … this dear, precious woman … was the person he wanted to spend all his days and nights with. Whatever time he had left to live, and he hoped that would be for a few more decades, he wanted to be with her.

"What … what are you saying?" she asked breathily.

"Will you marry me? Will you share my life? Our lives?" He deepened his voice. "This time I mean this proposal with every breath in my body. I'm asking you to marry me because I love you. No other reason."

Just then, his knee strength gave way. Flailing to grab onto anything solid, he toppled sideways, grabbing the railing at the last second. Otherwise, he would have crashed to the floor. "Sorry. Bum knee. Bad timing." Heat bled up his neck and cheeks.

"Here. Let me help you." Callie tugged up on the crook of his arm.

"I can do it." Embarrassment flooding him, he tried to reposition his foot.

"James, please." She clasped his hand firmly. "Let me help you. Our bodies have weaknesses, but we are both strong in spirit. Stronger together, don't you think?"

Was she saying what he thought she was saying?

"I most certainly do."

She stared down at him so earnestly he didn't resist her touch when she assisted him to a standing position. They clung to each other's arms.

"Sorry for the most unromantic proposal ever, second only to my last one."

"It was memorable, I'll give you that." She smiled.

He sighed, relinquishing his humiliation. So, he stumbled. It was bound to happen eventually. But during his proposal? Ugh.

Trying to regain the romantic mood he botched, he clasped Callie's hands again. "What do you say? Will you marry me and live your life with me as partners, friends, and connoisseurs of fine romance?" That didn't come out sounding quite as romantic as he imagined it would.

Her eyes moistened even more. "You're sweet for asking, James Weston."

"I mean it. Would a fool who bumbled his previous proposal so wretchedly try a daring attempt again if he didn't mean it?"

"I suppose not. I like the 'connoisseurs of fine romance' bit. It's unique." Her smile wobbled and she pointed toward the wooden roof. "Thank you for proposing in the gazebo. You fulfilled a girlish fantasy of mine."

"You're welcome. You probably never envisioned the guy falling over when he asked you."

"Falling for me, maybe."

"I have fallen for you, Cal." Letting go of her hand, he set his palms on her shoulders. She didn't say yes. But she didn't say no, either. He told her he loved her, and she didn't reciprocate. "Do you need time to consider marrying me? If so, I understand."

She leaned her forehead against his chest. "I've daydreamed of marrying you for so long I can't imagine telling you no."

"You mean it?" He set her slightly back from him and met her gaze. "You've imagined marrying me?"

"What do you think? I've had the biggest crush on you for fifty years."

"Fifty years?" Shocked to his toes, he stood there with his mouth hanging open, staring back at her. She liked him back in junior high? "Why didn't you ever tell me?"

"Pride. Doubt. I figured you'd never be interested in your friend's kid sister. I was nothing to you."

"Oh, Cal."

"You said you loved me." She took a trembling breath. "I've told you I loved you in my daydreams a hundred times."

"I never knew."

"Of course not. That's why I'm reluctant to agree to marry you now. It's brand new to you." She brushed her cheek gently against his. "But marriage? Living with each other? Putting up with each other's grumpiness and morning bad breath?" She chuckled. "I'm set in my ways, James. You are too."

"Sure, we are. But we'll get used to each other. Couples have been doing it since the Garden."

"Still—"

Was she turning him down? His heart thudded against his ribs. Why did he never realize Callie had a crush on him all those years ago? Talk about dense!

Chapter Thirty-eight

Callie had been home only a few minutes when Forest's text came through the family texting app. *Paige is in labor. Heading to the hospital now.*

Hurray! What should she do? Did Pauly have Piper? Was there anything Paige and Forest needed her to do?

Her phone vibrated with a stream of congratulatory texts and well-wishes.

Can't wait to meet the baby! ~Paisley

Praying for you guys ~Judah

You'll do great! ~Sarah

Cheers and good wishes ~Craig

Love you. Praying! Callie typed in.

A moment later, Pauly added, *Eager to meet the new one. Piper is fine.*

So Pauly was taking care of Piper. Everything was under control. Maybe Callie would make a pot of soup to have ready for when Paige came home from the hospital. That would give her a task to do instead of worrying. And while she cut up vegetables, she'd ponder James's second marriage proposal.

Why was he so eager to get married anyway? They'd been on only two dates. How could she agree to marry him? How could she not? Hadn't she imagined being his bride since she was twelve?

She pulled a package of frozen chicken out of the freezer and stuck it in the microwave to thaw. Chicken soup was her favorite fall food to make, so she would enjoy chopping all the vegetables and creating the homey scents of broth and meat cooking. All those veggies would fit right into her diet, too. She'd have to watch the salt. Add more spices.

After changing into comfier clothes, she set out onions, garlic, and an assortment of carrots, potatoes, and other raw veggies on the counter.

Kathleen entered the room humming. "Oh, Callie. You're back. I've been so preoccupied with my mosaics, I didn't hear a thing."

"Paige is in labor!"

"Oh, my goodness." Kathleen hugged her. "Congratulations, great auntie!"

"Thanks. I can't wait to hear that she and the baby are okay."

"So you're making soup for an army!" Kathleen pointed to the largest pan they owned.

"That's right. Some for Paige and Forest. Some for us." Callie peeled the skin off a garlic bulb. "I'm feeling anxious, so I thought I'd do something useful. I'm going to snack on vegetables instead of gorging on cookies like I want to do."

"Good plan! Did Paige have trouble with her labor before?" Kathleen washed her hands.

"Not really. I'm just being an old mother hen."

"I understand. Can I help?" Kathleen pointed toward the onions.

"Certainly. I'll gladly relinquish onion-chopping duties." Callie pushed the extra cutting board over to her.

"How was your date with James?" Kathleen asked in a singsong voice. "Is this soup-making binge a result of that outing, too?"

"How astute you are!" Callie fanned herself with a dish towel. "The man proposed to me again."

"Seriously?" Kathleen tugged the outer layer off an onion. "What did you say to him?"

"That I'd think about it." She lifted the cutting board. "Which I'm doing while chopping things and making soup."

"You'll figure this out, my friend."

"I hope so."

"Marriage is a big decision." Kathleen chopped the onion into small pieces.

"Especially at my age!"

Kathleen's hands stilled. "My dear, why does age have anything to do with your decision about marrying James? You both deserve happiness. Goodness, if a sweet relationship comes your way in your sixties, why not grab it?" She laughed. "Excuse me. Why not grab him and kiss him to the moon and back? You should marry him today!"

"Kathleen," she protested. But then she snickered. "I did kiss him to the edge of the universe."

"Good!" Kathleen shrieked with laughter.

"Humor aside. We moved into this house less than a year ago." Callie gazed around the kitchen she loved and got teary-eyed. "It's too soon for me to want to pull up stakes. Surely, you understand that."

"I do. But let's face it. If you marry James, you'll have to live with the man!" Kathleen's gaze twinkled toward Callie. "Such a terrible thing, living with a guy you've secretly adored for ... how long?"

"Don't rub it in."

Kathleen giggled like a teenager. "Doing husband and wife things ..."

"Kathleen Taylor!" Callie's blush bled up her face. "I don't want to discuss that with you or anyone else." She fanned her face again. "Goodness, it's warm in here."

"I don't mean to embarrass you. James is a sweet, good-looking man. You'd both be lucky to spend the rest of your lives together, loving each other." Kathleen shook her head slightly and smiled. "Nothing would stop you from spending lots of time here with us too. You'll always be part of our project house family."

"I love James. But I don't want to leave all of this. I want to keep helping the ladies who will come to live here."

"Oh, sweetie. Is that what's bothering you?" Kathleen settled her arm over Callie's shoulder. "Do you hate the thought of leaving our project house more than the joy of being James's wife?"

"What's wrong with me? I should be thrilled he wants to marry me. Now, my lack of an answer might be a setback in our relationship."

"The poor man put himself out there, twice, didn't he?" Kathleen returned to her onion chopping. "Was his proposal more romantic this time? More kissing?"

Tears burned in Callie's eyes. "Those onions are getting to me."

"Me too." Kathleen sniffled but kept chopping.

"He proposed at the gazebo. It was more romantic." Callie sighed. "He was sweet. I didn't doubt his sincerity one iota."

"That's a relief." Kathleen chopped about half the onion with tears streaming down her cheeks. "After you give yourself time to mull over the ramifications of marriage and love, you might have to ask him."

"Ask him what?"

"To marry you!"

"I will not!" Callie chopped a carrot ferociously, shedding her share of onion-induced tears. "Why would I do such a thing?"

"The man asked you twice, and you didn't agree either time." Kathleen scurried over to the door and opened it wide, fanning the strong scent of onions from the room. "Make him a chocolate cake with the words, 'I will!' 'Yes!' 'Marry me today!' written on top."

"I told him I'd think about it. So I am." Callie joined Kathleen on the porch to breathe some fresh air. "It's more complicated than I imagined a proposal being."

"That, my dear, happens to us at any age. Bring the man a cake and put him out of his misery."

"You think he's miserable?" Callie felt guilty for possibly making James suffer.

"By what you've told me, yes."

Callie groaned. Sighed. Then groaned again.

She stepped back into the kitchen that still reeked of onions and felt even more emotionally restless. She'd never been proposed to before. Now, James had asked her twice. She liked him a lot. Loved holding his hand. Enjoyed his kisses. When she was in his arms, all her doubts fled.

Hmmm. Spending *more* time in his arms might solve everything!

Chapter Thirty-nine

Late that night, Callie's phone vibrated. She was sleeping lightly anyway, waiting for news about Paige and the baby. She picked up her cell and peered at the screen.

Baby girl arrived. Adelaide Pearl. She and Paige are doing well.

"Thank the Lord!"

Callie sent a quick message. *Congratulations! Can't wait to meet her.*

More well-wishes and congratulations followed hers.

She sank back onto her pillow. Adelaide Pearl. What a cute name! Piper would be ecstatic to have a sister. Now Callie had two great nieces, one great nephew, and before long, a third great nephew or niece would be announced from Ketchikan, Alaska, where Peter and Ruby lived. Pauly was going from being a grandad of one grandchild to four in a short while. He must be so proud.

What if James had noticed Callie as someone other than Pauly's sister back when she was young enough to have children? They might have had kids of their own. She groaned. No reason to ponder what-ifs like that now. She was embracing her life.

Whatever maternal sentiments existed within her would go to doting on Piper, Tanner, Adelaide, and the Alaskan-born child, and whichever nieces and nephews came along in the future. That would be enough for her.

Yet even with her personal lecture, she wondered what a child born of her and James's love would have looked like. Would a girl have dark hair like Paisley? Would she share Paige's artistic flair? Maybe become an adventurer like Peter, heading off to Alaska when she turned eighteen.

Sighing, Callie scooted down under her comforter and shut her eyes. She prayed for Paige and the baby. One request led to another. She mentioned Lola and Micah to the Lord. Then she prayed for Paisley and Tanner. Ruby and her unborn child.

She thought of someone else who gave birth to a baby girl a long time ago. Sue Anne Whitley, a friend she knew many years ago, was forced to give up her child when she was young and unmarried. That baby grew up to be their own Sarah. How painful giving up her child must have been for Sue Anne.

After her old friend moved to the East Coast and got married, Callie lost contact with her. What became of her? Did she long for the daughter she gave up?

Callie pictured Pauly and his grumpy attitude. How different his life might have been if he married Sue Anne instead of Penny. She better not go down that slippery slope. Still, a thought stirred through her mind like a gust of wind rustling a pile of leaves.

What if Pauly and Sue Anne saw each other again after all these years? Would they still have feelings for each other? He was a lonely widower. Last Callie knew Sue Anne was married. But a lot of years had passed.

Of course, Sarah might not want to meet the woman who gave her up. But what if she did? What if Sue Anne came to Basalt Bay and—

Pauly would never forgive her if she stirred up old angst between him and Sue Anne. She must tread carefully.

But what harm would there be in asking Forest to find out Sue Anne's address? Callie could write to her and ask if she had any interest in meeting her daughter. That is if Sarah was open to the idea also.

If Sue Anne and Pauly just happened to run into each other in Basalt Bay, Pauly could hardly blame Callie!

Her thoughts roamed as they often did to thinking about her and James's kisses. The way his lips felt on hers as if they fit perfectly together. Why didn't she throw her arms around the man's neck and shout "yes" when he proposed? It wasn't like she didn't want to marry him. But why did he want to marry her now? Why didn't he notice her years ago?

She turned on her light. There would be no more sleeping tonight. Her restless thoughts whirled. First, a baby girl. Then, Sue Ann and Pauly. Now, James. Her James, if only she'd let love happen between them.

Is that what she wanted? To throw caution to the wind and marry the man she admired from a far for so long? To believe wholeheartedly that he truly loved her now?

Leaving the project house felt too painful. She just started the Caring Society. She knew the joys of welcoming younger women into her home. She couldn't let such deep feelings go easily. Yet she didn't want to let a relationship with James go, either.

This stressful pondering wasn't healthy for her. Not when her troubling thoughts made her want to binge eat in the middle of the night. More prayer. That's what she needed.

Lord, help me. She prayed for strength to not yield to temptation. Then she prayed for wisdom about her and James. She prayed for Sue Anne, wherever she was. She asked for God's blessing on Paige and the baby. She asked for the Lord to encourage Ruby, the sunshine who came into their lives and helped with the remodeling of the project house last year, and her unborn child.

Paige. Paisley. Ruby. Sarah. Alison. Teal. Lola. They each held a piece of Callie's heart. They were like the daughters she never had. How was she going to hold onto that and still say "yes" to James?

/ Chapter Forty

Callie and the other ladies' efforts to call friends and spread the word about their meeting worked well. Or maybe it was Alison's front page article in the local paper, entitled "Women Hope to Make a Difference," that brought more interest to their group. Whichever it was, the first session in the community room at City Hall was attended by twenty-five ladies, a nice step up from the ten who met at the project house five days ago.

Callie was thrilled with the turnout. "Thank you all for coming to the Basalt Bay Caring Society meeting! Seeing all of you here does my heart good. That we have a similar passion to help women in our community encourages me. We are more similar than we ever imagined."

She spoke for a few minutes about the outreach of women helping women in their town of eleven hundred. After sharing about the group and fielding a few questions, many of the same ones asked at the smaller meeting, she swayed her hands toward the display tables she and Bess set up at the back of the room. "I want you to peruse our information on the tables and consider what you might do to help. We've listed some areas of needed assistance, from donations to making calls to opening your homes for temporary housing. We'll take a break and then reconvene after everyone has a few minutes to check out the displays and literature. If you have questions, ask Bess, Kathleen, or me."

"Hot coffee and cookies in the back!" Kathleen called from where she acted as hostess.

"Good job, Callie." Sue Taylor shook her hand. "I'm surprised by the attendance."

"Me too. Pleasantly surprised."

"Now we'll see where the rubber meets the road." Sue nodded toward the women gathering around the tables at the back of the room. "Hopefully, some will sign up. Others are probably here out of curiosity."

"We all start somewhere." Callie patted Sue's arm and moved on to talk with some of the other women.

Bess stood at one table answering questions. Callie strode to the second table. Glancing down at the three lists on the tabletop, she saw that only one or two people signed up on each. Sue might be right about more than a few of these women being here out of curiosity.

After the short break, Sue explained the steps she'd taken toward establishing the Basalt Bay Caring Society as a nonprofit. She spoke of the group's need to choose directors and three people who would serve as president, treasurer, and secretary. "We want everything to be aboveboard in our record keeping and finances for our group. I'm willing to pitch in wherever I'm needed."

"Thank you, Sue," Callie said. "I appreciate your helping our group get started on the right foot."

Nominations were taken, followed by a vote. Callie would be the president, Sue the treasurer, and Sarah the secretary. Kathleen, Mattie, and Alison were chosen as the initial directors. Bess said she'd be a supportive member of the group, but due to already serving as town mayor, she declined her nomination to the board.

After the business portions of the meeting were concluded, Callie wanted to make a heartfelt call to action. "In closing, I'm thankful for each of you who joined us today, and for everyone who accepted positions in our group. Thank you for showing your support for the needs of women in our community and neighboring cities. We've all had, or will someday have, a need to reach out to someone else for assistance. We hope when the time comes, a family member will be there for us. But if that doesn't happen, a friend coming alongside us offering support during a crisis would be a great help."

She met the gazes of the ladies who seemed the most interested in her speech. "I hope this group of women will be the ones who raise their hands and say, 'I will help you! I am here for you.'" Callie pulsed her hand upward. Then lowering it slowly, she continued, "Some who have stayed at the project house needed shelter. Some needed a shoulder to cry on. It's been fulfilling to me personally to be there for them. If more of us did this, we'd be a blessing to more women. In turn, we will be blessed and encouraged too."

"I'm a naysayer!" Maggie stood abruptly. "I don't see any benefit in signing up for obligations you haven't been interested in up to this point."

Oh, dear. Should Callie ask her to air her complaints privately to her later?

"All this hoopla isn't my thing." Maggie toyed with a necklace around her neck, her hand gripping and releasing a medallion. "But I wonder if I've had it wrong."

What?

"We like to chat at Bert's and at functions, right?" She glanced around at a few ladies as if garnering support. "We share the best recipes, talk about the most handsome men in town, or belittle another woman's hair or clothing or what kind of house she lives in." Her tone changed. "But what if instead of nitpicking, we spoke positively? What a novel idea, huh?"

Knock me over with a feather! Maggie was coming around, after all.

"What if we yakked about ways to improve our friendships? Heaven knows we could all use some camaraderie and kindness. That's all I have to say." She sat down quickly.

Glory be!

"Thank you, Maggie. I couldn't have said that better myself." Callie was touched by her friend's words. Maybe change would come to Basalt Bay because of this group, even in the way the women met and chatted at Bert's. "If you have any other questions, stick around and ask. If you'd like to sign up to help with one of the sub-groups, please do."

Callie ended the meeting. A few stayed to help with cleanup. Some expressed great questions and enthusiasm for the Basalt Bay Caring Society. More names were added to the sign-up sheets.

It seemed she'd stirred some hearts to help. With this official start to their group, Callie believed good results would follow. Maybe their efforts would multiply like the bread and fish in the Bible story.

Chapter Forty-one

The next day, Callie was excited to be on her way to see Paige and meet the baby. She'd already sent her homemade chicken and vegetable soup with Paisley for the new mom and dad. But since Paige asked for a few days without visitors so she could rest and help Piper adjust to the baby, Callie waited until today to stop by. Thanks to James driving her, she was heading to the subdivision now, eager to hold Adelaide and chat with Paige.

"Did your women's meeting go well yesterday?" James asked as he drove.

"It went really well."

"That's great. Living in town would make it easier for you to get to the community hall for meetings." He glanced over and winked at her. "I'm still waiting for my answer, Cal."

"I haven't forgotten." She smiled at him but didn't want to get into a discussion about what her answer might be right now. Her thoughts had been so full of the women's group and then getting to see Adelaide, that she hadn't sorted through her feelings about James's proposal.

He stopped in front of Paige's one-story house. As soon as he shut off the engine, he got out and came around to Callie's side. He opened her door and held out his hand to her. Liking the feeling of his hand clasping hers, she let him help her out and didn't immediately let go.

"Shall I walk you to the door?"

"That's not necessary. Thank you for the lift. I appreciate it."

"It was my pleasure. Text me when you're ready to go."

"I will." She still held his hand, her purse hanging from her arm. "See you later, then?"

"That you will."

Their gazes met and held. Lightning flashing over her head wouldn't have surprised her more than the intense emotions rushing through her as she gazed into James's dark gray eyes.

"Let's make a habit of this, shall we?" He squeezed her hand slightly.

"Mmhmm." Even if she wasn't ready to declare her love for him, she knew what he meant. "I'll text you in an hour or so." She slowly moved her hand away from his, every sensor in her fingertips aware of the loss.

As she walked up to the front door, her heart hammered in her throat. She didn't hear James's car door open. What was he doing? She turned back, still affected by her recent interaction with him.

He stood in the same place, his hand lifted in a wave. She smiled and waved back. It felt like they were a couple in a storybook, and she was waiting to see how the tale unfolded. What would marriage to him be like? What would waking up beside him every morning be like?

She gulped.

Forest answered her knock and welcomed her in. A few minutes later, the sweet baby girl—Adelaide Pearl—lay cuddled in her arms. This dark-haired darling was the sweetest baby on earth. She didn't fuss or wiggle like Callie was holding her wrong. Instead, she leaned her chubby cheeks against her chest and kept sleeping peacefully. This was magical. Callie sighed and sighed again.

"Oh, Paige. She is so precious. Such a blessing."

"She's a dream come true." Paige sat on the couch with a couple of pillows surrounding her. She looked comfortable and relaxed.

"Sweet baby, I've waited so long to meet you," Callie cooed over the sleeping girl.

"I've had a lovely time getting to know her over the past few days. I love her so much."

"Of course, you do. How's Piper accepting the idea of sharing Mommy with a little sister?"

Forest had taken the three-year-old for a walk right after Callie arrived.

"She's being sweet with her, but jealous, too." Paige chuckled. "She wants all of Forest's and my attention. Thus my need to spend some exclusive time with the four of us working out any difficulties. At least trying to."

"Sounds like a wise decision." Callie smiled at her niece. "You are such a good mama."

"Thank you. A tired one, too."

"If you want to take a snooze, I'll gladly hold this sweetie pie for an hour or two."

"If I happen to fall asleep while we're talking, I know she's in good hands." Paige yawned and covered her mouth. "Excuse me." A few minutes later, she rested against the pillows and dozed off.

Callie rocked the tiny baby, thanking God for the blessing of another child to hold and love. She prayed for Adelaide to have a sweet and gentle spirit. A heart of service. A compassionate nature to those around her who were less fortunate. Her time of holding the baby in the quiet of the house passed all too quickly, but she cherished every moment.

Later, after James drove her back to the project house, Callie's heart felt full of all the tender emotions she experienced while holding

Adelaide. Maybe that's why she didn't balk when he asked if they could spend a few minutes talking in the car before he returned to his house.

He clasped her hand and toyed with her fingers. "Cal?"

"Hmmm?"

"I don't want to pressure you. If you really aren't ready to give me an answer, I understand. But I am curious. What do you think of my proposal? Do you hate the idea of marrying me?"

"I don't hate it. Goodness. I've loved you forever."

"What?" His hand fondling hers stilled.

Ohhh. Did she just tell him she loved him? She huffed out a breath. "You might as well know, I had the biggest crush on you in seventh and eighth grade. Then in high school. Through most of my adult life, actually."

"Callie Cedars, you flatter me!"

"I'm not trying to flatter you, James. It's the truth." She tugged her hand away from him and clutched her hands together in her lap. "It's why I haven't been able to say yes to your question. Marry the man who spurned me all those years?" The hurt in her heart barreled out in her words. She wanted to sob, but what good would crying over unrequited love do for her now?

"How can you not?" he asked softly.

"What's that supposed to mean?"

"Sweetheart, if you've carried such a crush in your gentle heart, and the man you've wanted to be with asks you to marry him, and when that man sits right here adoring you, won't you say yes, then?"

His words were like poetry and music to her heart.

"Let's have a beautiful future together, Cal. Will you embrace a future with me?" He swallowed hard. "Embrace me?"

Oh, James. Her heart fluttered and picked up an odd rhythm.

Embrace the man she had loved for most of her life?

Chapter Forty-two

James yearned to pull Callie closer and kiss her until she fully trusted his sincerity about wanting her for his wife. She confessed to having a crush on him. If she cared for him all those years, why wasn't she eager to marry him now?

Why didn't he notice this crush of hers? He didn't purposefully neglect her. Call it being dense or self-absorbed when he was younger. But he never knew how she felt! If only she'd said something. Had she taken those years of him not falling for her as a rejection?

How could he change her mind, her heart, so she knew beyond any doubt he loved her and wanted them to be happily married?

He held his hand out to her, gazing into her eyes. She didn't immediately clasp his hand. He didn't pull it away. She'd waited a long time for him to wake up to the possibility of them being a couple. He'd wait for her now. For whatever reason she held back from agreeing to marry him, he would wait as long as she needed. But he wasn't going to remain silent about it.

"I want to hold your hand. No strings attached. Is that okay?"

"All right." Her cheeks turned pink, but she clasped his hand. "I don't know why I'm befuddled over this. You're a nice man, James. I've known that about you since high school."

"Is that all you have to say to the man you've had a crush on?" He grinned cheekily.

"Fishing for praise?"

"Just wanting to hear the thoughts of the woman I love." He squeezed her hand lightly. "What bothers you about the idea of spending your life with me?"

"Oh, goodness. Where do I start?" Chuckling, she stared out the window, her face in profile to him.

He braced himself for the brazen honesty he knew Callie to have. Would she let him have it, both guns blazing, for his snail-slow realization of a love he could have had? For the years he wasted. Even if he was obtuse, he regretted those years too.

When Callie turned to him with a softer expression crossing her face, he sighed in relief.

"Marriage includes changes I'm not prepared for."

"Such as?"

"Sharing space with a man!" Her face hued a darker rose. "Deferring to his wishes. After sixty-three years, I'm set in my ways. I like what I like, and I say what I want to say."

James chuckled over her vehemence. "We are both set in our ways. But I like the thought of sharing my house with you. And my bedroom." He smiled as he addressed the delicate subject. He'd never said those words to any other woman. "I enjoy imagining what marriage to you would be like. Sharing our lives. Even the intimate parts of being husband and wife."

"James Weston, I'm shocked you'd mention such a topic to me! We aren't even engaged yet."

At least she said "yet."

"I may be an older man, but I'm not dead, woman!"

Callie chortled, whether over embarrassment or good humor he had no idea. However, he loved hearing the sound of her laughter. Her gazing into his eyes with such womanly intensity made his heart hammer like an anvil.

"What do you say?" He tipped his head, keeping his gaze on hers, hoping hers stayed steadily on his. "Do you ever imagine spending time with me, just the two of us?"

Callie coughed hard as if choking.

"So, the thought has never crossed your mind?"

"What it means is I have modest opinions about certain topics." Her blush made her cheeks even rosier.

Leaning toward her, he brushed his mouth against her warm cheek. When she didn't pull away, he moved slightly and touched his lips to hers, slowly, purposefully. He liked the sweet, eager way she responded.

"I've been thinking about spending time with you," he whispered.

"So, you're serious about wanting to marry me? I mean, really serious?"

She still doubted him?

"Yes, I still want to marry you."

"Not because of a laugh between you and Pauly?" Her voice rose.

"Cal, no! It has nothing to do with Paul."

"Get the sister to agree to marry you and then you both hoot and howl!"

James gaped at her. "You think I would be so cruel?"

"I hope you wouldn't be. I pray you wouldn't be. You are the one who started this romance because you thought pretending to like me would get Pauly and me to make amends."

He groaned. "That's not how I feel now. I love you."

She heaved a breath. "I love you, too, James. There. I said it. I want everything in a marriage and relationship, too. It's just—"

"You love me? Does that mean—"

"No! It doesn't mean anything."

"How can admitting you love me mean nothing?" He clutched the steering wheel with both hands.

"There's too much past between us." She put her purse strap over her shoulder and reached for the door handle.

"Callie, wait. After we kissed as we did, let's not leave things unfinished. What is so wrong with our past? We've been friends who—"

"Let's get one thing straight," she interrupted. "You and Pauly were friends. I was an observer of your friendship with him. A third wheel. The outcast sister. That's all."

"No, that's not—"

"Yes, it was! Admit the truth." She glared at him, cutting off his protest. "If you'll excuse me, this talk is over." She opened her door and exited the car. "Goodbye, James." She slammed the door.

Goodbye? What just happened? Stymied, he watched her walk up onto the porch of the project house without glancing back. How had their talk, and after their tender kisses, end so abruptly and with so much tension between them?

She said for him to admit the truth. Admit he was self-centered as a kid? What mattered was how he and Callie felt about each other now. Not what happened fifty years ago. But why was whatever happened a half-century ago bothering her so badly still?

He opened the car door and climbed out. Their relationship couldn't end like this. He had zero knowledge about fighting fairly with a woman. He'd heard communication was key in a relationship. But how to achieve common ground with Callie remained a mystery.

Didn't Paul warn him not to get involved with his sister? That there'd be trouble. James groaned. He wasn't taking advice from Paul about women! Not with his track record.

Closing his eyes, he prayed for strength and wisdom. Then he strode up the same path Callie took. He knocked on the door without getting the immediate response he hoped for. Tempted to try the doorknob, he waited like the gentleman his mother taught him to be.

Finally, Callie inched the door open. "Did I forget something?"

"You might say so."

Her eyebrows lifted.

"Or rather, I forgot to say what I should have said." He removed his hat, then gripped it between his hands. "Look, Cal. I admit to being stupid and obtuse in not seeing you cared for me as more than your brother's friend for all those years. Or for me not recognizing what a wonderful, eligible woman you were in your twenties and thirties. I was emotionally blind as a bat. I admit it! Okay?"

"Do we have to discuss this now?"

"Yes! We must discuss it. Please, step out on the porch. Or else let me in." His tone came out sharper than he meant, his agitation building.

"Since I don't want Kathleen hearing us, I'll come out. But that's the only reason!" She widened the door and stiffly stepped onto the porch.

"Thank you for agreeing to talk with me."

"Doesn't mean I've changed my mind." She crossed her arms.

"I understand." How could he convince her that he wasn't trying to wheedle his way into her heart because of Paul? He made a superbly bad decision when he tried acting as a mediator between those two before. Never again.

"Say what you want to say. Then you should leave." She lifted her chin toward his car in a defiant gesture.

"From the bottom of my heart, I love you, Callie. It has nothing to do with Paul. I think you're beautiful and special and a wonderful woman."

She bit her lip, eyeing him.

"I'm sorry for not being more romantic. I have little experience to draw from." A lousy excuse, but it was the truth. "I'll get better at romance and showing you how much I love you if you'll give me a chance. You like kissing me, don't you?" Since she seemed to be fighting a grin, he asked, "Well, don't you?"

"Yes. All right? I told you I speak my mind, so I'll be honest. I like kissing you, James Weston. I've imagined doing so long enough!"

"Good. Then why haven't you been more romantic with me if you've liked me for half a century?" He was being bold now.

"More romantic? I told you I've loved you forever. I've kissed you like you're the air I need to survive. What more do you want?"

"Callie Cedars"—he let a wide grin spread across his mouth—"that's a dangerous question for a woman to ask a single man. Especially if you don't want to talk about—"

"Never mind!"

"Do you love me right now?" James stroked his fingers down her soft cheek. "I'm not talking about some bygone crush."

Her lower lip wobbled. "Yes, I love you now."

"I love you right now, too."

They reached for each other's hands, fumbling slightly.

"I've been pushing you for an answer about my proposal. That's unfair to you. I'm sorry."

He wanted to kiss her. For them to lose themselves in smooching and living in the moment, wherever that might take them. But he had higher ideals. He wanted a wife and marriage and everything holy and beautiful about loving a woman.

"How about this? Whenever you're ready to talk with me about marriage, just tell me," James spoke quietly, his confidence building. "I'll wait as long as it takes for you to be convinced that I love you and want you for my wife. Until then, I'll wait patiently. I promise."

He turned abruptly and strode back to his car. He couldn't see her, but in his thoughts, he spoke to Callie, *I'll wait forever for you. But I sure hope it doesn't take that long!*

Chapter Forty-three

Callie closed the door and leaned against it like she imagined a teenage girl coming home from a prom might do. Her thoughts and emotions were in knots. James loved her! Not because of any shenanigans with Pauly, either. Not because he felt guilty about ignoring her in the past. Because he loved her now. And she loved him.

She wanted to dance and sing. But Kathleen would hear, and she'd have to explain the commotion. Instead, she sauntered into the kitchen to make some tea, still feeling dreamy and wistful.

Her gaze landed on an envelope propped against a mug on the island addressed to her. "Lola" was the only word written in the return address field. No street address.

Lola wrote to her? Callie clutched the envelope to her chest. Hands shaking, she sat on the barstool and tore it open as eagerly as any mama would.

"'Dearest Callie. I'm sorry for causing you concern. I had to see my husband. He needs me. Micah misses his daddy. Please don't be mad. My heart is thankful for how you welcomed me into your home. I will never forget your kindness. I hope we will meet again. Lola.'"

"Oh, Lola." Callie read the note twice, tears flooding her vision.

Lola didn't say she was safe. Or how she and Micah were doing. Only that Benjamin needed her. Were they eating well? Were they safe?

Lord, please protect Lola and Micah. Let Benjamin recognize his need for help.

If Lola was in any danger, she knew where to come for refuge and support. Callie and Kathleen would welcome her back. No questions asked. No condemnation. Loving her and keeping her and Micah safe and healthy would be all that mattered.

But it was up to Lola. Callie had to accept that.

She made herself a cup of peppermint tea. Sorely tempted to add two heaping teaspoons of honey, she added only half a teaspoon. She needed a little comfort food.

She'd gone from the elation of pondering a lifetime of loving James to the sadness of Lola's departure and current situation about which she could only guess. If she could make Lola's decisions for her—namely keeping her away from Benjamin—everything would turn out better. She groaned. Had she made the best decisions over the course of her life? Was causing trouble with Pauly and Penny wise or loving? Was gossiping about other people caring or grace-filled?

She'd made her share of mistakes. She remembered times when Pauly yelled at her to leave and stay away from their family home. How she determinedly came back, time and time again, trying to help her nieces and nephew. But all the while, she knew she was annoying her brother.

She wished she'd done better about taking Pauly's feelings into consideration. Maybe then, their past problems might not still be like a roaring forest fire between them.

She took a sip of tea. Delicious.

Her phone vibrated and she took the device out of her sweater pocket. "Forest" flashed on the screen.

"Hello. Is Paige okay?"

"She's okay. I have news about Sue Anne."

"Oh? I hope it's good news because I could use some."

"I have an address for her."

"Already? Good job! Where is she?"

"North Carolina," he said in his deep voice. "Her husband passed away ten years ago. No children."

So, she was single!

"Thank you for your help. Text me her address, will you?"

"Will do. Also, I have her email address."

"Forest, you are a treasure. Thank you for looking into this for me."

"That's high praise. You're welcome, Callie. Anytime."

"Give Adelaide Pearl a kiss for me. Piper too."

"I certainly will."

Callie ended the call and pressed her lips together. Sue Anne hadn't remarried. She and Pauly were both single. And she didn't have children after giving up Sarah.

That gave her a lot to think about.

After she put her empty teacup in the dishwasher, she went into her bedroom and opened her laptop. She'd sit right down and write Sue Anne a long email letter.

Would Pauly call this prying, too?

If she was meddling, it was for the best of reasons!

Chapter Forty-four

In the five days since James and Paul went to Eugene for their buying trip, they'd been busy doing the groundwork for their enterprise. For two of those days, Paul was watching Piper. However, James continued with the preparation work. They took inventory of the wood they collected, made sketches of garden benches and chairs, experimented with a couple of prototypes and worked out the kinks, and measured and cut boards for their first projects.

Fortunately, they came to an agreement on a simple style for their furniture. James's planer would come in handy to smooth down the aged barn wood and bring out the beautiful grains. They gathered plenty of stains and outdoor finishes for the projects, too.

Paul had been a handyman and household problem solver in the local hardware store for many years. James did carpentry work during most of his career. Combining their ideas and skills, they surely had the know-how to make a go of a homemade furniture business.

Today, they were going to make a garden bench—their first official piece of furniture. Each creation would be a design they planned to replicate in the days ahead.

"What do you think about a brand for our business?" James spoke over the sound of the sander he used to smooth out a cedar plank.

"A brand?" Paul huffed as if already out of breath. "We haven't finished our first piece and you want to make a brand for it?"

"I didn't mean a business logo. More like an identifying mark to show the furniture is our design." James buffed an edge of the wood that was sharp to the touch. "How about JPW for James and Paul Woodworking?"

Paul guffawed. "You decided on that?"

"Not decided. But it sounds right. J for me. P for you."

"What's wrong with PJ?" By his tone, he was already in a bad mood.

"Something bothering you?"

"Maybe." Using the power drill, Paul made a couple of holes where a notch would go between two boards.

James waited for the noise to cease. "What's happened?"

"It's my nosey sister! She called and asked if I minded if she wrote to Sarah's mother." Paul nearly snarled the words. "I called her a lowdown dirty snoop, which she is. She keeps digging into other people's business. Namely mine!"

"Why do you care so much if she writes to her?"

"She should let sleeping dogs lie."

Yet, the way he became angry must mean he still chewed on his past choices and hurts, letting them fester.

"Did she say why she was going to write to her now?" Maybe Callie wanted to invite her previous friend to their wedding. Was she thinking seriously about marrying him? Hallelujah!

"It's something to do with Sarah. I don't understand why she must meddle." Paul tossed the drill on the work counter, then strode for the door. "I need a break."

Obviously, things weren't going any better between Callie and Paul. Should James broach the topic of his and Callie's possible engagement? He'd been wanting to discuss it with Paul. But when he stormed back into the small shop, his face red, James had second thoughts.

"Are you still planning on marrying my sister?" Paul slammed his fists against his hips. "Because if you are, we might not be able to work together."

"What? Why not?"

"Because she'll try to run things! I'm not having that."

"She won't try to run our business, Paul. You've got her all wrong."

"Right. She's been my sister for sixty-some years. And I have her wrong?"

"Listen. Yes, of course, I hope to marry her."

"Of all the stupid ideas!" Paul tossed up his hands.

"Why are you so upset about this now?"

"Callie called and asked me what I thought about your marriage." Paul puckered up his mouth like he was about to spit.

"She did? That's great!"

"No, it's not! Why would you marry my sister at this point in your life? Are you nuts?"

"No." Slightly embarrassed over Paul's censure, James said, "It's great to be alive. Why not share that with someone? I think getting married and having a wife would be sensational. Marrying Callie isn't difficult. I look forward to our life together!"

"Geesh," Paul muttered and raked his fingers over his hair.

"What's so wrong with me that you wouldn't want me to marry her?"

"I didn't say anything was wrong with you. It's her. All her!" Paul picked up a raw piece of wood and set it in the planer. "She keeps bugging me to talk with her. Now my day is ruined." He turned the loud machine on, effectively silencing any other comments from James.

Finally, the power tool stopped, and James spoke up, "You don't mind my pursuing Callie, do you?"

"Of course, I mind! That's why I said we couldn't work together."

"But you want me to be happy, right?"

"Does she make you happy?" Paul asked in a scoffing tone. "If you must have one romance before you die, can't you pick up someone who's not related to me?"

"Pick up?" James snorted. "Love does what it wants, chooses who it wants."

"Come on! That isn't true."

"Didn't you have one true love?"

"We're not discussing me!"

"Why not? Maybe that's what makes you so mad about Callie contacting Sue Anne." James knew he was treading on dangerous ground. "Why not admit you still have feelings for her?"

"Leave that woman out of this! I'm warning you."

"You're the one who brought her up."

"No, I—" Paul groaned. "Callie did. If you want to get hitched so badly, use one of those dating services. Find some woman who wants to experience marriage, too. Stay away from Callie. She's trouble. And she's going to cause problems between you and me!"

James felt himself getting riled. "I don't want to use a dating service. I care for Callie. That's why I'm talking with you. I respect our friendship too much not to discuss this matter with you. But I'm not letting you discourage us, either. Callie and I love each other."

"I don't believe it," Paul growled.

"Even if you don't agree with my asking her to marry me, I want your support and friendship. Promise me that."

"You want all that—and her?" Paul's eyes bugged. "And for us to continue working together?"

"That's right." James grinned. "I want it all."

Paul stared upward, muttering as if asking God why he must endure such stupidity.

An idea came to James. "Would you come over for dinner this evening?"

"Why?" Paul scowled.

"I'm going to ask Callie too. I want the three of us to sit down to a nice meal together." James rubbed his hands together in anticipation. "Will you come to dinner and act polite around my girlfriend?"

"Girlfriend?" Paul let out a growl and sanded the wood forcefully, his face turning beet red. "I can't believe you'd call her that after what she said to me."

"What did she say?"

"That I should contact Sue Anne myself. Like I'm desperate enough to do that. Women!"

"Maybe she's right."

Paul gritted his teeth. "Don't you start."

"If you still care for her, it must show that love lasts a lifetime."

"Love." Paul spit. "Listen to yourself."

James chuckled, and he couldn't stop laughing. He bent over, his hand at his chest, and guffawed.

"Why are you laughing?" Paul demanded.

"You and Callie are the two most stubborn people I've ever met in my life. So much alike, yet you can't see it." James laughed again.

"Stop, already! We have work to do."

"Okay, okay." He forced himself to stop chuckling despite the humorous look on Paul's face. "So, will you come over for dinner and try to be polite to my guest?"

"I doubt that's humanly possible."

"As my friend and business partner, will you come to dinner?"

Paul's shoulders sagged. James was gaining a slight advantage over his resistance.

"Fine!" Paul jabbed his index finger in the air. "Don't expect much to come of it. Other than an ugly argument."

"And dress up a little."

"Are you kidding me? Didn't you hear what I said?"

"Sure. I chose to ignore it."

If an argument ensued between Callie and Paul, James might have to referee. Hopefully, his idea of a nice dinner and chat wouldn't bite him in the kneecap.

Chapter Forty-five

James asked Callie to dress up for dinner at his house, but she didn't know why. When he sheepishly informed her that Paul would be there too, she felt doubly confused. He better not be trying to play peacemaker at her expense again!

Although, the irony was humorous. Maybe James was as much of a meddler as she was! Maybe they had more in common than she even realized.

Since James was fixing dinner, Callie called Marcus for an Uber ride. Her nerves felt taut as she smoothed down the fabric of her red dress and then knocked on James's front door.

When he opened the door, his eyes lit up. "Callie, you look lovely. Thank you for joining me for dinner." He lifted her hand to his lips and kissed her knuckles softly.

"Thank you for the invitation." She gave him a once over, noticing his checkered tie over a cream shirt. His camel-colored cardigan looked soft and inviting for a hug, or for her hands to rest on during a long kiss later. "You clean up nicely too."

"Thanks. Come in. Paul's already here."

"Oh. He is?" She covered the disappointment in her tone. She hoped to snag a few minutes of alone time with James before her brother showed up.

After her call to Pauly earlier, and his negative reaction when she mentioned writing to Sue Anne, she didn't know what to expect from him tonight. Grumpiness and a bad attitude, most likely.

Taking a deep breath, she entered James's house. The aromas of delicious spices and meat smelled divine. "The scents wafting in this room are fantastic. Makes me want to eat the air."

"Save your appetite for the real thing." James chuckled, holding out his arms to take her coat. "Roast beef with potatoes and gravy. An old family favorite."

"I'm eager to try it. Your ability to cook is a boon." She winked at him.

"Good. My cooking skills will serve me well as a husband." He kissed her softly on the cheek, making her heart pound.

Pauly shuffled into the room and cleared his throat like their father might have done if he caught them smooching. "Callie."

"Pauly." She adjusted the waist of her red dress with white polka dots. The color was bold for her usual taste in clothes, but she felt like making a splashy entrance tonight.

She lost five pounds over the last two weeks. Five pounds! After she weighed herself this morning, she danced a victory jig. To some that might not sound like much. For her, it was a win! Surely her heart wasn't working as hard. She felt more energy. Things were looking up. Maybe she'd thank Doctor Isabel for pushing her to lose weight, even though that had been even harder than she thought it would be.

"Dinner's ready. Let's head into the kitchen." James swayed his hand for Callie to precede him.

His hand on the small of her back warmed her. She was becoming more familiar with his touch, his nearness that only a few days ago felt odd. His second proposal danced through her thoughts. Was she ready to say yes to him?

She met her brother's gaze. His scowl was deeply etched on his face. He must hate the idea of her being romantically involved with James. But why did she value his opinion, anyway? Other than she wished for a normal sibling relationship with him again.

As soon as she sat down at the table, she tried coming up with a polite, non-confrontational topic. She thought of the new baby. "I saw Adelaide. What a precious sweetheart!"

"She's a gem." Paul's voice swelled with pride. "I wish Penny were here to see her."

Now, why did he have to bring up his deceased wife? Callie regretted the unkind thought as soon as it crossed her mind. Of course, he thought of Penny. He'd married her. Maybe she would have been a better grandmother than a mother. Age may have helped her become a nicer person, too.

"She would have loved them." There. That kindness hadn't hurt her one bit.

"She would have been proud as punch of the great moms Paige and Paisley have become." He heaved a sigh.

Did Pauly still mourn the loss of his wife after four-and-a-half years? Was that why he acted grumpy and out of sorts most of the time? Maybe he'd loved Penny more than Callie ever realized. He stayed with her and took care of her faithfully throughout their marriage and then during her battle with cancer. He was sweet in his stodgy annoying way.

Taking in the lovely table setting of mismatched plates and glasses and the vanilla-scented candle in the center of the table, Callie appreciated James's efforts to make this dinner special. "Everything looks lovely."

"Thanks."

James said grace quietly, non-pretentiously. Callie sensed a strength in him when he prayed. Even in his attempts to get her and Pauly to communicate, there was integrity about him.

The prayer finished, James passed the potatoes to Callie before taking his own serving.

"Thank you." When their fingers touched, she felt a zing of attraction, a reminder of their previous kisses. She pictured herself spending the rest of her life with him—a giant leap from thinking of kisses to marriage. Still, she envisioned the two of them growing old together. Eating together. Sleeping together. Heavens, how her mind wandered.

What if she just said yes? Life was an adventure. Marriage would be an adventure too. She and James would be happy together, whether Pauly approved of them or not.

Dinner was peaceful as long as she didn't glance at her brother's grudging expressions aimed at her and James. She avoided troublesome topics—Penny, Sue Anne, or anything that might be perceived as her interfering in Pauly's life. If she invited Sue Anne to Basalt Bay and she came, would Pauly hold more grudges toward her?

She sighed and the sound vibrated through her.

"Something troubling you, Cal?" James asked.

Did he recognize the agony she was enduring, sitting next to her brother but not being able to speak freely? "Not really. You've outdone yourself tonight. This roast beef is tender and juicy. The gravy is fabulous. Your culinary talents surprise me." She had no idea he cooked this well.

A wide smile crossed his mouth, making him look even more handsome in the warm candlelight. His words replayed in her mind. *"My cooking skills will serve me well as a husband."* Indeed, they would. If Pauly wasn't present, she'd lean toward James and kiss those smiling lips. Maybe then, she'd be bold enough to answer his question about marriage.

"The better to win your heart!"

Pauly groaned.

Callie's face flushed, but she smiled at the man who held her heart already. That James said such things in front of her curmudgeon brother showed he was willing to risk everything to tell her he cared for her. That was spectacular in her book.

* * * *

James glanced back and forth between his dinner guests. While he grinned and flirted with Callie, by Paul's grumbling, he was uncomfortable. How would he ever adjust to James and Callie being a couple unless he saw them acting like they cared about each other?

How could James break the ice between Paul and Callie? His hope of them moving toward reconciliation during this dinner wasn't working.

Paul remained silent through most of the meal, answering in grunts or "Uh-huh." Callie was probably fearful of saying anything that might cause repercussions.

"Who's ready for dessert?" A homemade treat might soften their hearts where his roast beef dinner failed. "I made a batch of my famous brownies this afternoon."

"Wonderful. I'll try a small piece." Callie rubbed her hands together.

Hopefully, a miniature portion of the contraband would be okay for her and for Paul.

"Just enough to try my baking skills?" James winked at her.

"That's right."

"Paul?"

"I won't say no to brownies."

James stood and prepared the dessert. In his absence, he hoped Paul and Callie might converse. The room stayed quiet. A napkin falling to the floor would have made a louder sound. Those two were hard nuts to crack!

After setting a small piece of brownie on each of the three plates, James served his guests. Then he brought his plate to the table and sat down.

"Mmm. This is good." Callie held up a tiny piece of chocolate. "Brownies are one of my favorite goodies."

"Glad to hear it."

Paul gobbled down his dessert without commenting.

What could James say to nudge these siblings toward a significant conversation without being an instigator of trouble?

"Paul, is there anything you'd like to say?"

"About what?" Paul sent him a cross look.

Callie cleared her throat.

James didn't dare look at her.

"You've had time to consider Callie and me possibly getting married." He clasped her hand lightly. "Do we still have your blessing to proceed with a relationship?"

Callie kicked him under the table.

He stifled a groan.

She pulled her hand away. "This isn't the time, James. Besides, Pauly gave us his blessing, which I don't need."

"I take it back, anyway. You and James are as compatible as Fred Flintstone and Cruella Deville."

"Now, Paul—" James warned.

Callie threw her napkin onto the table. "You are insulting James by calling him Fred Flintstone."

"No, I'm not. I'm making a comparison between the two of you and two contrary cartoon characters."

"Are you still watching cartoons, Pauly?"

"That's not the point." Paul took a swig of water and then set his glass down hard.

In the silence, Callie's face turned red, and she squeezed her hands together so tightly, James figured she was restraining herself from saying something insulting.

Should he try to tamp down their hot tempers? Or let the chips fly?

"So, the fact Callie and I are different is what bothers you?"

"Different? Different?" Paul said in escalating tones. "Night and day. Ice and fire. Ocean and desert. She's my flesh and blood. But you are more of a brother to me than she's ever been my sister." The words tore from him like a burning rocket.

Callie's tear-filled eyes met James's gaze accusingly.

He did this. He caused this emotional explosion of words. *I'm sorry*. He hoped his gaze expressed his remorse. But while he ached for Callie's pain, he hurt for Paul, who carried this grudge for such a long time, too.

"Cal? What do you want to say to Paul?"

"That I'm shocked. He feels as if I'm not even his sister?"

"I didn't say that."

"Yes, you did. You said James is more of a brother to you than I'm your sister."

Paul shrugged. "Your sharp tongue has driven too many wedges between us."

"And your silence!"

Paul and Callie glared at each other, angry darts zinging between them.

James waited and prayed silently.

Suddenly, Callie sagged against the back of her chair. Her breathing came in thready gasps. "Oh, Pauly, I truly am sorry." Her softly spoken apology cut the tension in the room like a knife cutting through wedding cake and frosting. "I'm sorry for speaking harshly when I ... when I should have remained quiet. When I should have checked my injured heart before I said a single word to you. I'm trying to change. God knows I am trying to be humbler. And kinder. I've hurt you in the past. Said rude things. Even today, when I told you about Sue Anne, I should have let the matter go when you said you didn't want to discuss it." She took a noisy breath. "But I thought you should know I contacted her. I'm sorry if it offends you. Please forgive me for my wrongs?"

Paul's eyes glistened. Yet he didn't agree or say anything.

The stillness in the room became suffocating. If Callie's apology didn't soften Paul's heart, nothing would. In this moment of observing her tender spirit laid bare, James loved and admired her even more. After dinner was over and he apologized, and if she was still speaking to him, he'd tell her so.

* * * *

Callie held her breath, clutching her hands together so tightly, her fingernails gouged into her soft palms. She couldn't take much more of the tension in this room. She was half mad at James for making this painful conversation happen, and half thankful for him trying to open a door between her and Pauly.

She sincerely apologized to Pauly. Wanted to lay the hurt feelings from their past on the table. Then, if he still wouldn't accept her apology, she'd go on with her life knowing she tried her best to make things right. That's all she could do. Other than to continue loving him and praying for him.

"Can you and I have a do over?" She reached her right hand across the table, palm up.

Pauly didn't clasp it. But he lifted his moist gaze to hers. In that moment, she saw the big brother she'd been missing, the boy who used to play cards and have tennis matches with her, the one who used to sit by her and watch movies on the couch. She recognized the younger version of him in the stubborn set of his jaw that resembled their dad's. He blinked a few times. Then he stared tenderly at her as if seeing her for the first time in years.

"Pauly?"

"I'm, uh, sorry for holding onto this grudge." The words came from him stiffly. "I never tried to work things out with you. I didn't forgive or offer apologies. I have been brooding and silent. My actions probably fed your anger and hurts too."

Callie didn't agree. Whatever her brother said, she'd listen and not argue.

"The strife with Penny, with you and me, grew like a cancer." Paul gnawed on his lower lip, his front teeth showing in a grimace. "I want to let it go. So, yes, I do forgive you."

"Thank you, Pauly."

He drew a cloth hanky from his back pocket and blew his nose.

Beside her, James let out a long relieved-sounding sigh.

"Is there anything else you want to say?" she asked quietly. "Anything you want to get off your chest, once and for all?"

"Nothing else to say." Pauly shoved his chair back and stood.

Did this mean he forgave her but that was it?

When he held out his hand to her, her heart felt like it dropped to the floor. She settled her hand on his open palm lightly. With his other arm at her elbow, he assisted her to a standing position. Uncertain what he was doing or going to say, she waited.

Suddenly, he wrapped his arms around her in an endearing but awkward bear hug. Ages had passed since he hugged her. He held her and cried. Pauly crying! Tears flooded her eyes too. The protective, glacial feelings in her heart about their past melted. She held onto her brother as tightly as he held her. For a minute, it felt like they were five and seven again, playmates being rowdy then sitting arm in arm watching a scary movie together.

Pauly stepped back, patting her shoulder. "Even though I was angry with you all those years, I still loved you."

Shock and grief, the last of her twin towers of deep emotion, crumbled. "I love you too. So much."

Paul reached over and clutched James's hand, then he tugged James's and Callie's hands together until they were holding hands. He sniffled a few times. "You have my blessing to get married, whether you want it or not."

"Thanks, Paul."

James and Pauly shook hands and clapped each other on the back.

"Thanks for dinner," Pauly said. "I'll leave you two alone to talk over whatever else needs to be said. See you tomorrow."

After their goodbyes, he left the house.

Callie and James stared at each other. What just happened? A miracle, it seemed.

James's comforting arms surrounded her, and she leaned her cheek against the warmth of his cardigan. "This forgiveness and healing between Pauly and me wouldn't have happened if you didn't host this dinner. And if you didn't prompt us to talk. Thank you."

"Sure thing, Cal. Everything turned out better than I imagined."

"Me too. I thank God for it."

She had so much to say to James. But for now, being in his arms, standing close enough to hear his heartbeat, was enough.

Chapter Forty-six

The next morning, James stood in front of Callie's door holding a bouquet of yellow roses, shuffling back and forth in his shoes. Last night's dinner with her and Paul turned out well. Observing their reunion of hearts and forgiveness had been a beautiful and profound experience.

Now, he was here to find out what Callie thought about Paul giving his blessing for them to be married. James told her he'd wait for her answer. But by his eagerness to talk with her about it this morning, he might not be as patient of a guy as he thought. All morning he'd been chewing over what he should say to convince her to take a chance on him.

Paul expected him back at the shop in a short while. But before he could concentrate on applying a coat of stain to their first furniture efforts, he had something important to do.

The door opened. Kathleen smiled at him.

"Good morning, James." Her gaze danced toward the bouquet. "Those are lovely!"

"Morning, Kathleen. Is Callie here?"

"She sure is. Come in." Kathleen backed up and called, "Callie, you have company!"

James entered the dining area as Callie entered from the living room. "Hello, beautiful." He held out the roses to her.

"Why, James, I'm surprised to find you here so early. And bringing me flowers? You're spoiling me already." She clasped the bouquet and smelled them.

Already? His heart leaped. "I couldn't wait to see you."

"They are gorgeous."

"So are you," he said softly.

He loved her smile. Her sparkling gaze aimed at him.

"The man came by bright and early with roses that look like sunshine," Kathleen said in a merry tone. "I bet he's eager for a certain answer." She scurried out of the room, snickering.

"Kathleen!"

"She's right. I am eager to talk with you about that."

"Are you now?" Callie waved him toward the kitchen. "Let me do something with these roses."

"How are you feeling after last night?" He followed her, twirling his hat in his hands. Then he watched her trim the ends of the stems and put the flowers in a vase of water.

"Your dinner was lovely. Thank you for everything."

"I mean about what Paul said."

"Oh. About him forgiving me?"

Was she teasing him? "I mean—"

"I know what you mean, James." Leaving the pile of stem cuttings, she rounded the island and stood in front of him, the toes of their shoes nearly touching. Joy raced through him. He'd like to have Callie standing this close to him every day of his life.

He swallowed hard and kept his gaze fastened on her eyes. "Have you made a decision about us, Cal?"

"I have. I woke up during the night, pondering my conversation with Pauly." She smiled directly at him. "Thinking about you and me, too."

"You and me. I like that."

Unexpectedly, she pressed her lips to his. Sizzling fireworks shot through him. She kissed him intensely as if she was making up for all the years of kissing they missed out on.

"Callie. Oh, Callie," he whispered between the movement of their lips.

This smooching was unlike anything he'd experienced. Passionate, yet gentle. Demanding, yet yielding. Perfectly amazing and satisfying. Even so, the kiss ended too soon and left him hungry for more.

"Wow." He smoothed his hands over her shoulders and upper arms. "Wow," he said again.

"You wanted my answer?" She toyed with a button on his shirt. Did she feel his pounding heart? Her gaze met his with a soft look. "I will marry you, James."

"You mean it?"

"Yes," she said breathlessly. "I mean it."

"Oh, Cal." His arms still around her, he leaned her back slightly and kissed her. "When?" he asked as soon as their lips parted. "When will you marry me?"

"First things first. Where's my ring?"

"It's right here. I've kept the box close to me." Stepping back enough to reach into his coat pocket, he withdrew the small box. "Should I ask you again?"

"No. Just—" She held out her left hand toward him. "I still remember how sweetly you asked me to marry you before."

"Twice." He couldn't suppress the smile crossing his mouth.

"That's right. Twice." She grinned too.

He fumbled with opening the delicate red box. He lifted the ring out and held it toward her. "Please marry me?"

"Oh, James, it's lovely. Yes, I will marry you!"

Together, they eased the slim, solitary diamond engagement ring onto her finger. It was a little snug but looked gorgeous on her.

"You can have it resized."

"It's perfect."

He lifted her hand and kissed the place where the ring sat. "Thank you for saying yes, Cal. You make me happier than I've ever been."

"You make me happy too. I'm ecstatic to share our lives together."

"The best years of our lives are yet to come!" He kissed her with butterfly kisses across her cheek and down her neck.

A feminine throat-clearing sound made him pause. Catching the embarrassed look racing across Callie's cheeks, he shuffled back.

Sarah strode into the room, grinning. "Do you mind if I grab some juice out of the fridge? Then you two can continue making out."

James chortled.

"I have good news." Callie pulsed her hand with the engagement ring on it toward Sarah. "I said yes!"

"Oh, you guys. This is fantastic! Congratulations!" She hugged Callie, then James. "You will make the cutest couple ever. When's the wedding?"

"We haven't decided." Callie looked questioningly at James.

"Tomorrow?"

"No, silly." She batted at his arm.

"Let me know, and I'll save the date." Sarah grabbed a juice bottle out of the fridge and then left the room.

"I'd like a quick engagement," Callie said. "How about you?"

"Absolutely!" If he smiled any wider, his lips might crack.

"What about having a small affair right here?" She led him into the dining room. "Imagine the table set with reception goodies. Healthy options too."

"Of course." He'd agree with everything she said. She was going to marry him!

"Pastor Sagle will perform the ceremony." She led him into the living room, the biggest of the three main rooms. "We'll push back the furniture in here. Say our vows in front of the stairway with roses and greenery cascading down the handrail." She sounded excited and already had a plan in mind. "What do you say?"

"Yes! Everything sounds perfect. The best part is you're going to marry me! I want to kiss you and kiss you." And that's what he did.

Chapter Forty-seven

Two days after Callie accepted James's proposal, and with all the tasks to be taken care of for their wedding ceremony in four days, Callie almost forgot about the email she sent Sue Anne. When a notification pinged on her cell phone with her old friend's email address, she waited several minutes before opening it. What if Sue Anne wasn't interested in talking with her or seeing Sarah? She might even tell her to mind her own business. Pauly had told her that enough times.

Pauly. She thought of her brother accepting her apology and hugging her. Now they were going to be brother and sister in the way they should have been all these years. Oh, there would still be hurdles. Probably some arguments. But they'd be living across the street from one another. Sharing dinners and game nights. James and Pauly would be in business together. The two of them would hang out like the buddies they always were.

Callie would be a part of their friendship too. Of course, she'd be splitting her time with the project house ladies, leaving James and Pauly plenty of time to do their woodworking.

Staring at the email notification, Callie pondered what Sarah might say about this correspondence. She'd given her blessing for Callie to write Sue Anne. But whatever came next, whether the two of them met or not, would be up to Sarah.

If Sue Anne didn't want Callie reaching out to her again, so be it. If she wanted to meet Sarah but didn't want anything to do with Pauly, Callie wouldn't interfere. A lot of years had gone by. She couldn't blame Sue Anne for not having feelings toward him.

They had each made their choices. They must live with those. Or else leave them in the past where they belonged, as Pauly liked to remind her. But sometimes, it was only when a person recognized her need for forgiveness and grace that she could give grace and not hold someone else's wrongs against them. That's how Callie felt. She'd experienced grace. She wanted to extend it to others too.

Thank You, Lord Jesus, for what You are doing in my life. In James's and my life, together.

"You okay, Callie?" Kathleen walked into the kitchen and came to a stop. "Not bad news, I hope." She nodded toward the cell phone Callie was gripping.

"Just thinking." Callie took a breath then exhaled slowly. "I'm grateful for the journey God has brought me on to bring me to today."

"That's the spirit! Fill yourself with thankfulness. If you need anything, holler." Kathleen lifted her hand in a wave and then walked out onto the porch, giving Callie some solitude.

She tapped on the email icon and began reading. "'Dear Callie. It was lovely to hear from you. It's taken me a couple of days to ponder my response. My first reaction to your news was to jump on a flight and head west! Then I calmed myself down and spent some time thinking and praying. My dear friend, how have the years fled by so quickly? Yet at other times, it seems like it takes forever to pass through events or difficulties.'"

That made sense. Callie felt like she'd lived a long time. Yet the fifty years she admired James from afar were as gold dust evaporating in the air. Some days she felt like a girl of twenty, wishing the boy next door would talk to her. Finally, he had!

"'I'm sorry I didn't tell you about having a baby all those years ago. As my friend, you should have known my secret. I should have confided in you. But I was ashamed. I didn't want you telling Paul about Edward and me. I didn't want to hurt him any more than I had.'"

Callie gripped the cell phone tighter.

"'I wanted to keep my baby. However, my parents demanded that I let her go to a family who could provide for her better than me. Worst decision I ever made!'"

Callie's heart fluttered and sadness filled her. Sue Anne's parents probably meant well. Was the decision they enforced the best option for their daughter and granddaughter? Even for Edward? Although Callie would never wish a man like him on Sue Anne. She shuddered.

"'That she's in Basalt Bay is amazing news. I would love, love, love to meet my daughter … if she is willing.'"

Callie sighed. She'd hoped for this response from Sue Anne. Was Sarah ready to meet her birth mom?

"'I will gladly come to Basalt Bay. Thank you for telling me about Sarah. She sounds like a special person. I can't wait to meet her! Please, inform me when she's ready for a meeting or to correspond with me herself. I'm counting down the days and hours until that happens.'"

Callie closed her eyes. *Thank You, God.* She swallowed hard, subduing the urge to weep for joy. While she wanted to send an answer to Sue Anne right away, she'd respond only after she spoke with Sarah and got her approval to proceed.

Taking a deep breath, she focused on the day's tasks. She had a fitting session with the tailor to adjust the simple navy dress she purchased to wear for the ceremony. A puffy, frilly, white wedding dress was out of the question. She wanted something comfortable and simple, yet dressy.

She must check on the wedding cake without tasting too many samples. She'd schedule an appointment with Doctor Isabel before the wedding. And she needed to have a talk with Sarah.

Callie wouldn't be pushy about her meeting her birth mom. She'd be patient. Sarah would have her season to meet Sue Anne, if she wanted to. Maybe even for both to find love again. But none of that was up to Callie.

"'There is a time for everything.'" She quoted the verse from Ecclesiastes, thinking it applied not only to Sarah and Sue Anne but to her and James, too.

Chapter Forty-eight

Callie sat in the community hall with the other ladies of the Caring Society eager to hear why Sue Taylor called this impromptu meeting. She barely had time to get here between her dress fitting and cake tasting in Florence. Still, she wanted to give Sue her undivided attention.

"Ladies, I'll be brief." Sue stood in front of the group, her hands clasped. "I asked for this meeting to discuss a time-sensitive matter with you. Everything is set up for our nonprofit status, so I'd like us to kick off our group with a winter fundraiser."

Some oohs and aahs circled throughout the room.

Callie hadn't considered doing a fundraiser so soon, but she wasn't opposed to it.

"The main idea of our group is to help other women with temporary housing, providing food, basic needs, etc." Sue gazed around at the ladies. "But something has been churning in my mind."

Callie appreciated Sue Taylor's enthusiasm. The way she jumped right into the middle of this group, got the nonprofit stuff going, and wanted to be useful was encouraging. Hopefully, she was willing to lead the charge on a fundraiser. Because Callie was too busy to do anything other than marry James Weston!

"Sometimes women in crisis need something other than the women in the group can provide. They require services that cost money—doctors, lawyers, counselors, etc."

"That's right," Maggie said. "Even at my inn where I'm considering donating a couple of rooms as temporary shelters, my staff must clean the rooms. That's time and money."

Maggie was thinking of opening a couple of rooms for their project? Her tune had certainly changed since their first meeting. Tears filled Callie's eyes, but she blinked them away. This wasn't the time for emotional sentimentality. But her friend's change of heart was endearing.

"My idea is for us to have a fundraiser to generate some funds for those services." Sue lifted a flier with red and green lettering. "How about a festival in early December? That would give us a month to plan. I'm thinking there'd be music, food, booths, and kids' games. A fun day for all with proceeds going to the Caring Society." Sue spread out her hands. "What do you think?"

Several women jumped in with a buzz of conversation that lasted about fifteen minutes.

Sue was a natural leader. If Callie ever stepped down from leading the group, she knew who would make the perfect replacement.

"Callie, what do you say?" Sue asked.

"I think it's a fabulous idea. Maybe this festival will become a yearly event. And we'll need someone to lead this other than me." She held up her hand and pointed at her diamond ring. "I have enough going on with a wedding and a move. We can take nominations for a leader, but the idea is yours, Sue. Do you want to take the lead on this one?" Callie would be relieved if she did.

"I'd be delighted to direct this event. I'll need lots of help too." Sue gazed around the group and nodded at a couple of women who raised their hands to volunteer.

"I nominate Sue Taylor as our fundraising chairperson!" Kathleen said.

Bess seconded the motion. Everyone agreed with raised hands.

"Won't it be too cold for an outdoor event in December?" Maggie asked.

"Twinkling lights and a bonfire would be fun." Sue rubbed her hands together. "Although, it might be too cold for some visitors or booth operators."

"How about using this community room for booths with more delicate items or for venders and attendees who prefer to be indoors?" Bess suggested. "Let the hardier folks stay outdoors. Best of both worlds."

Another buzz of chatter ensued. The excitement and energy these women had as they discussed the possibilities of the upcoming event thrilled Callie.

What might the future of the Caring Society be like if all these women pitched in and helped other women so enthusiastically? Maybe the group would grow bigger than anything Callie had imagined. Perhaps her part was planting the seed. Starting the ball rolling. With these willing women and God's help, their mission would surely grow and blossom into a beautiful outreach. She couldn't wait to see how it all turned out.

Chapter Forty-nine

"You wanted to chat with me?" Sarah entered the kitchen quietly.

Callie swayed her hand to the other bar stool at the butcher-block island. She'd already set out hot tea and crackers with cheese for her. "Here's a snack, if you're interested."

"Sounds great, but I'm mostly tired." Sighing, Sarah dropped onto the stool. "Long day at the gallery. I love it, so I'm not complaining. Just beat."

"You're doing such a good job helping Paige during her maternity leave."

"I'm beyond thankful for the opportunity. That I can work with art and interact with the artists in Basalt Bay is amazing."

"God directed you here. I'm sure of it."

"I can't fathom a more perfect place to spend my life than with you, Bess, and Kathleen." Sarah gripped Callie's hand. "I already feel like you three are my favorite aunts."

Callie squeezed her hand back. "We love you too." Tenderness filled her.

"What did you want to talk about?" Sarah picked up her teacup and held it between both hands.

"I got a response from Sue Anne. She wants to come and meet you."

"She does? When?"

"Whenever you're ready. It's up to you. If you need more time to think about it, that's okay."

Callie really was changing. Before, she would have pushed hard for Sarah to do what she thought was the best thing for her. Now, she wanted to be patient and respectful of Sarah's feelings, even if waiting was still difficult for her.

"I see." Sarah dropped her gaze toward the island's wooden surface.

Callie tamped down the impulse to give unwanted advice. She sipped her tea and remained quiet, letting Sarah adjust to the news. The younger woman had already gone through enough trauma and struggled with losing her husband. The idea of meeting her birth mom must be overwhelming.

"I've imagined talking with her. I've thought of a dozen things I might ask her." Sarah made a nervous-sounding laugh. "It's weird meeting a mom I didn't know about when I'm now pushing forty."

Callie leaned over and gave her a motherly hug. "It'll be okay. Sue Anne is such a lovely person. I see her in you."

"You see Sue Anne in me?"

"Yes. In your eyes." Callie stroked back some strands of hair from Sarah's cheek like she remembered her mom doing to her. "In your caring heart. Even in the way you speak. I don't know why I didn't recognize the similarities as soon as I met you."

"Truthfully, I like hearing that I'm like her. I've been worried I may have inherited some of Edward's personality." Sarah scrunched up her face. "I'd hate that!"

"Judah turned out all right, didn't he?"

"Yes. But Bess was his mom. She's great." Sarah's shoulders sagged. "I'm nervous about meeting Sue Anne. But I'm a grown woman. Why should I fear meeting the person who carried me and birthed me?"

"If and when you meet Sue Anne is up to you. I did my part in contacting her. I won't intrude. And there's no rush." She gazed into Sarah's eyes, hoping she saw the love and concern she felt for her.

"I do want to meet her, despite my unsettled feelings. You'd be there too, right?" Sarah spoke quickly. "I mean if I meet her and it's wretchedly awkward, you'll step in and talk with her, won't you?"

"I'd be honored." Callie patted her arm. "This is going to work out. I feel it strongly within me."

"Thank you for caring enough to reach out to her." Sarah took a couple of sips of her drink. "When would she come, if I were ready?"

"I don't know how quickly she could get here. I wish she could attend my wedding, but that's too soon."

"I'll ponder this and get back with you, okay?"

"That's fine."

Sarah set her teacup in the sink, hugged Callie, and then left the room.

Callie felt a sense of relief. Her burden about Sarah and Sue Anne meeting, and even about Sue Anne and Pauly possibly seeing each other, eased. She took a leap of faith when she corresponded with Sue Anne. Hopefully, Sarah would meet her mother under the best of circumstances. In the days ahead, Callie would be praying for the mother-daughter duo.

She spent a few minutes praying silently for Sarah, Sue Anne, and Pauly, and for whatever the days ahead held for all of them.

Chapter Fifty

Last night during a phone conversation with Callie, James heard all about the winter festival the ladies were planning. Her enthusiasm was contagious. By this morning, his thoughts were leaping from one idea to another so fast he hardly knew what to do with them. What if he and Paul launched their furniture business during the event? They had a small assortment of products accumulating in the spare bedroom. Could they get enough furniture accomplished for a launch in December? He imagined the things they could make—benches, rockers, and garden tables. He was eager to talk it over with Paul.

"Good morning." Paul strode into the shop carrying two cups of coffee.

"What's this?" James accepted one of the cups.

"Brought my own coffee today."

"Smells good." James took a sip. "Mmm. Doesn't get better than that."

"Good old-fashioned black percolated coffee with two spoons of sugar in each." Paul took a noisy slurp.

"Two? Aren't you supposed to be watching your sugar intake?"

"Yeah, yeah. Don't mention it to Callie."

James snorted. "Are you watching it?"

"Sure am. Now, let's stop talking about it. We have five pieces of furniture finished. What are we going to tackle next?"

For some reason, Paul looked nearly ten years younger. Was he feeling better since he cleared the air with Callie? Or was it because of his enthusiasm over their woodworking tasks?

"What has you in such a good mood?"

"What makes you ask?"

"You're happier. Sprier. Or something." James took a drink of the sweetened brew and eyed his friend.

Paul shrugged a couple of times but didn't say anything.

"Well, alrighty then." Accepting that he didn't want to discuss it, James set down his cup on the work counter and pointed at a small wood pile. "Let's plan some more furniture. We need to make sure we have enough materials for, say, another five pieces."

"Five? Got a big order I didn't hear about?"

"Callie told me about a winter festival the ladies are putting on. What would you say to reserving a booth and displaying our wares there?"

"You mean the two of us sitting in some pauper's tent no one wants to look at?" Paul grimaced. "Why not have a sale on your front lawn?" He clicked his fingers. "Like a garage sale! If no one shows up, and they probably won't, we won't make fools of ourselves."

"Is that what you think?" James asked, perturbed that Paul would think so little of their hard work. "That no one will be interested in our furniture? Why? Because we're old and just starting out? I happen to be proud of what we've created! Those two benches are fabulous. So is the rocking chair and garden table we made."

"Okay, fine. I'm proud of them too. Putting ourselves out there for all of Basalt Bay to stare at and criticize? No thanks!"

"It's not like that." James picked up a piece of distressed wood and ran his palm over it. "People like stuff made from wood, especially barn wood. Our furniture is good craftsmanship. Let's do this thing right, Paul."

"Can we even make money building furniture? With the simple stuff we've put together?" Paul stared at the piece of wood and gnawed his lip like he tasted sugar on it.

"I think so. Let's work hard. Give a booth a try. Make it a grand opening! Then we'll find out what people think about our stuff."

"What about your marriage?"

"What about it?" James shrugged. "Callie is fine with us going into business together."

"I mean, isn't it coming up in three days?"

"Yeah. So?" James scratched his head, not understanding where Paul was going with this.

"So, when are you going to have time to make five more pieces? With Callie calling the shots—"

"She isn't calling the shots." James snorted. "We're going to support each other's dreams. Besides, there's still a month before the event. Plenty of time to get five or ten pieces finished."

"Ten? Good night! We'd better get started now." Paul set down his cup firmly.

"Okay. But are you going to tell me why you were whistling when you walked into the shed? Got a hot date?"

"Yeah, right. If you must know, Callie called and said Sue Anne is probably going to come for a visit."

"That so?" James turned on the planer, preparing to work on the piece of distressed wood he thought would make a lovely garden tabletop.

Paul held one side of the board. "I suppose the news started my day off nicely."

"You must be looking forward to seeing your old flame." James grinned, rubbing it in a little.

"Now, now. That's old business. But Sue Anne coming back made me realize something." Paul's gaze remained on the wood in front of him. "This project of ours has given me a reason to wake up in the mornings. New creations to think about and sketch. I'm not sitting around watching TV all the time." He adjusted his grip on the board. "Seems I'm living again. Maybe that's what put a spring in my step."

A wash of moisture flooded James's eyes. "That's good news, Paul. Real good."

They ran the board through the planer, and the loud sound of the machinery stopped any further comments.

Later, Paul withdrew a crinkled, folded sheet of paper from his flannel shirt pocket. "Here is my latest sketch."

"My word, Paul. This is fantastic!" James perused the drawing of a headboard with intricate latticework. "Buy a sketch pad, man. Stop drawing on paper and scrunching it up like this."

"Aww. It's nothing."

"You're wrong. It's extraordinary." James shook the paper in the air. "Let's work on this one next."

"Seriously? You like it?"

"It'll be a great showpiece for our booth at the festival. Maybe some folks will want to buy things like this for Christmas gifts."

"I didn't think of that." A wide grin crossed Paul's face. "Let's check our wood supply and get cracking."

They spent the rest of the day working on the headboard design. When their work stalled because the planer overheated or they needed a coffee break, they talked about the furniture pieces they'd like to make in the future.

"Maybe we should rent a bigger space." Paul nodded toward the ocean waves. "Fall storms are coming. Your shop isn't big enough to hold all the pieces we'll make between now and Christmas."

"Plenty of room in the house."

"Your wife will have an opinion about that!"

James grinned. He liked Callie being called his wife.

"She'll be fine with us using the extra rooms for storage."

"You sure?"

"She's supportive of what I'm doing. The same as I'm supporting her in her causes. Our marriage will be about teamwork. Not a ball and chain around my neck."

"If you say so, buddy." Paul patted his shoulder like he didn't agree with him.

James wouldn't argue. But with the way he and Callie called each other morning and evening, and sent texts throughout the day, he felt like he knew the woman he was about to marry quite well. They'd make a great team. Partners who had waited a long time to be together.

He had only one regret—that he didn't fall for her when he was younger so they could have shared even more of their lives together.

/ Chapter Fifty-one

With two days left until the ceremony, James was more nervous than he imagined he'd be. He wasn't anxious about whether he wanted to marry Callie. He wanted that more than anything. But he kept having the feeling he'd forgotten something. Did he overlook a task?

He bought the rings. Even though they were having a small ceremony at the project house, he rented a tux. Arranged for Pastor Sagle to direct the service. Asked Paul to be his best man.

What could he have overlooked? As he tidied up his bedroom, making more space for Callie's belongings in his closet and emptying a dresser for her, the question nagged at him.

His phone buzzed. Pastor Sagle's name crossed the screen. Hopefully, nothing was amiss.

"Hello."

"Pastor Sagle, here. Can you and Callie come by for a counseling session this afternoon at one o'clock?"

"Counseling? Why?" James's shoulders tightened.

"I agreed to do the wedding on short notice since I've known you two for so long." The pastor took a noisy breath like he was walking and talking. "I have an opening in my schedule, so I'd like a chat with the bride and groom."

"Chat about what, exactly?"

"Premarital counseling. I usually require six sessions."

"Six?" James's voice shot up.

"We'll start with today's session. Resume after the wedding."

Was the pastor serious? Would Callie even go along with attending counseling? What if she refused and the pastor wouldn't marry them? Would they have to cancel everything? James bit back a groan.

"See you at one o'clock?"

"I guess."

"Both of you," the pastor reminded him.

"Uh, yeah. I'll call Callie and make sure she's available."

The call ended and James pressed his fingertips against his forehead. Now to break the news to his fiancée.

At one o'clock, they both sat stiffly across from Pastor Sagle. Callie let James know she wasn't happy about squeezing a marriage counseling session into her already busy day, but she agreed to the impromptu meeting.

"First, let me say congratulations to both of you." Pastor Sagle beamed. "That you found love in your Third Act is marvelous!"

Third Act sounded more like he meant their Finale.

"Thank you, Pastor," Callie said. "What's this about? I have an appointment this afternoon. Lots to do."

"I'm sure you have a full plate." Pastor Sagle linked his fingers together and rested his hands on the cluttered desktop. "It's a pre-wedding discussion. I assume you two have talked about many things together. But I want to make sure you've explored interpersonal topics that might have been uncomfortable to broach."

"Uncomfortable?" Callie gaped at the minister. "Surely, you don't mean—" She stared at James with accusation. "I thought this was about the wedding ceremony. We'll keep it simple. Traditional vows." She gulped. "That's not what this is about, is it?"

James shrugged, his face scorching from his chin to the roots of his hair.

"No. It isn't," Pastor Sagle said with a kind yet matter-of-fact tone. "I felt we should discuss some things you might not have considered."

James didn't dare glance at Callie.

"You've both been on your own for most of your adult lives," Pastor Sagle said as if they weren't aware of that fact. "You're both set in your ways."

"That's for sure," Callie muttered.

"So, tell me what you plan to do to incorporate your lives together. How are you going to combine your bachelor and bachelorette statuses to embrace communal living with your spouse?"

Communal living? At least he didn't bring up sex. James wasn't about to discuss that here.

"I will be moving into James's house if that's what you mean." Callie eyed the minister with a perturbed look. "We'll work on getting used to each other as time goes by. This is new for both of us. Sharing space, I mean." Her cheeks reddened.

"Sure, sure." The pastor unlinked his fingers and swayed his hands toward her. "It hasn't been that long since you moved from the house you lived in for a long time to go to the house you're in now."

"We call it our project house."

"Right. How do you feel about leaving the project house where you've opened your home to women in need, in exchange for living with James?" He tilted his head slightly, glancing between them. "That must be hard on you to step away from."

Tears welled in Callie's eyes. Was she thinking of Lola and Micah? James clasped her hand gently, comfortingly, he hoped.

"It was hard to imagine leaving at first, especially after Lola left us." She smiled sweetly at James and his heart melted a little. "But I've been fond of James for a long time. We are in love. I want to be with him as his wife." She turned her attention back to the pastor. "Not to say I won't miss the other ladies. I will. But I plan to stay involved with the work at the project house and with the Caring Society after the wedding. It will be my volunteer job."

"That's right." James nodded. "With my blessing."

"Good, good. And James, how do you feel about making space for Callie in the family home where you've lived your whole life? Planning to share your bachelor's domain must be challenging." Pastor Sagle chuckled. "I'm protective of my privacy and house."

Callie met James's gaze, her eyebrows lifting. Was she concerned about how she'd fit into his lifestyle and his home? He needed to put any of those worries to rest.

"I have lived in my house for a long time. But I look forward to Callie being there with me and my home becoming her home too." James brought Callie's hand to his lips and kissed the soft skin over her knuckles. Her eyes widened. He liked taking her by surprise and putting an extra sparkle in her irises. "I'm ready to share my life with her—every nook and cranny. It's like we're getting a new lease on life, together."

"I like that too." Callie squeezed his hand.

They smiled at each other, and he felt the bond of their love and their commitment to marry each other simmer through him.

"All right." Pastor Sagle clapped once then clasped his hands together. "What about arguments? Let's discuss your argument plan."

"Argument plan?" James felt aghast at such a suggestion.

Why was the pastor bringing up troublesome topics two days before their wedding? Here James was excited to share his life with Callie. They didn't need to discuss disputes already.

"I've surprised you both." The pastor scooted forward to the edge of his chair. "Arguments happen. You should have a plan for when they do. Will you talk things through immediately? Agree to never go to sleep with harsh words between you? You might take a break and talk later. Or each stomp off to your own space." He nodded toward Callie, one of his eyebrows arching high on his forehead. "You will be adapting to new surroundings. Maybe you'll seek refuge at the project house. Or head over to your brother's house?"

It seemed like the minister was trying to cause an argument right here. James felt riled enough to disagree vehemently until he noticed Callie patting his hand. The warmth of her skin brushing his soothed him, calming him. He met her gaze. She winked at him. All the frustration he felt building in him withered away.

"We have argued already, Pastor Sagle," Callie said in a serene tone. "We've known each other our whole lives. When we have a disagreement, we'll talk things out. Yes, there may be some stomping off. But we'll come back to each other. That's what marriage is about. Working through things. Coming to common ground. Loving each other no matter what."

James let out a long sigh. Callie was right. They had disagreed and survived. In the future, they'd work through problems and figure out how to communicate. They both had their faith. They'd rely on God's grace and guidance. Praying together too.

"James, you want to add anything?" Pastor Sagle asked.

"If Callie gets mad at me and heads over to her brother's house, that's okay." He shrugged. "Another time, I might go over to Paul's house as I've done for decades. Truth is, I'll always come back to Callie. I'll find her and work things out. Paul's my friend. But she and

I are marrying each other. We're opening the door to each other's hearts, for better or for worse, for all time, and clinging to each other." He squeezed her hand. Her answering squeeze put his heart at peace.

"Right. Good."

"Did we cross all the Ts, Pastor?" Callie let go of James's hand and moved forward as if to stand.

He was more than ready to end this counseling session too.

"There's only one other thing I must mention. Doing my due diligence as your shepherd, you understand."

James groaned, fearing the pastor's one other thing.

Callie settled back into her chair.

"What are your expectations about intimacy?" Pastor Sagle leaned his forearms against his desk, glancing between them. "Have you discussed the private side of your marriage?"

Why was he bringing that up now? Did he put all couples on the spot like this? James felt like a bug under a science lab microscope.

Callie coughed and patted her hand over her chest. "Really, Pastor—"

"I discuss these issues with every couple whose marriage ceremony I'm going to perform. You two are no exception. James, have you prepared the bedroom for Callie's arrival?"

"Y-yes, I have." His face felt on fire with embarrassment.

"Callie, have you prepared yourself to share a bedroom with James?"

"Prepared? Pastor, this is a personal matter between James and me."

"That's right," James concurred.

"So then, have you discussed intimacy together?" Pastor Sagle eyed them sternly as a teacher might do to a couple of six-year-olds.

"No." Callie twisted her hands in her lap. "Of course not!"

James shook his head and gazed at the floor.

"Then let's have a chat about it, shall we?" The pastor settled back in his chair like he was getting ready for a long discussion.

"Just peachy," Callie muttered.

Crawling out of the room was a sore temptation. But for Callie's sake, and for the hope of a blessed marriage and future with her, James faced the pastor. He tried to listen to him with an open mind. And prayed Callie wasn't embarrassed out of her socks!

Chapter Fifty-two

Callie had just returned home from her doctor's appointment when Maggie and Patty showed up at her door clutching gift bags. She welcomed them in, hugging them both. "Come in. What's this? What's going on?"

"We wanted to throw you a big bash before your wedding." Maggie dropped her gift bags on the kitchen island and heaved a sigh. "But your niece said you didn't want any hoopla. Is that true?"

"That's correct. We're having a quick wedding. Besides, we have plenty of stuff between us. No reason for showers."

Patty dropped her package beside Maggie's and settled onto a bar stool. "A little fun with friends wouldn't hurt, though, would it? Maggie and I got you some cutesy lingerie."

"Lingerie?" Callie felt the heat of a two-hundred-watt bulb crossing her cheeks. Leave it to these single ladies to push for that kind of "fun." After the lecture she endured at Pastor Sagle's office earlier, then her personal discussion with her doctor, she was sensitive to husband-and-wife topics. Lingerie, indeed!

"How about some tea?"

"Yes, thanks." Maggie sat on another bar stool.

"Would love some," Patty said.

Callie went to work getting tea and snacks ready.

"I guess you'll be serving your husband his morning coffee from now on." Patty snickered. "Coffee in bed, hmm?"

Callie groaned.

Maggie whooped. "Look at her blush!"

"I'm not blushing!"

"Yes, you are. It's hard for me to imagine you and James Weston as a romantic couple. The two of you sharing a house and—" Maggie cleared her throat. "You're a braver woman than I am."

Not brave. Hopeful. And thankful.

Callie put Kathleen's recently baked scones on a plate. She placed them and two saucers on the island. "Help yourselves, ladies." When the tea was ready, she set out the cups, spoons, and the sugar bowl. Then she took a seat herself. "Now, what's this foolishness about?" She gazed between the two who had mischievous expressions on their faces.

"Open mine first." Patty scooted a red and pink package with heart decorations across the wooden surface. "It was a hoot picking these out in Florence."

"You girls are sweet to get me some things. But you didn't have to go to all this bother."

"No bother," Maggie chirped.

"James is going to like this one," Patty said in a singsong voice.

Callie sipped her hot tea, controlling her agitation, then slowly pulled a box out of the gift bag. The way these two smirked and giggled, she feared a frog might jump out at her. Instead, a delicate, shimmery sky-blue fabric lay perfectly folded in the box, catching the light like glistening stars.

"Oh, my. It's so beautiful." She touched the edge of a matching nightgown and thin robe set, admiring the smoothness of the silky material against her fingertips. She never wore anything like this. Never handled anything so soft and filmy. The fabric caressed her fingers. She tried imagining what wearing such a garment might feel like on her body.

"It is gorgeous," Maggie said. "Callie Cedars, your leaving us mature-age single gals in the dust is an abomination. We were going to hold onto our independence to the grave!"

"Now, we're a duo instead of a trio," Patty said mournfully. "A sad duo."

"Now, now." Callie dropped the fabric and reached out, clutching both women's hands. "I'm not leaving you. We'll always be here for each other. Friends forever, right? My marital status doesn't change that."

"Yes, it does. Go ahead. Open mine." Maggie pushed her bags toward Callie. "I wish I had time to make a wedding quilt. These will have to do."

One by one, Callie opened the presents—slippers, another shimmery nightgown, this one mint green, and two cinnamon-and-spice-scented candles. She oohed and aahed over each item. At least there wasn't anything truly embarrassing in the packages. The gifts were kindnesses extended by two dear friends who cared about her.

"Thank you both. This was so nice and special of you to come by and share these beautiful gifts with me."

"We're happy for you, Callie. Really, we are." Patty met her gaze with moisture in her eyes. "No one deserves happiness more than you. I hope James will make you happy."

"He does. I hope I will make him a good wife."

"He better appreciate you, that's all I have to say." Maggie harrumphed. "If he makes you cry even once, I'm coming over there and bopping him on the nose. I will too!"

"I believe you." Callie chuckled. "I'll be sure to warn him."

"You'd better."

They chatted and laughed, reminiscing about days gone by when they were young, full of hopes and dreams for happy futures and families. Callie stored the memory of their friendship in her heart like a treasure box full of precious things she could take out and think about in the future.

Chapter Fifty-three

After yesterday's discussions about married life, Callie didn't know what to think when Pauly texted her that he wanted to talk with her. He'd better not assume she needed marital advice from him! He was the last person on the planet she wanted to discuss marriage stuff with.

As she exited Marcus's Lexus, she glanced over at James's house, soon to be her house too. Was he watching her? Did he know about Pauly wanting to talk with her?

Her brother answered the door quickly and invited her into the kitchen. That was a huge change. He usually ignored her knock. Refused to get her tea. Bygones. She sighed. She wasn't holding those things against him anymore.

He swayed his hand toward the table where mismatched mugs rested with hot tea in them. He answered the door *and* was serving her tea? Miracle of miracles.

Callie sat down and sipped her drink. Fortunately, Pauly refrained from putting his usual two heaping teaspoons of sugar in hers. "Thank you."

"Sure." Clearing his throat, he set a long narrow antique-gold jewelry box beside her cup before sitting down. "I should have given this to you years ago. It belonged to Mama."

"You kept her jewelry?" Hands trembling, Callie picked up the vintage-looking box. Slowly, she opened it. "Ohhh." Inside the box, a delicate gold rose pendant with a slim chain lay nestled on a bed of white satin. She faintly remembered her mother wearing this necklace on special occasions when Callie was a child. "It's gorgeous. Thank you for saving this jewelry for me, Pauly." She touched the rose, imagining her mother doing the same thing.

"I thought you might like to wear it for the wedding." His forehead wrinkled. "You know the 'something old' bit." He took a couple of long swallows of his tea. "If you want, that is."

"It would be an honor to wear Mama's necklace. Thanks for thinking of it." She clasped his hand and squeezed gently.

"It's not doing me any good up in my drawer," he said gruffly as if covering over his emotions.

"Nevertheless. I appreciate your thoughtfulness. It's like Mama is smiling down on me from heaven, giving me this token of her love." She slid the gold box into her purse for safekeeping.

They sipped their drinks in silence for a couple of minutes.

Should she bring up Sue Anne again? Had Pauly thought any more about talking with her when she came to Basalt Bay? Maybe today wasn't the best day to mention their past.

"I've been thinking about what you suggested about my seeing, or, er, talking to Sue Anne." He coughed.

"Oh?" His bringing up the subject surprised her. "That would be great. I'd love for you two—"

"Hold on! I didn't say anything about us getting back together."

"Of course not. I'd love for you to talk. That's all." She patted his arm.

"Yeah, well." Pauly grumbled and picked up his cup, circling it in his fingers. "I never forgot her."

"I figured."

"Have you heard anything about when she's coming?"

His question confirmed he was looking forward to Sue Anne's arrival, despite his gruff tone.

"Not yet. It's up to Sarah. When I hear which day it is, I'll text you. Okay?"

"Oh, uh, sure. If you think of it." He shrugged like it didn't matter.

She nudged his arm. "Thanks for being okay with James and me."

"Yeah, yeah."

"I'm thankful you're going to walk down the stairs with me." She smiled, imagining herself dressed in her navy dress, walking down the stairway decorated in garlands.

"Why wouldn't I?"

She didn't react to his baited words. "I'm just thankful things are better between us."

"Okay. Fine." Pauly let out a huffy-sounding breath. "Do you need anything for tomorrow? Any words of advice about marriage?"

"No thanks. I've had enough advice to last me for the rest of my life." She rolled her eyes, dousing any thoughts of Pastor Sagle's marital pearls of wisdom from her mind. She might never be able to listen to one of his sermons again without thinking of his discussion about intimacy. "James and I will get along just fine."

"See there. If it hadn't been for me, you two might not even be getting married tomorrow." He thumbed his chest and stood.

"Wait. What do you mean?" Her suspicions on alert, she stood and faced her brother. "How are you responsible for us getting together?" Was he pushing for one final argument between them?

"Didn't James tell you that he and I bet on whether he could get you to marry him?"

"What?" The word exploded from her. "You bet on—"

"Don't take it the wrong way. I was just saying—"

"Why shouldn't I get upset to hear that my future husband and my brother bet on my answer to marry a man I've—" She bit down on her lower lip. She would not talk about this with Pauly. Her feelings for James were not up for discussion with him.

"Hey, sorry. I didn't mean to stick my foot in my mouth." Pauly pressed the heels of his hands against his forehead. "I thought you knew. Honest, I did."

"I didn't. But I know now!" She marched to the front door, steam roaring up her pipes. She couldn't wait to get out of her brother's house. Oh, he made her mad! James too!

What was she going to do with this information? James bet on her answer to his proposal? The nerve. The gall of those two men making a joke out of something precious. Idiots! Thoughtless clods!

Tomorrow was her wedding day. Could she even go through with it knowing her fiancé wagered with her brother over whether he could get her to marry him? Hadn't she feared their engagement might involve some underhanded mischief between James and Pauly?

Chapter Fifty-four

The loud banging at James's front door sounded like Paul's heavy-handed fist. But his friend would just barge in. Who else would knock so forcefully?

"I'm coming!"

He opened the door and tension shot through him. Callie stood on the porch glaring fiery darts of rage or accusation at him. Her face was beet red, and her lips were clenched so tightly together they turned white around the edges.

"Callie, come in. What's wrong? What's happened?"

"How could you?" She marched stiffly past him into the living room. "How could you do this to me? I trusted you!"

"How could I do what? What have I done?" He started to close the door and noticed Paul standing over on his porch shrugging, his hands palms up as if he were apologizing. Had Callie been at Paul's house? Now she was here and mad at him?

"Everything was going great." She trudged across the small room, swinging her arms. "Pauly was treating me like a human. Like he cared. Was that real? Or fake too?"

Fake too? Uh-oh.

"He gave me Mom's necklace to wear tomorrow," her voice took on a softer quality.

"That's fantastic."

She scowled at him as if he were to blame for all the wrongs in the world.

"Isn't it?"

"You ruined everything. Everything!"

"How did I do that?" He took three steps toward her.

She backed up as many steps and thrust out her hands toward him. "Look. I'm shaking so badly, I can't control my tremors. I'm so wretchedly angry at you and him, I could just scream!"

"Please. Tell me what happened. What did I do that has you so upset?"

He wanted to hold her, comfort her. They'd assured the pastor that when arguments came, they'd talk and work things out together. Little did James know such a time was going to happen so quickly, the day before their wedding.

Callie pulsed the air between them with her index finger. "You bet my brother over whether or not you could get me to marry you, didn't you?"

A pain seared up his chest. "Oh, um. Yes, but Cal, that was before."

"Before you convinced me that you loved me? Before you acted contrite about the first proposal?" Her voice escalated. "Was it all fake? Did you ever love me? When were you going to tell me about this dishonorable wager?"

"I don't know." He gulped hard. His throat hurt. His heart hurt. "I sort of forgot."

"Sort of?" she shouted.

"You and I got real. Our feelings went deep. True feelings. Not fake." He kept his voice calmer than he felt. "Yes, I do love you, completely. But I can't deny making the foolish bet. It was before we expressed our love for each other. It was an offhanded, stupid comment I made to Paul." He reached out to her, but she crossed her arms, letting him know she did not want him to touch her. "Please, Cal. I made a mistake. An unwise mistake I regret. Don't let this become a wall between us."

"A wall? Is that what you think this is?" Her voice rose. "If it is, it's a fortified, six-foot-wide brick wall!"

"I'm so sorry." He clasped his hands together, wringing them. "I should never have made that challenge with Paul. He mocked me, and I—" He groaned. He wouldn't pass the blame onto Paul. "Never mind about that. It was my fault. Callie, you matter to me. You're my whole world now. I love you. I want you for my wife." At her sharp intake of breath, he continued quickly, "I admit again that I didn't see you like I wish I would have in the past. It was wrong of me to joke with Paul about getting you to marry me. I see that now. If I could take it back, I would."

Her jaw looked so clenched it might be locked.

"I'm bound to make some blunders." He shrugged. "I'm human. Fallible."

"That's no excuse!"

"No, it isn't. My second error was not talking to you about this and explaining what I did. I was embarrassed." He dared to walk closer to her. "Not in a million years would I have wanted you to hear about my ridiculous deal from Paul. Please, forgive me?"

She still glared at him. "Do you think you won?"

"Won you? Yes." He smiled tightly.

"Not that. Won the bet. What do you get out of it?"

"You. All I want is you!"

She stared up at the ceiling, tapping her foot in a heavy beat. Like a drumbeat foretelling doom. A death knell. He was waiting to hear his judgment. Would his thoughtless comment to Paul ruin everything between him and Callie?

He was going out on a limb that might break beneath him, but he asked, "Did you ever think unkind thoughts about me?"

"What does that have to do with anything?"

"It has to do with forgiveness. With letting an offense go." He lifted his hands in a helpless gesture. "Did you ever think something rude or mean toward me?"

"Yes! I've been thinking bad thoughts about you ever since Pauly told me about the bet."

"See there. I forgive you for those unkind thoughts."

"I don't need your forgiveness for my thoughts, James Weston!"

"No, I don't suppose you do. Still, I wish you would forgive me. Please have mercy on me?" He clutched his hands together. "I love you, Cal. I want to marry you. I'm sorry for what I said to Paul. Will you forgive me? Will you still marry me?"

After about thirty seconds of her not meeting his gaze, she asked, "Do you realize how embarrassed I was to hear about that from my brother?"

"I can imagine." And if Paul mentioned the bet at some point down the road, maybe in front of friends or family, it would have been even worse. Man. He'd made a mess of things. James could only hope and pray that Callie would forgive him.

"All this time, up until the moment I confessed that I loved you, I feared you were only pursuing me because of some joke between you two."

"Cal—"

"When Pauly told me about your bet on whether I'd agree to marry you"—she met his gaze with moisture in her eyes—"that's exactly what it sounded like."

"Sweetheart, it isn't like that. Honest. It was something stupid between two old friends who like to get the better of each other. I never meant it to hurt you. I see that it has, and I'm so sorry." He clasped her hands and was relieved when she didn't pull away. "What can I do to assure you of my love?"

"I don't know. I still feel hurt."

"I'm sorry for being careless with my words. Can you accept my apology?" He brought her hands to his lips and kissed each one softly. "If we can't get past this, maybe we should call Pastor Sagle and ask him for another—"

"Absolutely not! I'm fine without any more of his sessions." A slight smile crossed her mouth. "There's always Maggie."

"Huh?"

"She told me she'd come over here and bop you on the nose if you ever made me cry."

"Ah, Callie. I'd deserve that too. I'm sorry for making you sad."

She heaved a sigh. "All right, James. I forgive you. But if you want out of this marriage, tell me now."

"I don't want out."

"If this deal with Pauly is still floating around in your brain, or you feel like you have something over him because you won that bet about me, we can call off the ceremony."

"Callie, no. I promise you, I haven't thought of that discussion in weeks. It's so far gone, I don't even know why Paul brought it up today." She got a look on her face, and he rushed to say, "But it's good that it's out in the open. For both of us."

She exhaled loudly. "I wouldn't have wanted to find out after the wedding. I guess this proves one point. Pauly's got a big mouth."

Chuckling, James tugged her into his arms. "That it does." She leaned her cheek against his chest, and they held each other. He sighed. "Is this what our arguments are going to look like?"

"Hopefully, it's how they end."

He set her back slightly and held out his hand. "Here's a deal between you and me. I promise to hold you in my arms after every argument."

She stared at his hand. "Always?"

"Always."

She shook his hand slowly. "After our arguments, which there might be plenty of, we will always do this, too." She kissed his cheek softly.

"I like that." He kissed her cheek also.

They took a walk through town and talked about less volatile things. By the time they said goodbye with promises to see each other at the altar tomorrow, even though there wouldn't really be an altar, a sweet peace and excitement for their future together had been restored.

James thanked God that Callie had been willing to forgive a foolish man for saying something ridiculous. It wouldn't be the last time one of them had to apologize or offer forgiveness to the other. But he was grateful for the grace they shared between them now and in the future.

Chapter Fifty-five

Later that day, feeling so thankful that Callie was still going to marry him, James ticked off the things he needed to have ready for the wedding—shoes, tux, rings. The bedroom smelled clean and fresh. The closet had plenty of room for Callie's things. He stocked the fridge with fruits and vegetables. He bought five boxes of teabags since his bride liked tea so much. Ought to last for months.

Then, wham! Out of the blue, the thing he'd fretted about forgetting struck his brain like a sledgehammer hitting a fence post. A honeymoon! He forgot about a romantic getaway! They hadn't even discussed one.

Was planning a honeymoon his responsibility? Was Callie expecting to go somewhere special? Did he want to bring her here to his family home for their first married night together? The same place his father brought his mother? Groaning, he raked his fingers through his hair.

What arrangements could he even make at this late hour?

Panic escalating, especially after their argument earlier where he felt like they might break up, James dropped into the living room rocking chair and covered his face with his hands. How did he overlook such an important detail of their wedding as to completely skip over honeymoon plans? He muffed this as badly as he messed up his first proposal and that horrible wager with Paul.

If he called Callie, she'd probably say it didn't matter. But after all that happened today, he didn't want to disappoint her again. Maybe there was still time for him to come up with a plan. Just because they were an older couple didn't mean they couldn't spend a couple nights somewhere special like other newlyweds did.

He'd call Kathleen. She knew what Callie liked. He needed some ideas fast!

"Kathleen," he said as soon as she answered her phone, "I have a problem."

"What's wrong?"

"I didn't think to plan a, well, a—" Suddenly embarrassed to admit this to anyone, he went silent.

"What did you forget? How can I help, James?"

He should have called Paul. Or Judah.

"Is Callie within earshot?"

"No, she's in her room. What's going on?"

"I forgot to make arrangements for a getaway," he said quietly. "A honeymoon."

"Ohhh." She chuckled. "Don't fret, James. I'm sure Callie isn't expecting anything grand."

Her comment hit him hard. Why wasn't his bride expecting anything 'grand' from her groom? Like Kathleen thought he wasn't the type of guy to give her a nice honeymoon? Did Callie possibly confide in Kathleen about their tiff? Stuffing down a grumbling attitude, he was even more determined to figure out a surprise destination for his soon-to-be wife.

"Do you have any idea where Callie might like to go? Preferably, a place that's reservable today?"

"No. I'm sorry. Why don't you ask her?"

"I'd like this to be a surprise."

"Okay. Maybe go to a nice restaurant along the coast?" She sighed. "Why don't you ask Paisley or Paige?"

"Yeah, okay. Thanks, Kathleen. Don't mention this to her, okay?"

"I wouldn't dream of it."

He called Paisley next, feeling foolhardy. He should have thought about a honeymoon before today.

"Hello," Paisley answered. A baby whimpered in the background.

"It's James. Did I catch you at a bad time?"

"Not really. Tanner is in my arms. What's happening? Is everything going okay for the wedding?" Her voice had a bouncing quality like she jostled the baby while she spoke.

"That's my problem."

"The wedding?"

"No, the, uh, honeymoon. We never discussed where we'd go. Or if we'd go anywhere." His words came out fast. He didn't try hiding the anxiety rippling through him. "Now I'm worried as all get out that I failed to do the one thing for her I should have done!"

"Don't panic. The one thing you need to do is marry her. You still plan to do that, don't you?"

"Of course!"

"Then don't sweat the other stuff. I'm sure Aunt Callie doesn't have any expectations of being whisked away to Hawaii."

"Hawaii!" He hadn't imagined such a luxurious place. Did she dream of going to a faraway destination? If so, they should have put off the wedding for a few months.

"You could still do something meaningful and sweet, but local."

"Like?"

"Um. It's late in the season. Maybe go on a boat charter?"

"We already did that for one of our dates."

"Okay. How about booking a room in Florence overlooking the bay? The views are fantastic. And romantic," she added softly. "Order dinner in. Dance on the balcony. That's where Judah and I went to get married and had our short honeymoon."

"Really? Okay." His panicked feeling eased. "That sounds feasible. Close. A room with a scenic view of the ocean for a couple of days would be nice. Dining in sounds … romantic."

"It sure does. Don't forget dancing."

"I won't forget. Thank you." He ran his free hand over his chin, picturing dancing with his bride.

The baby whimpered and Paisley made cooing sounds before speaking again. "Being together after the wedding is what counts. Not where you go. But it's sweet of you to want to give my aunt a wonderful wedding celebration. Thank you for that." Paisley sighed. "She deserves happiness. So do you."

Whatever anxiety he felt when he made the call dissolved. "You're welcome. I want her to be happy too. I'd better go and make a few calls. Tomorrow will be here before I know it."

James ended the call, but his thoughts whirled with imaginings about him and Callie getting married tomorrow.

Chapter Fifty-six

On her bridal morning, Callie awoke feeling both nervous and filled with wonder that her girlhood dreams and fantasies of marrying James Weston were coming true today. Even though she had entertained thoughts of canceling the wedding yesterday, she was glad she and James talked the situation through. Marriage was about trust and commitment. She believed what he said—he made a stupid off-handed bet with her brother. No doubt Pauly was as much to blame.

She was choosing to live a life of grace as much as possible. Surely, that was a better way to walk on this earth, a better way for her heart to get stronger, than remaining angry and resentful. She wanted to be more peaceful and loving, starting with forgiving James and believing the best in him. After all, they were getting married today!

"Callie Weston." She tested the name. "James and Callie Weston."

She liked the sound of their names together. The guy she dreamed about for a lifetime was going to be her husband. *Her husband!* She clutched her hands together and made a squealing sound.

The knock at her door didn't surprise her. She had imagined one of the ladies in the house might want to chat with her first thing. Hopefully, none of them offered her any advice. Today she wanted to relax and ponder marital bliss. No worrying about getting along with a husband when she'd been single for such a long time. No contemplating sharing a one-bathroom house with a man. No worrying over the bedroom-sharing part of their relationship at all!

She'd fill her thoughts with picturing yellow roses in her bouquet, the cute hat with a big flower on the side that she bought instead of a veil, and kissing and laughing with the man she was going to marry.

"Come in," she called, almost as an afterthought.

Unlike Kathleen's usual calm persona, she rushed into the room frowning.

"What's happened?" Emotions clogged Callie's throat. "Is it James?"

"No." Kathleen scurried to her bedside and clasped her hand. "I'm sorry to have to tell you this on your wedding day, but it's Lola."

"Lola? What's happened to her? Tell me."

"She's here."

"She just arrived?" Callie scooted off the bed and quickly donned her robe. Kathleen helped her get the fabric over her shoulders. "Is she okay?"

"Come into the dining room and see for yourself. She doesn't look good. But she and Micah are here. That's what matters." Kathleen's wide eyes filled with tears. "I think we should call Pastor Sagle. Hurry. I'm afraid to leave her long for fear she'll run again."

Callie shuffled out of her room, tying her belt along the way. In the dining area, one tattered backpack rested on the floor. Lola's back was turned toward Callie, her shoulders slumped as she pointed at something outside the large expanse of windows. The way Micah dangled listlessly on her hip must mean he was tired, or else he hadn't been eating well. That possibility burned anger right through Callie.

Lola left full of hope. What was she returning with?

"See the bird flying over the trees." Lola sounded stuffy like she had a cold. Or else she'd been crying. "I think it's an eagle."

"Lola?"

She turned slowly. Her gaze met Callie's. Tears flooded Lola's red-rimmed eyes. Her face appeared gaunt. Her lips trembled. She was obviously feeling sad. Maybe had a broken heart.

Callie gulped back her desire to weep. "Oh, my dear." Arms wide, she rushed forward and hugged Lola and Micah. "I'm so glad you've come home. I'm so sorry for whatever you've gone through. But you're here now. Safe."

Lola sniffled against her shoulder. "I'm ashamed of how I left. I thought, I thought—"

"Shhhh. It's all right. You're home."

Lola cried softly.

Callie met Kathleen's gaze and mouthed, "Call the pastor."

Kathleen hurried out of the room.

Lola jostled Micah and whispered to him in Spanish.

"Come. Sit down. I'll fix you some tea. That makes everything a little more tolerable." Callie pulled out a dining room chair. "What would Micah like? Milk? Cereal?"

"Yes, please," Lola whispered. "He, we, haven't had much to eat in the last week." She touched her stomach, bringing attention to her loose-fitting shirt.

The poor dears.

Taking a deep breath, Callie hurried into the kitchen and prepared a tray of tea, toast, and fruit for Lola. Then she dumped cold cereal into a plastic bowl and poured milk over it for Micah. All the while she worked, she prayed for Lola and fought against the angry feelings she felt toward Benjamin. He must have abandoned his family again. All for what? An old girlfriend? His alcohol indulgence?

Fortifying her emotions and her willpower to have a more grace-filled attitude, she brought the tray to the table. Kathleen entered the room and helped Micah get situated in the high chair. Callie's and her gazes met. Kathleen nodded slightly.

"Lola, Pastor Sagle will be here in a few minutes," Kathleen said.

Lola lowered her gaze and sighed. "All right."

"You're welcome to stay here for as long as you want. You are welcome to live here and be a part of our family." Callie hoped her words conveyed the depth of feeling she had for Lola and her son. "You and Micah are both welcome here as much as my own nieces are. You can even have my room."

"What? No! That would never do."

"Today is my wedding day. I'm marrying James and moving into his house, so I won't be needing my room here." Callie took a long deep breath. "It will work out better for you to not have to go up and down the stairs with Micah. I'm serious about my room."

"What perfect timing!" Kathleen clasped her hands together. "The Lord has provided beautifully."

"Yes, He has," Callie agreed.

"I don't know what to say. Other than thank you. And congratulations." Lola's lips wobbled like she was fighting crying. "I'm so sorry for the trouble I've caused you."

"No trouble, sweetie. Worry, yes, because we care for you." Callie clasped Kathleen's hand in a unified gesture. "All of us at the project house care about you and Micah. We are standing by your side—Kathleen, Bess, Sarah, and me. We are your family. You are one of us now."

Callie let go of Kathleen's hand and they both hugged Lola.

"Thank you. It was beautiful when I went back to my husband. Like a honeymoon." Tears spilled down Lola's cheeks. "When he apologized for his wrongs and promised never to do those things or drink again, I fell for it. I believed him. But his promises were lies."

"I'm so sorry," Callie said.

"It's okay, dear one." Kathleen hugged Lola again. "After you talk with the pastor, you can decide what you want to do next. If you want to sleep for a week, I'll help you with the little guy. If you want to binge-watch TV, that's okay too. I'll make lots of comfort food."

"You are too kind. Both of you." Lola's sad-looking gaze swept the room, her eyes widening when she glanced at the flower arrangements and the wedding cake on the other end of the table. "You are getting married here?"

"Yes, I am. I've waited a long time to marry James Weston. We love each other."

"You are lucky. He's a good man, yes?"

Callie knew what she was asking. "Yes. He's a very good man." Despite her anger at him yesterday, James was trustworthy. He was honest with her and apologized sincerely. She was glad she chose to forgive him and move on from the offense. Maybe she was already walking in grace more than she realized.

"I'm glad." Lola adjusted Micah onto her hip. His head leaned against her shoulder like he was dozing off in her arms.

"I'll finish getting my things out of my room." Callie nodded toward the decorated stairway. "Until then, rest and get some sleep in your old room. It's all ready. I've kept everything dusted and cared for since you've been gone."

"Thank you. Your kindness means so much to me."

"I'll do a deep cleaning in Callie's room in the morning," Kathleen said. "Then the two of you can move in there tomorrow afternoon."

"It's more than I hoped for. More than I deserve." Lola took a tired-sounding breath. "Sleep and rest are what I need. I will talk to the pastor. Then I must speak to a lawyer."

"We can help arrange that. Come. Let's get you settled." Kathleen picked up Lola's backpack then led her toward the stairs. "When the pastor arrives, I'll watch Micah while you chat."

Callie followed them to the stairway. "No matter what, we are here for you, Lola."

"I won't go back to Benny. It's over. For Micah and me, this is the last straw."

Callie didn't comment, even though she was glad to hear it.

"You deserve much happiness in your marriage." Lola took a couple steps back and kissed her on the cheek. "You will make a beautiful bride."

"Thank you." Callie fought tears. "The wedding is a small affair. You can attend if you want. Or just relax in your room."

Lola nodded and trudged up the stairs, moving slowly as if coming here had taken all her strength.

As Callie prepared for her wedding, she prayed for Lola. While her heart ached for her and Micah, thankfulness filled her too. God had brought them back to the project house today, back to her and Kathleen. Her new family.

Even though Callie wouldn't be living in this house, she'd spend as much time as possible here. Helping women who needed refuge during a storm, people like Lola and Micah in dire need of support, was a priority to her. A calling. She was thankful James understood and accepted that about her.

Chapter Fifty-seven

James clutched the wedding ring in his pocket, terrified of accidentally losing the jewelry as he stood in front of the small group gathered in the project house living room. Folding chairs were lined up in short rows between the couch that was pushed back to the wall and where he stood. Flowers and foliage were draped along the stairway banister that served as a backdrop to their ceremony.

Any minute, Callie would stroll down those steps toward him. He was so excited for his first glimpse of her descending the stairway in her wedding finery. She told him she wasn't wearing a traditional gown or veil. Whatever she chose to wear on this festive day would be perfect. She was perfect and beautiful to him in every way.

It was a good thing they invited only a few friends and family. Otherwise, James would be even more nervous standing in front of a church full of people. Already, his armpits were sweaty. His tux felt too tight around his middle. The over-starched and ironed slacks made him itch. Still, he would put up with anything to be marrying Callie and to look his best for her.

He nudged Pastor Sagle's arm and whispered, "What's taking so long?"

"The bride being a few minutes late isn't unusual."

Maybe not. But Callie being late meant James had to stand in front of the guests acting like he wasn't worried. When in fact, he was fretting that she might have changed her mind. What if after all the years of his not noticing her, she turned the tables on him? What if after his betting with Paul—

Callie wouldn't do that. She loved him. He loved her. They were meant to be together in their Third Act, as Pastor Sagle called it. Hadn't James told her that on the phone last night? She'd whispered that she was eager to start their lives together. *"Every part of it."*

He took a deep breath and glanced at the wall clock. Ten minutes past starting time. Then fifteen.

He shuffled from foot to foot, tempted to tromp up the stairs and hunt for his bride. He met a couple of worried glances—Paisley's, Paige's, Sarah's. Did they feel sorry for him?

Earlier, Callie texted him about Lola's return. She said the younger woman arrived brokenhearted, but she was relieved to see her come home. Is that what was causing her delay now?

Maybe he should go find her. See if anything was wrong. He took a step. Pastor Sagle clutched the crook of his arm and shot him a warning glance.

Just then, the wedding music started. James gazed upward.

In a light green dress, Kathleen strolled down the steps with a soft smile and a twinkle in her shining eyes. Next, Bess walked down the stairway in a light blue dress. Both women took their positions on the opposite side of the pastor.

A slight gasp went up from the crowd as Callie stepped into view at the top of the stairs.

Oh, Cal. She was gorgeous! James's heart kicked up a rapid beat. She looked so beautiful dressed in a navy dress and a darling vintage hat with a large rosy flower on the side. Their gazes caught and danced as she walked slowly down the stairs with her hand linked around her brother's elbow. James didn't break eye contact with her.

She hadn't deserted him. She didn't run from him to prove a point. They were going to love each other for the rest of time. Today was the beginning of their fantastical Third Act!

Callie smiled at him like she knew exactly what he was thinking. He grinned back at her, fighting the tears flooding his eyes. With each step she took closer to him, his heart pounded faster. She was a beautiful bride. His bride.

He swallowed the lump in his throat a couple of times. She let go of Paul's arm and reached for James. Their fingers touched and linked together. It felt like she was coming home to him. And he was coming home to her. Peace. Amazing peace filled his soul.

Paul took his place beside James. The wedding party turned slightly, all facing Pastor Sagle.

"Sorry I was late," Callie whispered near James's ear.

"It's okay. I would have waited all night."

They both grinned at each other. He'd ask about the delay later. For now, he loved the way her eyes twinkled. The way they gave him unspoken promises. *I'll love you forever. Can't wait to be in your arms.* He grinned wider.

Wait until he told her about his honeymoon surprise. How he rented a suite for three days overlooking the water in Florence. Hopefully, she loved his idea and the plans he made for dinner on their balcony. Three days away to focus on his bride and their new start in life. Three days of dancing on the balcony in the moonlight.

"Do you take this woman—"

James hardly heard the prompts on which he was supposed to be focused. All he thought about was him and Callie getting married and living together as man and wife.

* * * *

Callie felt her heart trembling. Happiness and joy fluttered through her emotions. What was she supposed to do with these loving, natural, and passionate thoughts she had been contemplating about James today?

She recognized the worry on his face as soon as she stepped onto the stairway. Was he concerned she wouldn't show up? Because of a few minutes of tardiness? After all the years she waited and prayed for this day? Silly man.

Later she'd explain to him about the last-minute visit she made to Lola's room. Since she decided not to attend the wedding, Callie wanted her to see her wedding outfit and fasten the necklace Pauly gave her from their mother.

"Will you take this man—"

Would she take James Weston to be her husband? In a heartbeat!

"Yes! I do!"

James chuckled. She loved the sound of his laughter. Would never tire of hearing his tender, masculine voice when he spoke to her. Their hearts were joining together in a love that would last them the rest of their lives. The beauty of intimacy between a husband and wife was still a mystery to her, but she was eager to experience all married life. Thankfully, her doctor had given Callie her blessing to live life to the fullest, as long as she followed her other advice, too.

Callie had waited for James for fifty years. Her waiting was over.

"Do you promise to love him and honor him for the rest of your lives?"

"I do. I do!"

Pastor Sagle grinned. "Then by the power vested in me by the state of Oregon, I pronounce you husband and wife. James, you may kiss your bride."

Finally! Anticipating this momentous kiss for half a century, Callie was more than ready to meet her husband's lips in an earth-shattering kiss.

James gently cupped her cheeks with his palms and gazed into her eyes. "My sweet, beautiful Callie. It feels like I've waited for you forever."

"Same with me." Only for her the words were literal. She felt like she had waited for him forever. But the wait was worth it for the chance to marry her childhood crush, her adulthood dream, her present love.

His warm lips brushed hers softly but briefly. He linked her hand into the crook of his arm and turned her toward the dining room. Wait! She barely tasted his kiss! It was over already?

Their crowd of friends and family clapped and cheered.

James probably didn't want to make a spectacle of kissing her dramatically in front of their small audience, but this was their wedding! She wasn't letting one more second pass before she got her foot-popping, spine-tingling, husband-wife kiss she'd been waiting for!

"James?" Grinning, she stepped in front of him and fingered his tie.

"Yes?" He smiled too. "I love you, Cal."

"Love you too."

A few whistles went up in the room.

Callie gazed intently into her groom's eyes. No one else mattered. Just him and her.

"Cal? Is something wrong?"

"Nothing's wrong. I've learned if I want something to happen in life, I'm going after it. I set my cap for you fifty years ago. Right now more than anything else in my whole life, I want to—" She grasped his tux lapels, and she went for it! She kissed him deeply and passionately and with all the love she had in her heart for him.

The crowd whooped and hollered.

Chuckling warmly, James wrapped his arms around her and pulled her against his chest. He kissed her back as amorously as she kissed him.

Now that was a wedding kiss!

"Whooee!" James grinned.

"Lots more where that came from," she said flirtatiously. "I think I'm ready for our honeymoon!"

"You and me, both."

They strolled arm in arm into the dining room where Kathleen had set out a feast of cold cuts and cheese, fruit bowls, veggie trays, nuts, and desserts.

"After the reception, I have a surprise for you," James whispered in Callie's ear.

"You do?" Her heart had barely settled down before it revved back up.

"I reserved a few nights' stay in a honeymoon suite in Florence." He trailed his fingertips along her dress neckline near her shoulder. Tingles shot up her spine. "Us having a little getaway sounds romantic, doesn't it?"

"I'll say!"

An unexpected honeymoon destination sounded incredible! She loved it even more because James, her sweet, adorable husband, had planned it for them.

Chapter Fifty-eight

Callie felt like pixie dust had been sprinkled all over her and James. Like they were glowing in happiness all through their reception.

Paul gave a toast and talked about his lifelong friendship with James. He said he was looking forward to his and Callie's silver years of friendship as siblings. Callie hoped for that kind of relationship with her brother, too.

Paisley and Paige both spoke of their love for their aunt, especially in the absence of their mom, which made Callie cry.

Sarah commented on the blessing Callie had been to her, emphasizing her role in contacting her birth mother. How she'd been like a beloved aunt over the last nine months, making a huge difference in her life.

Each kindly spoken word blessed Callie and made her extra thankful to be alive and healthy enough to enjoy this day with her friends and family. She wished Lola felt well enough to come downstairs, but she understood why she didn't.

Nearing the end of the reception, James clasped her hand gently. "Ready to start this journey with me, my love?"

"Am I ever!"

Callie hurried into her old bedroom and changed into casual clothes. Tomorrow, Kathleen and Sarah would clean this room and help Lola and Micah get settled in here. Knowing they needed her room made leaving easier. In her absence, Kathleen would watch over both like a mother hen. Callie had no doubt about that.

The guest room upstairs would be available for another person, and after her honeymoon, Callie would work on the planning-room bedroom conversion. That meant the project house would soon be ready to open its arms to two more women who needed support and friendship.

A tapping sounded at the door, then Sarah entered. "Hey, Callie. Need anything?"

"I'm almost ready." She patted her short hair and smoothed her hand over her waist, thankful for the pounds she lost so far. "I'm all set. I'm even going to wear this." She placed her vintage hat back on her head, tilted it slightly, and smiled at her reflection in the mirror. Her cheeks were rosy. Her blue eyes sparkled. She had so much hope for the future.

Thank You, God.

"You are a beautiful bride." Sarah hugged her. "I love you."

"Love you too. Your comments warmed my heart." Callie inhaled deeply, controlling her urge to cry again. "I shall miss being here for morning tea and chats."

"I'll miss that too." Sarah clasped her hand. "I want to tell you I'm ready to meet Sue Anne as soon as she is able to get here."

"Oh, Sarah. That's wonderful news! I'll contact her when I get back."

"That would be great."

"Good will come of this for both of you. You'll see."

"I hope so." Sarah drew in a long breath. "I feel like I must talk with Sue Anne before I can truly move forward with my future."

"I understand." Callie picked up her sweater and purse off the bed. "I'm proud of you for being willing to take this step."

"Thank you for all you've done to help me."

"It's been my pleasure." Callie grabbed hold of the suitcase she had prepared to take to James's house.

"Have a lovely honeymoon. Anything you want to ask me about marriage? Remember, I had a husband before."

The younger woman's rocking eyebrows made Callie chuckle.

"James and I will be fine, but thanks for the offer." The heat of a blush crossed her cheeks. "I'm new to being a bride, but I'm eager to experience everything about marriage." She rocked her eyebrows too. "Maybe before long, you'll be ready to find love again, also."

"You never know." Smiling, Sarah slipped out of the room.

Callie took one last look around the space she loved, letting all the warm remembrances of this room, this house, encompass her. Then, with a prayer of thankfulness in her heart, she walked into the dining room to join her groom.

"James, I'm ready to walk out the door with you as Mrs. Weston."

He met her with a soft kiss. "Then let's hit the road, Mrs. Weston."

Mrs. Weston sounded nice. Romantic. Inviting.

The group called farewells and well-wishes.

"Ready?" James's gaze locked magnetically on hers.

"I am ready to go anywhere with you."

"Then let's go, sweetheart."

Hand in hand, hearts in tune with each other's, Callie strolled beside James to his car. They were on their way to begin their honeymoon, in their sixties and going strong! Callie thanked God for the precious gift of getting to be this man's wife, and for him to be her husband.

For the amazing blessing of living life to the fullest, together.

Finally.

Thank you for reading *Callie's Time*, Basalt Bay 1!

Look for Sarah's story in 2024.

The Basalt Bay series is a spin-off from the Restored series that also takes place in the fictional town of Basalt Bay.

Author's note:

Callie's story isn't meant to be any kind of medical advice. It's simply her story. However, writers tend to include glimpses of their own journey in their writing. Two years ago, I was encouraged by a medical professional to go on a month-long whole foods diet. During the first two weeks, I went through sugar withdrawals, including the jitters, headaches, and crankiness, like Callie did. But by the end of the month, because I felt so much better, I decided to continue avoiding gluten, dairy, and sugar. Over the next year, I lost a surprising twenty-five pounds! This was part of my inspiration for *Callie's Time*.

Here's wishing peace, health, and a blessed Third Act for all of us!
~Mary

A special "Thank You" to …

Paula McGrew … for helping me hunt for deeper emotion and better wording in this story. Thanks for your encouragement and cheers. I appreciate your help so much.

Suzanne Williams … for another sweet cover. I appreciate your artistic design and the way you let me have some input into the process.

Mary Acuff, Kellie Griffin, Joanna Brown, and Jason Hanks … for reading this story with open minds and hearts and giving me honest feedback. I appreciate you so much!

My family—Jason, Daniel & Traci, Philip, Deborah, Shem, Lala-girl, and Little Cowboy—Hugs and love to you all!

(This a work of fiction. Any mistakes are my own. ~meh)

Other books by Mary Hanks

Liv & the Preacher A Marriage of Convenience for a Good Cause Novel

The Preacher's Sons

Lake, Hud

Restored Series

Ocean of Regret, Sea of Rescue, Bay of Refuge, Tide of Resolve, Waves of Reason, Port of Return, Sound of Rejoicing, Shores of Resilience

Second Chance Series

Winter's Past, April's Storm, Summer's Dream, Autumn's Break, Season's Flame

If you are interested in hearing more about Mary's writing projects, sign up for her newsletter at

www.maryehanks.com

About Mary …

Married for 40+ years, Mary Hanks loves to read and write Christian fiction, especially ones where the couple is married. She has written thirteen books in the second-chance inspirational Christian fiction genre. *Liv & the Preacher* is her first standalone novel. *Callie's Time* is her first book in the mature-aged Christian romance genre.

Thank you for reading the Basalt Bay series!

www.maryehanks.com

www.ingramcontent.com/pod-product-compliance
Lightning Source LLC
Chambersburg PA
CBHW051135190726
48290CB00006B/1861